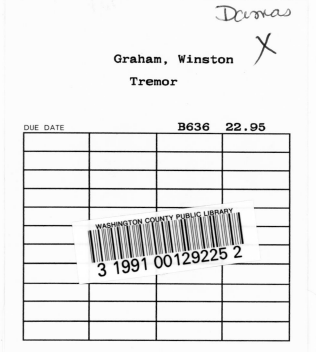

Damas

X

Graham, Winston

Tremor

TREMOR

WINSTON GRAHAM

TREMOR

St. Martin's Press ✖ New York

Library of Congress Cataloging-in-Publication Data

Graham, Winston.
Tremor / by Winston Graham.
p.   cm.
ISBN 0-312-14056-8
1. Earthquakes—Morocco—Agadir—Fiction.
2. Hotels—Morocco—Agadir—Fiction.
3. Agadir (Morocco)—Fiction.   I. Title.
PR6013.R24T74   1996
823'.912—dc20   95-39345   CIP

First published in Great Britain by
Macmillan General Books

First U.S. Edition: February 1996
10 9 8 7 6 5 4 3 2 1

For
Gwen, Robin and Tina

TREMOR

PROLOGUE

SOME FOUR thousand million years ago the Earth came into existence as a sphere of whirling gas and molten dust, circling its parent, the Sun. In the next thousand centuries it began to cool and form a crust, and in another thousand the crust hardened and came to contain within itself, and to suppress, the explosive gases, the white-hot fused rocks, the molten metal and the solar energies seething at its centre.

Passing millennia have strengthened and thickened the crust. But the crust is still only a thin shell relative to the size of the Earth. We build our flimsy structures of concrete and cement upon a frail surface. We strut on thin ice. Thirty miles down the temperature is still a thousand degrees centigrade.

Now and then the sedimentary rocks, with their covering of soil and vegetation, on which we live and on whose sustenance alone we depend to live, shift themselves under pressure from below. They buckle or slide. Small movements adjusting to a slow squeeze, settling or contracting, yielding to or resisting elemental force.

The human ants living and multiplying on the thin surface suffer and are disturbed or disorientated by these shifts. If the shifts occur in or near centres of population there is a heavy loss of ant property and life. To them it is a major disaster.

The most famous of these disasters, because it was the most publicized, occurred in San Francisco on the 18th of April, 1906. Most of the damage was caused here by the fire that followed the earth tremor. Deaths were minimal: fewer than five hundred. The worst earthquake this century was in Kwanto, Japan, in September, 1923, where more than a hundred thousand people died.

In 1960 Agadir, in Morocco, was almost levelled, with some twelve thousand killed, of whom two thousand were Europeans. Many of these were French residents, but many also were British, Americans, Swiss and Germans, holiday-makers who had come to escape the winter and enjoy the new hotels, the fine bathing beaches, the balmy sunshine.

It happened on the 29th of February, the day of the Leap Year and the third day of Ramadan.

CHAPTER ONE

I

THERE WAS no flight from London to Agadir. You took the
13.40 flight to Bordeaux, changed there and then again at
Casablanca. On Friday the 26th of February, 1960, the plane
was ten minutes late taking off.

News had reached Air France that a bus bringing eight
of their passengers had been involved in an accident, but
they would be arriving shortly. Had the plane been nearly
full it is likely it would not have waited. But it was less than
half full.

The eight relevant passengers had no means of knowing
this, and spent half an hour in a fever of anxiety.

Among them was Matthew Morris. Tall, cheerful, not-
ably good-looking, twenty-eight, artistic, unreliable, humorous, emotional, having just left his wife. Another was Jack
Frazier. Tall, thin, thirty-six, nervy, chain-smoking, talkative,
half-French, having just left his friends.

The bus had hit a taxi, or the taxi the bus, and a steering
track put out of alignment. After the usual exchange of
insults, a long and exasperating wait for a relief bus. When
it came, the too slow change from one bus to another, then
the luggage, and finally they had lumbered off on what
seemed certain to be a lost cause. The two men, sitting next
to each other, had got into conversation. Then the older
man, in an obvious fever of impatience, had left the bus and

3

taken a taxi, but in fact had arrived at Heathrow at almost the same time, to discover, as Matthew and the others discovered, that their plane had not yet left but was about to take off.

So a sprint down endless corridors, and they had all gasped their way onto the plane, with the doors slamming behind them, and the engines instantly started.

At Bordeaux Matthew found that his solitary bag was missing and it took twenty minutes to locate it. It was retrieved just in time from a plane about to leave for Nice. Not a propitious start to a holiday. The two men had not shared seats next to each other on the first leg, but Frazier dropped into the adjoining seat on the flight to Casablanca and Matthew, explaining about his bag, said he thought there must be a voodoo on this flight. Frazier, too talkative most of the time, grunted and coughed at this and kept his eye on the *défense de fumer* sign, waiting to light a cigarette. He carried a small suitcase which he kept on his knee all the time.

Rona. It was a funny old thing, Matthew thought, to leave your wife. Rona Ellison, she'd been; twenty-eight now, with dark, short cut hair, trimmed to chin level; a round face; pretty and full of common sense. Abounding with common sense; a solicitor's daughter; qualifying herself; a good brain. They had married four years ago, just before his first novel was published. So her husband was a rising young novelist of twenty-four, who already had one book in production and a brilliant future.

It hadn't quite worked out that way.

All the same, it might have worked. Incompatibility? Did the lawyers still use that dreary term? A £500 advance hadn't lasted long. He'd spent freely and enjoyed it, and hadn't bothered about another novel, expecting much of the first.

Anyway, music was his chief love, the basic love of his life. But you couldn't live off it. Two years in Paris – he'd squeezed the concession out of his mother – had proved that. Played the piano well – always had – but not good enough. Played the bass sax well, also the guitar – not good enough. Sang moderately – not good enough. He'd had a talent with words, quite amusingly, so he wrote a comedy thriller about his years in Paris.

Third publisher took it. 'Refreshingly different', he called it. So had some of the reviewers. But not the public. If they wanted thrillers they went to Chandler, if comic they went to Wodehouse. Never the twain should meet. Or so it seemed. The book hadn't earned its advance.

It hadn't been an angry parting yesterday. He still found her attractive, and she him. But a second novel written and published last year had hardly sold as well as the first, and he was discouraged at the thought of trying a third. For three years they had received a subsidy from both fathers but that had dried up. Now that she was qualified she was keeping him. Not a happy situation.

He knew she was mainly in the right. It seemed likely that had he beavered away in fairly regular hours scribbling away like Mr Gibbon, or even tapping away like Mrs Christie, Rona would have given him all the support she could. She didn't like, and she made it plain she didn't like, coming home to find him plucking at a guitar or moodily preoccupied reading an article on Diatonic Harmony, and to be told without apparent embarrassment that he hadn't done any work, any real work, that day.

The tiny flat in Hampstead was hers. Aside from a piano, a mass of records and a lot of art books, so were the contents.

He didn't know what to do now. Most of his clothes

he'd left with his mother. 'Two weeks in Morocco?' she'd said. 'Will that solve anything?' 'Not much. But I need a holiday. Maybe something will happen. Inspiration – I'm thin-blooded.' 'But it's really over between you and Rona?' 'I reckon so.' 'Pity. She's such a nice girl.' 'I think the same.' 'Your father doesn't want me to lend you any more money. Says it's unfair on Dorothy and Jean.' (His half-sisters.) 'Thanks, no, I've an overdraft that can still stretch a bit.'

This second Caravelle was nearly full, passengers almost all French. The hum of talk matched the hum of the engines.

Last Tuesday, he'd supposed, had helped him to make up his mind. He was not a quick mind-maker-up, and without it he might have dragged on a while longer.

Rona knew Eileen Patterson, the successful woman novelist, and at a recent meeting of something called the Women's Guild had scraped an acquaintance with the famous Hannibal Scott, who was there as a guest speaker, and had invited them both to dinner. At it there had been much talk of writers and writing: of Virginia and Leonard Woolf, of dear Morgan Foster, of Tom Eliot, of Aldous and Wystan, of Christopher Isherwood and Marcel Proust.

Matthew had been quite out of his depth: he read Graham Greene, Evelyn Waugh, Kingsley Amis, Raymond Chandler, et al. If, on the other hand, the subject had turned to music, he could have held his own pretty well whether it was on Schoenberg, Stravinsky or Fats Waller.

Neither of the two eminent authors had read either of Matthew's novels, but towards the end of the meal, when writing habits came up (could this, he suspected later, have been Rona's doing?) they were both emphatic that Matthew's idea of an author's life was really the romantic public's idea of how an author operated. In their own cases, and in the case of nearly every other professional writer they knew, the very reverse was the case. To wait for inspiration was fatal. Inspiration, they insisted, was the product of work, of regular writing at regular times, and every day, irrespective of the ultimate value or amount of the work produced.

At this point Matthew had added visibly to Rona's irritation with him by explaining that he didn't really like writing at all. He had no fervent wish to make it his permanent career. He was really only writing novels, he said, in the hope that one or another would hit the jackpot and enable him to retire.

It had been rather a brutal thing to say – its brutality born out of his own irritation at being patronized. Afterwards, after they had gone, he was sorry because he knew of Rona's efforts to get these eminent people to their unpretentious flat in the first place. And all for him. As she said coldly, when he tried to apologize, it had all been done for him.

A two-hour wait at Casablanca. There were a few English books on the bookstall and, as if to cheer him out of his depression, he was surprised to find his first novel among them. *Chance Medley*, by Matthew Sorensen.

The jacket had a small tear in it, and the tops of the pages were yellow from exposure to light and heat. He suddenly felt proud of it, and then sorry for it, representing him as it did so far away from home. He almost bought it out of sympathy, but the price in francs was inflated, and after all if he bought it he would be withdrawing it from someone else who might eventually fancy it and buy it for themselves.

This third plane was a much smaller one, and quite full. Matthew and Jack Frazier, having shared a coffee together, boarded the plane together. Matthew took a window seat and Frazier sat next to him, the suitcase firmly between his knees. The stewardess had wanted to stow it in the luggage compartment above, but Frazier refused.

Next to Frazier was a blowzy woman of about fifty, over made-up and in a girlish outfit that didn't suit her at all. She had two younger women friends in the seat in front, and they had made a fuss because they could not have three seats together. The two friends were also floridly dressed and chattered away in loud voices in provincial French. Again almost everyone on the plane was French.

Frazier, who had a nasal Birmingham accent when he spoke English, and an accent Matthew couldn't place when he spoke French, was back at his most talkative and was soon chattering away to the three Frenchwomen, shouting to make himself heard above the roar of the engines.

Presently he turned and offered Matthew a Gauloise. Matthew smilingly refused.

'I hate catching bleeding planes,' Frazier said. 'That panic this morning! Phew! I doubt I could've felt more in a muck-sweat if I'd been the last Jew leavin' Hitler's Germany!'

Matthew smiled. 'Lucky they waited. And lucky we got away when we did.'

'What? How d'you mean?' Frazier's voice had sharpened.

'I mean, once you lose your slot at Heathrow it often takes time to get another.' Matthew opened a newspaper he had bought in Casablanca.

'I suppose you paid in francs for that,' Frazier said. 'The Moroccan franc has just been devalued, you know, and they've a thing called a dirham that's worth a hundred old francs. We'll have to watch it, especially in the hotel. Someone always tries to overcharge you when these currency contortions happen.'

Matthew said: 'You can't get the dirham outside

Morocco. Or so I was told. They say the French franc will still be legal currency.' After a minute he added: 'D'you come here often?'

'Nah. It's years since I been over. Just came to do a bit of business, then I'm off again. And it was a good excuse to see the sun. Know what I mean?'

Matthew folded the paper open. There was a report on the Channel Tunnel project. It was recommended that it should be a rail tunnel system only, and cost estimates were it would be upwards of a hundred million pounds. A pipe dream? They had talked about it so long.

'And you?' asked Frazier.

'What?'

'You. You just on holiday?'

'More or less. I needed a break.'

'But you read French.'

'Yes, I spent two years in Paris.'

Two years not very profitably occupied, he thought now. Except to come to terms with his own shortcomings. Chiefly he had studied life. And he now spoke fluent and colloquial French. (He might be a bit out of date in the latest fashionable phrases: French argot altered and changed its meaning every few weeks.) And some Dutch he knew from a girlfriend who came from Leiden. Not exactly a portfolio of learning and achievement to bring home to England as the product of two years. But of course he had enjoyed it. And there had then been the novel.

His companion now turned back to the blowzy Frenchwoman, who it seemed was called Laura Legrand. Frazier introduced Matthew to her, and then to the two younger women. It seemed they were just 'friends', meeting together in Bordeaux after a long absence and taking a three-week vacation together. Where were they staying? The Hotel

Saada, of course; it was very *luxe*. Me too, Frazier said: a happy coincidence. And Matthew? Yes? So they were all to be at the same hotel.

Matthew's custom was always to stay at the best hotel his overdraft could afford, and the agent he had booked through said he thought he would profit from the devaluation; but he did not join in the mutual congratulations because his eye was caught by a girl in a green linen suit, two seats forward on the opposite side of the aisle.

Thick warm red-brown hair shoulder length. Clear, clean young profile. Nose a bit tip-tilted. Thick lashes that were not stuck on; what colour would her eyes be? Green, blue, brown? Fine skin. Her arms were bare to just above the elbow. A long slim hand raised a glass to her lips. She drank with the bottom lip slightly forward: a suggestion of appetite. Matthew knew that many French girls had poor skins, but those that were good were very, very good, poreless, like alabaster.

He had had no particular thought of finding that sort of comfort while he was away. Susceptible enough to good looks, and being himself attractive to women, he had nevertheless been faithful to Rona throughout their marriage. Rona was pretty and, until disillusion set in, ardent. But this girl was a stunner. He watched attentively but could not see her speak to the woman beside her. Could it be so lucky that she was on her own? And staying – who knew – at the Saada?

The plane droned on over the desert. Presently the girl he was watching got up and walked towards the loos at the back. Sometimes sideviews are deceptive; a full face brings disillusion. Not so here. The eyes in the half-lit plane looked grey-green, which meant her hair was probably not its natural colour. Perfect oval face, good cheek-bones; she didn't look more than twenty-five or -six. He thought their eyes met as she went past, but she glanced away. She must be used to glancing away; a lot of men would look at her as she passed.

'What?' he said to Frazier.

'I said, what d'you do? What's your line of country?'

'I'm a writer.'

Frazier blinked. 'Writer, eh? What sort of writer?'

'Oh, novels chiefly.' He laughed.

'Don't think I know the name. Matthew Morris? But then I wouldn't, would I, eh? Not much of a reader myself. Just a newspaper man myself. Or a *Playboy* mag.' The thin man coughed through the cigarette smoke.

'I write under Matthew Sorensen. But I don't suppose that means anything to you either.'

Frazier brooded. Eventually he turned the issue to what he found more interesting. 'Why change the name?'

'Habit of writers.'

'Trying to dodge the brickbats, I suppose. Or does it help taxwise?'

'I was born Sorensen,' Matthew said. 'My parents were divorced when I was two, and my stepfather thought it more convenient that I should take his name.' (Had insisted, in fact.)

Frazier eased the suitcase between his knees and lit another cigarette from the butt of the old. 'The fuzz always reckon it's suspicious if you have two names, don't they. Up to no good, they reckon. Well, there you are, one name's always been good enough for me.'

'Doing what?'

Frazier blinked. 'Me? Oh, I'm a sort of writer too. An underwriter, as you might say.'

'Insurance agent?'

11

'You could say that ... You on holiday, looking for material, I suppose?'

'Not really. Not unless it comes my way.' As it might well – now, Matthew thought. Have an affair with this girl. Two passionate weeks. Wonder what colour her intimate hair is. Very dark probably. Two weeks of lubricious adventure, then go to Paris for a bit. Write a steamy novel. There hadn't been enough sex in his two previous novels – too much humour. You had to be shocking to sell.

'Plenty of odd things in this country to give you inspiration. Odd bods and odd jobs. Last time I was over here, about four years ago, I was in Beni Mellal. Know where that is? Between Fez and Marrakech. In the desert. Real town to give you the heebie-jeebies. I got talking to a man in a bar. He'd a British passport but could hardly speak a word of English. Can you beat that?'

Matthew didn't try.

'This feller was born in Malta of Italian parents, see. Lived in Morocco now. Commercial traveller. Drove around Morocco on business. Know what he travelled in?'

'No.'

'I'll give you three guesses.'

'Couldn't.'

'Brassières.' Frazier laughed and coughed. 'D'ye know, I hardly bothered to wonder before what women here wear under their kaftans. But you only need to look in the souks: there they are, rail after rail of 'em, all sizes, shapes, colours, styles, lace, cotton, silk, fancy, you name it. French women don't wear 'em so much, do they.'

'No,' said Matthew. 'They think it's healthier without.'

'Well, they certainly wear 'em here. Reckon this man in the bar was on to a good thing!'

The girl in the green linen suit was returning to her

seat, but she had her back to him. Just the right sized hips.

The plane lurched a bit, and Matthew's ears crackled. They were coming down.

The two younger women were twisting their necks and leaning over talking to Laura Legrand. They both had big mouths. But if he were writing of them he wouldn't have used the word 'generous' to describe them. 'Mercenary' maybe. But, then, you could so easily be wrong. For all you knew, these three women might be charity workers travelling to succour the victims of infantile paralysis.

Other people were stirring, and the seat-belt light came on. The two women slumped back into their seats. A stewardess passed by and asked Jack Frazier to put his cigarette out. Papers were being folded. A couple of people pinching their noses and blowing.

Susie at the travel office had suggested Morocco to Matthew because it was probably the warmest place at this time of year if one didn't want the expense of going as far as Kenya or the Caribbean. Though it was not his nature to be depressed, he had asked himself as they boarded at Casablanca just what he intended to do with his days. With tomorrow, for instance. Sit on the beach all morning, or by the pool, and read and swim? Or walk around the town. He had only brought two books and a notepad. The thought of actual work was enough to bring on an allergy.

Through the porthole the lights of Agadir showed as the plane banked for its approach landing.

II

THE HEAT struck you as you came out of the plane and trooped with the others towards the airport building. In Casablanca it had been warm air with a light breeze: hardly enough to make you shed a coat. Warm for February in a latitude still north of the Canary Isles. But Agadir was different.

Nadine Deschamps had been in Agadir in February three years ago making a film and was astonished. Last time there had been a cool wind every day from about noon, and chilly when the sun went down. She remembered after the shooting sitting in the Saada with the director and a few of the other actors, and the women had all worn capes or stoles or coats over their shoulders.

Not so tonight. The air clung hotly, soggily round you. It could have been the tropics.

An impulse decision to come now. Get away from Paris and a failure of a sort. Not a failure in a part but a failure to get a part. That and Réné Brandin. But the first was the main reason. Réné had become impractical in his demands, but that of itself had not driven her away.

She had had her sights on the lead in an English film. Through a friend, who was a publisher, she had met the author of the novel, a rather ingenuous but charming young man; and they had struck up what was literally a friendship. He had said he wanted her to play the lead in the film which was shortly to be made of his novel, and that he would do his best to get the part for her. She'd liked the novel, which was set in the days of occupied France, and thought not merely that her appearance as lead in a Rank production, with probable release in America to follow, would advance

14

her stature enormously, but that she could do the author proud by acting the part of a girl whose husband had been shot by the Nazis and thereafter worked for the Resistance herself and helped to infiltrate the German occupying forces. It was a lovely part and she dearly wanted to play it – and had expected to.

There had been objections in some parts of the Rank Organization to making a film in France and about France, it being argued that with the British film industry staggering to survive in the first and worst post-war slump, it was more to be desired that the films made should mirror England and the English way of life – like the Ealing films – rather than try to put on a partly French subject with mainly French actors. (The leading man was to be an Englishman caught up in the tensions of the French Resistance.)

However the 'ayes' had it, and the film was to be a prestigious one, no expense spared. Nadine spoke fluent English, so the tide ran in her favour.

But the director, Mortimer Morton, a plump, elegant man of forty, then at his peak because of the runaway success of his last film, had come over with the producer and the author and had held court at the Scribe. He had a list of eight French actresses he wanted to interview, and he exercised, as most directors do – once they are appointed – dictatorial powers. Out of courtesy the producer and the author were consulted, but Mort, as he was called, must have his way.

And his 'way', it was soon perceived, was influenced by certain criteria of his own. He perhaps rightly assumed that all the actresses had been put forward by their agents with suitable CVs and the strongest possible recommendations. Therefore any one of them, in a sense, would do. So he wanted the one who would interest him most. He wanted the one who would be most likely to please him when he got her into bed.

Such was the prize that probably most of the applicant actresses would have given favourable consideration to the general idea. But the other seven were not given the opportunity. Though watched over by a duenna of a mother, a girl called Maria Antoine took his fancy, and from the glances they exchanged, even under the lowering gaze of Mama, it did not seem that his fancy would be unrewarded.

At her own interview at which only the three men were present Nadine of course knew nothing of this. Queries were made; she was asked to read a little of the script, photographs were proffered and accepted, compliments exchanged; it was all over in fifteen minutes. Only the next day, her publisher friend was informed of the outcome by the author and passed on the message to her.

It had been a bitter pill for Nadine. The prize of a lead in an important Rank film was gone, and all the latent possibilities of Hollywood to follow. Depressed and angry, she had turned down a secondary role in a good French movie and had decided to sit back and take a holiday from films, from metropolitan France, and, in particular, from Réné. They had been appearing together in a farce at the Théâtre Gramont and, when it folded, so had their association. She could well afford the break.

Passports had been stamped at Casablanca but there was the inevitable wait for luggage at Agadir, and eventually she followed the porter out to the waiting bus. The sky was sulphurous with cloud, which was lit at one edge as if by a setting crescent of moon. No stars showed. She heard a woman greeting another and saying that this exceptional heat had begun only yesterday.

The bus filled up, and presently a tall good-looking young man sat down beside her. She had seen him on the plane a couple of rows behind her. Dark enough for a Frenchman, but his colouring was English, and so were his clothes. Then she heard him talking to an older man on the opposite seat.

Handsome, she thought, and his voice had a better accent than the man he was talking to, who had a nasal oscillating voice that she found difficult to follow. They were not friends, it seemed, had only met on the plane. Both spoke fluent if accented French.

She was aware that the younger man was secretly observing her; probably his choice of seat had not been accidental, but she ignored him, preferring to stare out at the approaching lights of Agadir.

He had excellent hair, Castilian brown, curling like a mane, cut expertly to brush his collar, fine hands with a single gold signet ring, big bright sensitive eyes, a mouth that naturally wanted to curve into a smile.

This bus, rather than depositing its freight at a central terminal, stopped at the main hotels of the town, and she discovered that both of the Englishmen were getting off at the same stop as herself, in front of the great illuminated glittering sign of the Hotel Saada.

This was beyond the main town and was built along the new esplanade bordering the beach. A white lip of surf could be seen beyond the lights.

Seven passengers for the Saada, among them three sloppily dressed women she had seen on the plane, who talked in voices which varied between the blatant and the subdued. Friendships, it seemed, had already been struck up on the way, for the older Englishman was talking and joking with them while they waited for Nadine to hand over her passport and sign the register. She thought, I don't want to be caught up in that group.

As she moved away in the wake of the bellboy who was to show her to her room, the younger man came across.

'Mad'moiselle, pardon me, did you drop this?'

This was a lace handkerchief he held out. She looked at it and thought: how original.

'No, m'sieur. It is not mine.'

'I beg your pardon.' His dark eyes sought hers. He had beguiling dimples in his cheeks as he half smiled. She did not smile back at him because of the company he was in. But she inclined her head gently, since there was no point in being discourteous, as long as he was prepared to keep his distance.

She passed on.

CHAPTER TWO

I

THE HOUSE had belonged to a well-known violinist and his artist wife. Mr Artemis bought it from their son when they died. Near the top of Hampstead village, Georgian, square-built but elegant, well-proportioned rooms, a tidy but otherwise uncultivated garden, all surrounded by a high brick wall which keeps out the sound of traffic.

Mr Artemis is entertaining. He is a substantial, soft-spoken man, going grey, heavy eyelids, a blood blister on his bottom lip.

Four men in the room with him: Big Smith, Jonnny Carpenter, Joe Rooney and Greg Garrett. They have not been here before and are not entirely comfortable in these discreetly elegant surroundings. All tall men – except for Greg – and all casually dressed as for a pub – except for Greg, who likes to be thought of as dapper and affects tight trousers and fancy waistcoats.

'Should be here by now,' says Mr Artemis, glancing at the clock. 'You said eight, didn't you.'

'Yeah,' from Big Smith. 'He'll be 'ere. Last thing he says to me: "I'll be there, spot on." ' Taking a gulp of Scotch that his host has provided. Big Smith is about fifty, big-stomached, badger-hair slicked back and thinning, cockney accent, looks a bruiser, and was once.

Others are all younger. Johnny Carpenter is middle

19

thirties, lean, narrow-faced, known often for some reason as Jacques or Frère Jacques. Bright-eyed, devious, always with a crumb of cigarette stuck to his lower lip. (They quickly get to that stage and then stay there a long time.) Joe Rooney is the heavy, a bit slow of movement and brain, but you can always rely on him in a crisis. Sweats in a thick jumper even on a warm day.

This is not a warm day, being Wednesday the 24th of February, 1960.

On cue the discreet manservant comes in with the fifth guest, Fred Prosser.

Prosser is a weasel of a man, greying, lined, spotty, blinking too much, as if surprised by the light. It seems only Big Smith has met him before.

Smith does the honours. 'This is Mr Artemis. Meet the rest of the boys, Fred. Get him a wet, Nosey. D'you mind?' to Artemis. 'What d'you like, Scotch, brandy, gin, vodka? . . . This is best single malt. That suit?'

After a minute Fred Prosser is sitting on the edge of a cane-bottomed chair, clutching a glass and having a cigarette lit for him.

Big Smith says heartily: 'I've told the boys most of what you told me, Fred. How I went round this morning to Benson & Benson, seven o'clock this morning, dressed respectable; you let me in, showed me round afore anyone else was there, so I could see it all for meself: safes, offices, alarm switches, the lot, so I got a good picture of how everything works. Right?'

'Right.'

'And I've told them how you'll do the same for any of 'em, so in case we like to move, we know just what we're moving into. Mr Artemis can go too if need be.'

'That should not be necessary,' says Artemis.

'Anyway the others can go, smell out the lie of the land, if they so wish. Right, Fred?'

'Right.' Fred sips experimentally at his drink and has to take a short breath.

'Any questions?'

The others are eyeing Fred, who eyes them back. He looks not so much like a member of the underworld as one of the underclass, the underprivileged. You can see him in a dole queue. He does not look a strong character, one you would necessarily rely on.

'Are you employed by the bank?' Artemis asks.

'No, sir. It's this cleaning company. Zenith Cleaning Co. I been with them three years. But only on this job two months. The bank's got this contract, so I go there every morning, see. I go at six thirty every weekday. Bachelor, the caretaker, lets me in. He lives on the top floor, and as he comes down he switches off the office alarms and then lets me in.'

Johnny Carpenter coughs through the smoke of his cigarette. 'Sounds bit too easy to me. Why can't anyone ring the bell, knock the caretaker off, walk in? Where's the catch?'

'First off the caretaker has to recognize me through the grille, see? Then when he lets me in there's damn all to take. All the cash and securities are in safes and vaults. And there's all the other alarms.'

'What other alarms?' asks Artemis, settling on a pair of lightly tinted spectacles.

'Good stuff. All modern stuff.'

'Such as?'

'Well.' Fred Prosser shifts. 'The AFA Central Alarm

System, with air-pressure differential detectors. You wouldn't have a chance, not without them being switched off. Not a chance. The bulls'd be round pronto.'

'What time do the staff come?'

'About nine. Some a few minutes before that. From seven to eight thirty I have the place more or less to meself.'

'How many staff?' Johnny Carpenter asks.

'Fifteen and a doorman. As soon as they've checked in they go to their offices. It's a merchant bank, see. Not men sitting behind grilles.'

'But cash?'

'If you know where to look for it.'

'And you do?'

Prosser looks at Big Smith. 'And he does,' says Big Smith.

Prosser blinks rapidly. 'There's two safes and three vaults. Safes are on the ground floor; vaults are in the basement.'

'How do you deal with these alarms?' Mr Artemis asks.

'Switch 'em off.'

'So I would have supposed. But are there not keys?'

'Yes, Mr Railton, the manager, and Mr Leeds carry 'em between 'em.'

'When do they come?'

'About a quarter after nine. Mr Leeds is always first.'

Big Smith, receiving a nod from Artemis, passes the whisky bottle round. There is the clink of glasses.

Johnny Carpenter coughs again. 'Don't know as I all that fancy a merchant bank. Too much doing deals on paper. Cash is what you want.'

'Cash is what we all want,' says Big Smith.

Greg Garrett has pale blue eyes that seldom seem to blink. Though the one small man among them and the quietest of them all, he is the most dangerous. He's the sharp-tempered one who might pull a trigger at the wrong moment. Now he squints down at his yellow-patterned silk waistcoat and flicks away some ash that has floated across from Johnny. 'Personally I'm a bit agin it too . . . Course you never can tell. These fancy jobs. You play the black and the white goes in off. Who'd have thought that Twickenham job would have come up roses?'

'Someone got killed on that Twickenham job,' says Big Smith. 'Awkward accident. You want to avoid that. When folk get killed it makes it all more serious, like.'

'I would not want any of that,' says Artemis, his eyes yellow behind his glasses, but suddenly alert.

'No, no, of course not,' says Smith. 'Sure thing not.'

There is silence for a few seconds. Nimbus clouds of tobacco smoke hover above them.

'Merchant banks,' says Johnny Carpenter again, folding his long arms, 'merchant banks never carry that much *cash*. You can't expect millions. What *can* we expect to make it worthwhile? What would you say, Big? It's your idea.'

'What would you say, Fred?' Big passes the buck.

'Oh.' A shrug. 'Couple of hundred grand.'

'You seen it?' demands Garrett.

'How can you expect him to have seen it?' Big is exasperated. 'It's always a bit of a toss-up, as you've just said yourself.'

'One good thing.' Johnny Carpenter sniffs. 'These merchant places, security's not so tight. And they *do* have some cash. Often gold. What have you *seen*, Fred?'

'I know there's plenty about. I seen the empty bags. And the bands. Often as not they're thrown out with the waste.'

'Bands?'

Johnny sighs patiently. 'You never seen used banknotes in packets, Greg? Course you have; what about Bournemouth? Those brown-paper bands says fifty-pound notes, and then the number in the packets. Makes 'em easier to deal with and count. That's what you meant, Fred?'

'That's right.'

'Right.'

They all listened to a sports car accelerating up the hill.

'Might come round tomorrow,' says Garrett. 'See for myself.'

'OK.'

'What about guns?' says Big. 'You arrange that, Mr Artemis?'

'I would prefer not.'

'Then Greg can, I know. Greg's got his own estate, Greg has. Shoots his pheasants regular. Aside from his Twickenham doorman.'

Greg says: 'Keep your wit for them as appreciate it.'

'If more of you want to come round in the morning, come,' says Prosser. 'But I wouldn't want to wait long.'

'Why not?'

'Zenith Cleaning rotate their cleaners. Never been more'n three months on any one job.'

'Are you the only cleaner?' Mr Artemis asks.

'Yes, sir. I work a five-day week, like the rest of the bank.'

After another silence Big Smith says: 'If it's up to me I'd go in as soon as poss. Any more questions? What about you, Joe?'

'I'm for going in. But it'll be a long wait.'

'Could be. I suppose we could go in at eight. Cut the waiting.'

'Nah,' Prosser says. 'Postman comes about eight. Bachelor signs for the letters. Must be inside before that. Anyways, I'm supposed to leave at eight thirty. Bachelor shows me out. The doorman comes just after.'

'So who's going to take in the letters when the postman comes? We got to handle him as well?'

'You can't. He's got a mate in his van. But you won't need to. It'll take no time to deal with Bachelor after the postman's been, and I can be trussed up in two minutes dead.'

'Or not dead, as the case may be.'

'You will have your fun, Big,' says Prosser uneasily.

Mr Artemis takes off his glasses and looks at the little man more closely.

'Have you got any form, Prosser?'

'Form? Me? No, not on your life!'

'They'll grill you, you know.'

'Oh, a bit. But not, I reckon, if I'm tied up proper. Why me more than anyone else?'

'He don't look like a robber, I must say,' Johnny Carpenter says with a mocking grin. 'More like the type that gets robbed.'

Big Smith says: 'I can bring in Ron Oller for the cars. You can rest on him.'

'The cars will be seen to,' says Mr Artemis. 'I don't think we need to split off another share.'

'OK.'

Johnny Carpenter is staring at the small stiff figure of Garrett. 'But if Greg don't like the deal . . .'

'Course he does. Or will when he's seen the territory. Who'll go with him tomorrow?'

Prosser said: 'Two's company, three's a crowd. I'm not sure—'

Mr Artemis interrupts. 'I think if Big has seen it, that

should be enough. I wouldn't want too many of you hovering around. People might see you going in and out. If Greg's agreeable I think you should go in tomorrow or Friday.'

'OK,' says Greg, pulling down his waistcoat. 'I reckon I'll go along with that.'

II

BENSON & BENSON were a small but influential private bank whose offices in St Mary's Gate were on the ground and first floors of a narrow concrete building put up during the boom after the war. The offices followed the fashion of the day, with concrete pillars, inside too, lots of glass, black square-shouldered vinyl furniture, flush doors, ficus and palms, and discreet trellis work. The firm had moved here after being bombed out and had maintained its reputation as one of the solid, old-fashioned merchant banks that could be relied on to uphold the reputation of the City. On the floors above them were corporate financiers and insurance brokers; and, on the top floor of all, John Bachelor, the caretaker, and his wife had a small flat.

Double doors led into the ground-floor reception hall and office of Benson & Benson, and to the stairs and the lift. A small desk left of centre in the hall was occupied by Higgins, the porter general and receptionist.

St Mary Gate is only five minutes from Liverpool Street Station, but at six thirty on Friday the 26th of February the daily rush had not begun. The latter part of February had been mild, with a lot of rain, but today was dry and windy. A man walking here and there, an occasional car accelerating down the street, were the only signs of the traffic to come.

No one took special notice of a white Ford Zodiac Estate that parked a hundred yards down the street, leaving its sidelights on to welcome the approaching day. There was room enough in the back of the car for Greg Garrett and Joe Rooney. Johnny Carpenter was driving with Big Smith beside him. From here they had a clear view in the semi-dark of the alley running beside the bank, in which the side door was situated.

Presently Fred Prosser walked down the street, having come from the station, pressed the bell of the side door, was examined through the grille and allowed in.

It was the signal for the four men to reach behind and take out stocking masks. Then a roll of sacking was pulled forward, unwrapped, and the sawn-off shotguns distributed. Johnny Carpenter alone carried a French Army revolver. They did not at once put on the masks, but sat and waited. Big Smith whistled through his teeth. He whistled 'Mighty Like a Rose'. When he was a boy he had seen a play in which the murderer whistled 'Mighty Like a Rose' before his next killing.

No one had any intention of killing anyone if it was possible, but if you went in *feeling* like killing someone it gave you just that extra frightfulness. They were all on Benzedrine.

It wasn't long before the side door swung open and then closed again. That was the signal. One by one they pulled on their stocking masks and slid quietly out of the car, across the street in the half dark, down the alley, to find the door ajar, edged in. The last of them closed the door behind them.

Big Smith led the way along the passage into the entrance hall, thence to the ladies' lavatory. The four men, two of them very big, filled the room.

It had been arranged that as soon as the mail came and Bachelor had signed for it and put it on the porter's desk, Fred Prosser should tap on the lavatory door to say they could come out. But time went on and the tap did not come.

It was hot and uncomfortable standing here. They were all wearing heavy sweaters so that they should look bigger and more frightening. Greg Garrett wore built-up heels. Fortunately they could relieve themselves, even though it was forbidden to pull the plug. At ten past eight the door opened an inch and Fred Prosser hissed: 'Post's late.'

In a straggling chorus, necessarily hushed, they cursed the Royal Mail. The first of the staff, the doorman, Higgins, was due at eight thirty. It was cutting it fine.

'Not sure whether we shouldn't call the whole thing off,' snarled Garrett, always the one to panic, the one most likely to blow up in an emergency.

'Shut up,' said Big. 'We got twenty minutes.'

'For Chrissake,' muttered Rooney. 'We got to move soon.'

The stocking masks had been half lifted so that they could smoke. Johnny Carpenter took a flask from his pocket and handed it round. At eight fifteen the tap came. They burst out.

III

HIGGINS, AN ex-sergeant in the Military Police, whose daily job it was to unlock the main doors, came in by the side door at eight twenty-nine. As he closed it behind him he was confronted by two big masked men brandishing shotguns. A wise soldier knows when the odds are against him, and he did not put up a fight. Bound and gagged, he was dragged sack-like into a corner of the reception hall and dumped alongside Prosser, the cleaner from the Zenith company, and Bachelor, the caretaker. Wide-eyed, he stared around. Men with shotguns everywhere. In his testimony later he said there were at least seven of them. (The testimony of others reduced it to five.)

Waiting in robberies can sometimes be the greatest strain – waiting interspersed with sudden bursts of violence. Fifteen people had to come. But was it just fifteen? And which was which? Prosser couldn't be consulted, or it would blow his cover. All would have to be in their offices before ten, when Benson & Benson were officially open to do business. There were six or seven – Prosser could not remember – for the firms on the upper floors, but they came in through a separate entrance.

A man called Davies was the next to arrive. His first job was to sort the mail and take it to the various offices. When he came in he saw that Higgins was not at his desk and that the mail, an unusually heavy one, had slid onto the floor. As he went across, tut-tutting to himself, something was thrust into his back and he turned to see a masked figure urging him to submit quietly. He submitted quietly.

Next two typists. One gave a little squeal and almost fainted; the other, quick as a flash, turned and darted for the door. But Johnny Carpenter was there to grab her and stuff a cloth into her mouth. She was then passed back to Joe Rooney, whose special talent was tying people up without strangling them.

Another wait. Then came Mr Leeds.

He was treated like the others, but more gently, for he carried the keys. As they were taken from him he had the defiance to say: 'They won't do you any good.'

'We know that, cock. Waiting for Mr Railton now, aren't we.'

'You won't get in even then. You'd best give it up.'

'What're you on about?'

'Collins is needed as well.'

'Who's Collins?'

'The cashier. He's not here yet.'

A gun was shoved in his face. 'What the hell does he do?'

'He's got the third set.'

'So what? You mean one lot won't work without the others?'

'That's right. You'd be better to go now before somebody raises the alarm.'

'I'll blow your bloody head off!'

'Ask anyone here. Ask Railton when he comes. I'm only telling you the truth!'

When Railton came – and he was early – they took his keys and tried the two lots together, but the safe doors did not budge. Irritatingly the keys were stamped ONE and THREE.

Settle to wait, silently cursing Prosser while careful not to look at him.

Settle to wait. Not easy in a large reception hall with not much cover and seven – eight – ten – eleven trussed-up bodies in the alcove beside the lift.

Traffic increasing now. The reluctant daylight had arrived and showed up the long narrow street outside. From here you could just see the Zodiac with its sidelights on. Other cars were stopping near; a taxi discharging its occupants.

One of the girls began to moan and retch, and Johnny Carpenter was compelled to go over and loosen her gag. He waved his revolver and put its cold muzzle against her temple. 'One scream and I'll do for you.' She rolled her eyes and stayed very quiet, glad only to be able to swallow again.

Five more men, rapidly and efficiently dealt with.

But Collins was late.

His train to Broad Street had been held up with a points failure. He didn't hurry, for he was a phlegmatic man. He had no special expectation that his keys would be needed in the first fifteen minutes of business. As he turned out of Bishopsgate into Camomile Street a first flurry of rain came round the corner spraying him like an impudent child. He stopped to raise his umbrella. February Fill Dyke. But they had had enough. His garden, which was on heavy clay, was waterlogged.

Young Benson, barely fifty, senior partner since his father died, was off skiing, and had left it all to the other two, also youngsters in Collins's perspective. All the partners were too much like whiz-kids these days. Old Alfred Benson had been the ballast, the stabilizing influence, the upholder of the firm's tradition for solidity and careful judgement. Collins thought: I've only five years to go. A fair pension, of course, and I've put a tidy bit aside. Just have to tell Mavis to draw in her horns. Sometimes she frittered money; nothing to show for it; just frittered.

There was a traffic jam as he came into St Mary Gate; it started into motion again as he went up the three steps and walked into the offices of Benson & Benson, as he had done man and boy for the last thirty years.

They were waiting for him, this strange reception committee. They treated him with less courtesy than they had the early arrivals. Bruised and shaken, he joined the assembled group of twenty people lying on the floor. Only Mr Leeds and Mr Railton had been given the dignity of chairs. Hands reached in his pockets, rudely searching, keys withdrawn. Lying on his face, he could only guess what was now going to take place.

IV

IT DIDN'T take long then.

Mr Leeds alone was taken down and forced to supervise the opening of the vaults. Big Smith and Johnny Carpenter ransacked them, while Garrett and Rooney stayed in the reception hall standing guard over the prisoners and on the *qui vive* if anyone else came in. Rooney's nose had begun to drip as it often did in a crisis, and he kept sniffing and raising his arm to wipe his mask on his sleeve.

Five minutes they'd reckoned, once the vaults were opened. Into the waiting bags everything that was likely to be of negotiable value. Much cast aside at a glance, but when in doubt take and sort later. Some drawers in the second vault were full of *money*; grab those, empty those; urge to be gone.

Five full bags they carried up the stairs. Greg Garrett had been searching the safes, contents in another bag.

Big Smith said to the prisoners: 'Listen, you lot. Nobody's going to get hurt so long as you do what I say. Right?'

No one answered.

Smith said: 'We gonna leave you now. One of us is gonna stay outside the side door to make sure we get clear. If someone gets in our way we shall shoot 'em down. Right? So it's five minutes by that clock. When the clock says five to, you can move. Not before. If you move before, if we hear any screamings or trying to set the alarm off, my mate will come in again and empty his gun at the lot of you. That's a promise. As God is my judge we'll do for the lot of you. Right?'

No one spoke.

'Here, you,' Smith said to Leeds, who'd been thrust back on his chair. 'You're manager so you're responsible. If anyone sets up a racket my mate's been told to finish you off first. Right? Understand?'

Leeds nodded. Then from between parched lips he muttered: 'Yes.'

Two of the men had gone. Big jerked his head at Johnny, who was locking and bolting the front entrance. 'On your way.'

It had been a long time since they went in. A street crowded with cars, inclining down towards traffic lights at the end. People, chiefly men, pushing along the pavements, hurrying to work.

As each man came out he pulled off his mask and, carrying their dark bags, they sauntered out into St Mary Gate, mixing unremarked with the rest, crossed the street to the waiting car. The boot was not big enough for six bags, so two went on to the back seat with Garrett and Smith following.

At that moment a woman called Elsie Wardle, who was selling flags on behalf of the Red Cross, approached them. She was an enthusiastic collector and had reasoned that by being out early she would catch a lot of people going to work.

'Support the Red Cross?' she said, rattling her tin and smiling.

They took not the slightest notice of her until Big Smith, stepping back to open the rear door, trod on her toe and nearly upset her tray of flags.

'Well, really!' she shouted. 'Some people! Some people haven't got the manners of pigs!'

Johnny Carpenter was driving, and as he saw a gap in the traffic he prepared to pull out. Big Smith was sliding into the back, and as Miss Wardle was somewhat in the way he gave her a shove in the chest.

'Go stuff yourself, dear,' he shouted.

V

MAKE TOWARDS Houndsditch, then south with the flow, cross Aldgate and turn into a car park in the Minories. There they changed cars for a Mark 9 Jaguar, thoughtfully provided by Mr Artemis, and left the Zodiac in its place. Mr Artemis had insisted that all the cars they used should be 'clean', so there was no risk of being held up at some embarrassing juncture. In the Zodiac they left masks, some clothing, what was left of the rope, rubber gloves, etc. The guns were too precious to abandon. Greg Garrett, who had provided them, said he could cope with them. It was not as if any of them had been *fired*.

They crossed the river at Tower Bridge, made for the Old Kent Road, stopped again in a side-street near the Thomas à Becket. Here on wasteland two more cars were parked; their own.

Greg went off first in his MG, the guns wrapped in sacking in the boot. He was giving Joe Rooney a lift to Borough, where he would take the Northern Line to Camden Town. Johnny Carpenter was to drive Big Smith as far as Waterloo and then take the money bags to Mr Artemis's respectable home in Hampstead. There a safe would be waiting open for him to put in the money. When it closed it could only be opened by Big Smith, who had last night chosen his own private combination and set the numbers. (There was honour among thieves, but everyone was being careful not to put it under too great a strain.)

Cautious telephone calls would be exchanged tomorrow, and if there were no alarms they would assemble after dark tomorrow evening, the safe would be opened in the presence of all, and the haul examined, estimated, divided. Mr Artemis had various channels for laundering or making the best of the less negotiable bonds and securities. Anything too risky would be burnt. It was a good plan.

VI

IT WAS a good plan but it had its flaws. When Big Smith disappeared into the Waterloo tube Johnny Carpenter looked at his watch, licked his lips and took a deep breath before lighting another cigarette.

This was the moment of decision. Either he crossed the Rubicund or he didn't. (Was it Rubicund? Something like that. For him it might well be the River Styx.) He had made all his plans, but the job had taken at least half an hour longer than he had estimated. Since then he had made up a few minutes on his calculated schedule. But it had been cutting it fine even to begin with.

All his private arrangements could be cancelled. He would have wasted a few quid, but so what? There'd be a nice little pay-off from this job. Why not be content? Wait till next time.

But would there ever be a next time? He had listened, hardly able to believe his luck, when the plans were made. Of course he'd known Big Smith and Greg Garrett for years. And everybody knew him, Frère Jacques. A clean slate since he was twenty-odd. Always around, Frère Jacques, always up to something but always able to keep out of trouble. And Samuel Artemis he'd known on and off, at the ringside, on the racecourse, on and off where there were dealings.

As soon as his cigarette was alight he pulled out into the traffic. His uneasy mind, the timid streak in his mind, told him he could put off a decision another half-hour, see how long it took him to get to the West End and his own flat in Bulstrode Street. It could still be yes or no up to that moment. Though not a moment longer than that.

Although he quailed at the thought, something told him he was going ahead.

He was driving an old Sunbeam Alpine he'd had a couple of years. Shabby but fast. Traffic was not heavy for a Friday. Cross Waterloo Bridge, dodge round Aldwych and up Kingsway into New Oxford Street. Quicker than he'd hoped. Ten minutes saved now from the original plan.

Flat was over a shop. Two journeys for the six bags, upstairs, fish for the key. In.

This is it. The damned river, whatever it is called, crossed now, no return. Open the bags on the floor, everything in a great pyramid, bundles of notes sticking out here and there. Not hard picking the wheat from the chaff. Artemis, no doubt, would have wanted to sort the stuff carefully; with time you could assess what could be made profitable use of. The one thing he had not got was time. It would be an hour at least, maybe two, before anyone began to worry.

Lovely stuff here: English, French, German, Italian, American currency. All could be packed safely in one small suitcase. Regretfully he left the rest behind. Three copies of

The Times to lie on the top lest someone flipped the case open.

Change of suit, grab up two passports, air tickets to Marseilles and Bordeaux. To catch the second of these he had to be at the West London Air Terminal by noon. The Marseilles alternative left him another half-hour's leeway but didn't have the ongoing flight he wanted. (He had given up his earlier idea of driving or being driven to Heathrow, because he thought it would be more conspicuous.)

Pause, look around the room; the empty bags, the mountain of tumbled paper scattered over the floor; spectacles on, old trilby hat, raincoat, cigarettes, all as anonymous as you could get.

He knew he also had to fear the police. Collecting woman might give description, but more likely to be of Big Smith, who had pushed her. He himself was not a man with characteristics easy to remember; it had been an advantage all his life.

Taxi to West Brompton, leaving his too easily identifiable Sunbeam outside the flat. Check in, board the bus, which was nearly full, sit next to tall, rather loose-jointed, handsome young chap who seemed to be travelling alone. Suitcase containing his clothes in the luggage compartment of the bus, the other case comfortingly between his knees.

Well, that Rubicund was crossed finally now. No going back. Onwards Frère Jacques, who was tired to death of the small-time robbery, the small-time con; enough to live well off for maybe three months; then all the stress and hassle of planning and the risks of carrying out something new. This, this Benson job, had been the biggest of his life. Now he wanted to live off it – in South America, or maybe Australia or the United States – for a nice piece of the foreseeable future. One big coup, and this was it: and all in one pocket, not split five ways. To hell with his friends and comrades. Let them stew.

Traffic was slow, but plenty of time now. Plane for Bordeaux did not leave until 13.40. Having carried his two cases as far as Manchester Square, to make it more difficult for any bloodhounds who came sniffing and asking questions, he had again been tempted to tell the taxi he hailed to go to Heathrow. But caution prevailed.

Now the worst tensions were over he felt a great need to talk to someone. He always had been a chatterer, and was known for it. Just talk. Meaning nothing. No time to change his under-clothes. The sweat of the morning had dried on him, broken out and dried again. Nothing to read, so he kept glancing at his companion's *Daily Mail*. Nothing new. When would news of the robbery break? Later editions of the *News* and the *Standard*. Big headlines or small? Stop Press or Front Page? No one had been killed or hurt. Not too much of a sensation. Depend on what competition there was.

Would the police already be at airports and stations? It figured. But with no descriptions to go on, they could hardly hold up the arteries of the world while every passenger was stopped and searched. It was the last big risk. You took your chance.

The young man next to him was probably going on holiday somewhere. (Certainly not everyone in the bus was going to Bordeaux.) Johnny could not see the name on the BEA travelling bag. Ah, yes. Morris. M. J. Morris. Looked comfortably off. Good cuffs. Good links too. Johnny always noticed good cuffs. For a short time he had worked in a tailor's in Wolverhampton in his youth, before going into the motor industry. No shirt sleeve showing meant socially dispossessed; too much meant socially insecure.

What would the lads be doing now? Greg Garrett no doubt would be back at his farm, leaving the guns in the boot of the car until after dark. Johnny had seen his place once, and very nice too. Greg was smart: happily married, two boys at prep school, two hundred acres, better spoken than most of his kind, mingled with the gentry, shared their shoots, fussed over their wives, no one had the slightest idea that he had gunned down the doorman in cold blood at the jewel robbery last November.

Joe Rooney would be busy at his garage in Bromley, changing brake pads or adjusting clutch travel or whatever. Respectable man too; his wife a bit of a shrew who ordered him about, four kids all at the council school, noisy, unruly lot of little bastards. Joe was the only quiet one in the family. But he wasn't as slow as he looked. You never did to underestimate him.

Big Smith had been a boxer and couldn't keep away from it. Ten to one he'd be up at Haverstock Hill, where the weigh-ins took place, getting seen about there so people'd remember. Or maybe he'd go back to the Thomas à Becket, which had a gym on the first floor, and hang around in the hope of seeing Henry Cooper or one of the other top heavyweights.

And Samuel Artemis, always with money, the perfect manager, womanizer, four wives; third one in the witness box in the Divorce Court had said: 'When my husband was circumcised they threw away the wrong piece' (shocked the judge); a backer, a promoter, a fixer, not lightly to be crossed.

None of them lightly to be crossed. They wouldn't take kindly at all to thin, nervy, chain-smoking, talkative Frère

Jacques letting them down, double-crossing them, playing the three-card trick twice in one day, now off to the sun with the proceeds of a job they had all risked their liberty to do. The unforgivable sin of the underworld; one degree worse than grassing.

The bus had been on the move about twenty minutes when the driver stamped on the brakes and they were all jerked forward. Johnny bumped his head on the seat in front as there was a jarring of metal and they came to an abrupt stop. Shoutings at the front. A taxi slewed across the road.

The passengers, till then passive like sheep on the way to market, were standing up, rubbing bruises, picking up bags, talking to each other and to the other passengers as if the jolt had loosened their tongues. The driver had climbed down and was shouting at the taxi-driver.

'My cripes!' said Johnny to the young man. 'That's torn it. We'll miss the bleeding plane.'

The young man was licking his knuckle which he had cut on a window ledge. 'Hope not. What time's your plane?'

'13.40.'

'Same as mine. Are you going to Bordeaux?'

'Yep.'

'I've a connection to make too,' said the young man.

'On to Morocco?'

'Yes. Agadir.'

'Same here. Name of Frazier. Jack Frazier.'

'Mine's Morris. Matthew Morris.'

They talked for a few minutes. Johnny suddenly wanted to go to the lavatory and could not. His bowels were turning to water.

The taxi had come out of a side-street and tried to squeeze into the flow of traffic: he'd expected the bus driver to ease off to give him room, and the bus driver had expected to be given the right of way. A policeman now came, and the taxi, with a badly buckled wing but its yellow light still bravely shining, was reversed into the side-street. But something was wrong with the left front wheel of the bus. The steering rod had been put out of true, and when the clutch was let in the bus steered into the kerb.

More consultation.

The bus driver climbed back into the bus. 'Laze and gennelmen, regret to say because of mishap this vehicle is now unserviceable. The police are telephoning to the terminal for a relief bus, which should be along very shortly. Thank you.'

'That'll be half an hour,' said a short stout man standing in front of Johnny. 'At least. My flight goes at one twenty-five. Not a hope.'

'Laze and gennelmen,' said the driver, 'please return to your seats to await the relief bus. It should be along very shortly.'

People began to sit down, in various attitudes of impatience or resignation. A light rain was falling, and nobody wanted to stand outside on this dismal February day.

Matthew looked at his watch. 'Hm. Well, it'll be a close call. We might just make it.'

Johnny thought not. He felt sure his number had come up. A thousand-to-one chance had ditched his scheme. By now, or very soon, not only would the police be looking for him but his friends too. Mr Artemis would have rung Big Smith. The others would have rung or been rung. They would ring his flat and get no reply. When would suspicion become a certainty? As soon as someone went round to his flat and forced the lock.

'Excuse me,' he said to Matthew. 'I'm getting out.

Mother nature calls. One of them shops over there'll oblige, I expect. Then when I come out I'm going to see if I can get a taxi.'

'Doubt if you'll get one in this rain. But good luck.'

CHAPTER THREE

I

WHEN LEE Burford's wife left him he felt it was almost the end of the world. They had been married for thirty-five years, and it had been an unblemished union. Completely opposite in temperament, they had yet become kindred spirits, sharing differences of opinion as if they were an excuse to come closer together, reacting to troubles and pleasures with a sort of family unity which could hardly have been greater if they had had children.

She had shared and always been interested in his cases. He often took briefs home when he might as well have dealt with them in his office: her sharp, intuitive but totally unlegal mind would sometimes go straight to the heart of a problem and point him in a direction he might not have taken. He himself had a practical level-headed mind which served him well in the law. But although successful he was not a flier, and he was passed over once before becoming head of the old-established firm of Thorogood, Cohn & Levinson, of Milk Street, Boston.

Their home was in Oakbridge, a hamlet adjoining the pretty and historic small town of Concord, a few miles out of Boston. A substantial cedar-built house – always too big for them – forty years old, flanked by woods of birch and maple and a hundred yards from the main road to Lexington. The ground just here rose sharply, and the builder, advanced for his time, had constructed the house in a modern style, semi-open-plan, on two floors, with the big living-cum-dining-room on the upper floor where you were almost on a level with the tops of the trees. There was not much conventional garden but a greensward ran away in front of the house, flanked by trees, many of which Ann had planted herself: hickory, ironwood, aspen, hackberry and American beech, and most of which turned a flamboyant bronze or crimson in the fall. Ann never wanted a living-in couple, but two dailies coped with the housework. She always cooked him an evening meal, and they shared a bottle of good wine.

An amicable, happy home, a happy life. The one disappointment was that they had no family. She had conceived once and then had a miscarriage. Doctors and surgeons had been consulted, and she had insisted against his wishes on having an operation, but nothing had come of it. They had shared their disappointment, and in a way it had brought them closer together.

They had lived in this district so long that they knew many people, but most of them were acquaintance-friends rather than close friends. In a world in which marriages broke up at the drop of a hat, the very success of theirs, the uniqueness of their continuing preoccupation with each other, set them a bit apart. Also the lack of children meant the lack of a common interest that brought many couples into closer contact. He had business friends enough in Boston and was a member of the Tavern Club and the Algonquin. Although she knew so many people, a few special friends only formed an afternoon bridge circle noted for its good play and its good humour. Bridge, in her view, should be played well but for amusement, and those who came or those to whom she went shared that opinion. If there was an evening session he sometimes joined in.

They avoided drinks parties when they could, but about once a week went to the Golf Club. Sundays he played golf with a regular group, but she had given up. A dinner party once a month, and opera at the Met when it could be arranged.

The Burfords were an old Boston family, and Lee looked like one, dressed like one and behaved like one. Some people mistook his reserve for snobbery. But his father had been a Doctor of Philosophy, and they had not been at all well off in the early days. Until his aunt died Lee had been dependent on his law practice – though this was now highly prosperous. Sometimes, in other parts of America, people took him for an Englishman. Although he had no desire to be an Englishman he was not offended.

Ann came out of the same class, only more so, she being herself a direct descendant of the Paul Hayward who came over in the *Mayflower*. Her father still lived at Dartmouth near New Bedford, a retired Democratic Congressman who had established a reputation for unimpeachable integrity. Now that he was retired he complained that he also had become somewhat impoverished, and cynics attempted to connect the two.

It was a Friday in April 1959 that Lee drove in about six and whistled as he usually did when he came into the house. There was no reply but he heard a stirring in the kitchen. He went in expecting to see Ann but confronted Hannah, their Irish maid.

'Oh, Mr Burford,' she said. 'Mrs Burford has gone away.'

He stared. 'Gone away? Where?'

'I don't know, sor. She left this morning, about eleven it would be, I'm thinking. She said I was to come in this evening and see to your dinner.'

'Oh.' So far there was no alarm in his thoughts. 'Oh, very well. Did she say when she'd be back?'

'No, sor. But she says to me, she says, she left a message for you in the bedroom.'

'Ah.' More satisfied but a little irritated, he poured himself a drink before going to the bedroom. There was a pleasant little legal problem which had cropped up in a case today, and he had hoped to tell her of it. Unlike her to go off suddenly. He hoped her father was not ill. But then surely she could have telephoned his office.

The big bedroom had a wonderful view of the bare trees. All the buds were swelling but as yet the weather was too cold.

It was a big envelope and he tore it open and put on his spectacles.

Darling, darling.

I don't know how to say this, or how you will take this. There's no way I can lead up to it tactfully. I'm leaving.

I'm leaving you and leaving Concord and leaving Massachusetts and leaving America. I'm sure you'll think I'm crazy, and maybe that's true, but I'm not certifiably crazy. We've had a *wonderful* life together, Lee, *really* wonderful – thirty-five years and hardly a harsh word. People have said it's too good to last, but it *has* lasted, hasn't it. And now I'm breaking it up.

I'm going to New Zealand, Lee. How about that for a lunatic idea? I'm going out to join my cousin Althea. For years since her husband died, she has been running their small boatyard and living on small boats. You know how I adore small boats. Always when I have a week with Daddy in the summer we muck about in cutters and yachts of all sizes and even dinghies. You know all this. I've told it you so often. And I know you hate it.

There's always been that tug of the sea in my blood, and a sort of yearning. I've been a good wife, haven't I? Traveling all over the world with you. Going to conferences with you, talking over difficult law cases with you. Don't think this has been any sort of a chore for me. Darling Lee, promise you will not think that. I've really loved it, as you must know. But I have no belief in an afterlife, and I want before it is too late to lead a totally *different* life. With luck – with luck I shall have a bit of time, a bit of *active* time to live another way.

I shan't come back. I *know* that in my bones. I have a little money, and it will do me well enough. I hope you will be able to live a comfortable and cheerful life without me. Please, please, don't grieve. Please, please understand. Please, please forgive me. I am leaving all my things behind me, which also has been a wrench. You are the only man I have ever loved and you are the only man I ever shall love. But I have to take this step.

Believe me, your ever devoted
Ann

II

ANN WAS a healthy, robust woman, nearly as tall as he; apart from her inability to have children and an operation she had had three years ago, she had enjoyed perfect health. She had kept her good looks and her good spirits; tall, blonde, very feminine, very practical. Every year, of course, she had gone down to Dartmouth, spent as long as she could be spared with old Simon Hayward, and Lee had always

47

been happy to listen to her adventures when she came home, and happy that she had enjoyed herself. But this . . .

This was *impossible*.

The telephone was answered at the third ring. Living alone as Congressman Hayward did now, he was not often far from a telephone.

'Lee? Ah, I was expecting you to ring. Yes . . . Only this morning. She rang me about nine . . . No, of course I had nothing to do with it! Except that she has talked about it often during the last few years – how she'd love to do it. It wasn't *my* suggesting, I promise you. She never mentioned it to you? . . . Well, it was a pipe dream, wasn't it. That's what I thought. Once you stop condemning her, you can't help but admire her . . . No, I suppose not; not yet. It's a terrible reason to break up a marriage, I guess. I mean, one as good as yours, Lee. But she was always crazy about the sea, though she saw so little of it. Don't forget her grandfather and her great-grandfather were both in the US Navy. I can't explain it better than that!'

Lee could picture the old man, dressed as he always was in a blue reefer jacket with brass buttons, denim trousers, sandals, open-neck shirt with big black tie tied so loosely that it was like a cravat, grey hair cut very short, gold-rimmed spectacles; rather a 'character' in the district, now trying to explain the inexplicable, to justify the unjustifiable.

'Althea? She's not really a cousin but she grew up in Massachusetts, they went to school together; she married a guy from New Zealand and she's been living in North Island ever since. She's been back twice. Apparently they own a boatyard. Of course you can see the appeal . . . I don't know. Obviously Ann hasn't been there, but she must have seen photos and home movies, that sort of thing. Sure, Lee, she may come back, but not for a while, I'd say. Anyway we can't stop her, can we; she's kicked up her heels and gone. Which way was she travelling, d'you know? No, I guess she wouldn't tell you, would she. She certainly didn't tell me.'

The old man coughed and listened. 'No, I certainly wouldn't go after her. Look, Lee, I'm real sorry this has happened to you. You're a fine guy, and you've done really well by Ann, and now she's played you what may seem to you like a dirty trick. But you've got to think you've had thirty-five years together, and that's a fair crack of the whip ... No, I certainly don't see it as any sort of reflection on you. As I expect she said to you, she wants to lead a totally different life, a sea life, an *active* life, with boats. She hasn't got all that long – though maybe looking at myself, I'm eighty-three, and I still muck around with boats and the like – she's got a fair time. What shall you do? ... No, I'm sure, you've hardly given it a thought yet. But take it easy, boy, there's a lot of water still to flow under the bridge. Like me to come over and see you? No, well, any time, just lift the phone ... I suppose she's travelled pretty light, so there'll be a lot of her stuff around. I should try to carry on for a while and see how the dice roll. Of course I'll tell you if she rings.'

When he got off the telephone Hannah came back into the room. 'Will I bring in the supper, sor?'

'Not yet. I'll take another drink first. I'll ring the bell when I want you. Is Della here?'

'No, she's went long since. Mrs Burford specially asked me to be here this evening. She seemed to think it would be better.'

'OK. I'll not keep you too late, otherwise your husband will be getting anxious.'

'Oh, no, sor, he knows. I said I'd be home by eleven.'

Lee didn't ask if her husband knew why she'd been called in or knew that Ann had left. Anyway it would soon be all over the village.

'Oh, sor, before I leave you, Mrs Heinz is downstairs. She said she'd like to see you.'

Was this another link in the chain? 'Of course. Send her up.'

III

LETTY HEINZ said: 'Yes, I knew about it, Mr Burford. But only since Wednesday.'

'What did you know?'

'That she was thinking she might leave. It was not till she came back from Concord and said she had been to the travel agent that I supposed she was in real earnest.'

Letty Heinz was a recent friend. One of Ann's peculiarities – for Ann had none of Lee's reserve – was a tendency to take a sudden fancy to someone she had just met and make a fuss of them. It sprang from goodwill and a genuine interest in other people's lives. When Letty had first appeared at their bridge table Lee had not been taken with her. He looked on her as one of Ann's lame ducks, and a not particularly well-educated lame duck at that. She seemed to know nothing about music or to be even reasonably well-read.

Letty Heinz was half Norwegian, half English, it seemed, and had come to America during the war, had married Carl Heinz, a long-distance truck driver, and they had a son called Leon; she was separated from her husband, and her son, instead of going on to college, had fallen for one of the new

50

psychedelic beliefs while still at his state school and was now a drop-out, living in a commune in New York.

She didn't seem quite the companion for Ann – never had – but when Ann had to have an operation for removal of a cyst she invited Letty to come to the house and look after her for a few days, and this had been a success. Letty unexpectedly turned out to be a good bridge player, so she had stayed a month. Thereafter she had quite often come in for an afternoon's bridge, and had also partnered Ann at duplicate – a form of bridge that Lee disliked.

She was a pretty woman, slim, almost petite; and partly because of her slightness she looked younger than thirty-eight, which she said she was. He had felt once or twice in the last year or so that Ann and Letty had confidences between each other that they did not share with him. His resentment was vague and unspecified and certainly not a reason for any complaint. Anyway his trust in Ann had been complete. But he looked at Letty now without warmth.

'Why have you come?'

'Come? Here, you mean? I came to see you, Mr Burford.'

'For some reason?'

'Well, yes, I heard what had happened and I thought I might be of some help in this – this trouble you are in.'

'You can only help me by telling me anything you knew of her plans, what she has said to you.'

Letty shrugged her shoulders. 'Oh, we have talked of it now and then. Yes, I must say that. But there was never any hint of criticism of *you* in this talk. You have always been the good husband, the kind, thoughtful husband, and she, I think, I think Mrs Burford has always been the kind, thoughtful wife.'

Lee nodded.

'I guess,' she said, 'there's often articles in magazines

giving reasons why this sort of thing can happen: middle age, change of life, but . . . But I do not believe it was that with her. It is a – a dream which she has wished to realize. You know? Now, perhaps, with God's help, she will be able to realize it.'

'But not with my help,' said Lee bitterly.

'It is hard for me to say the right thing,' Letty said. 'I have only known Mrs Burford a few years – you also that long, but you mainly at a distance. But I think you have given Ann a wonderful life, have given her every comfort and all your affectionate attention.'

'I believe I did.'

'Now she has gone to do something else. But do not say you have not helped her. She is carrying your love with her. If you continue to give her that love you will be helping and supporting her in the way she now most wants.'

'And when she returns?'

Letty Heinz wrinkled her eyebrows. 'The way she spoke, Mr Burford, I do not think she will return.'

IV

'OF COURSE she'll be back,' said Henry Hayward heartily. 'I give her six months maximum. Why, it's outrageous, what she's done, and before long she'll realize it and return to the fold.'

Henry Hayward was Ann's elder brother; he had been with the Federal Reserve Bank but was now retired. He came over the following day, with his wife; they had been almost due for their annual visit and presumably this crisis, this outrageous defection on the part of his little sister, was reason enough to accelerate their arrival. Lee had never been close to Henry. He always felt in his bones that Henry thought Ann had married a bit beneath her by not marrying someone who had been to Groton. Henry seemed to remember his school and college days with a sort of retarded affection. Even at sixty-eight he still referred to his membership of the Hasty Pudding Club. Lee, on the other hand, so far as he ever thought of it, recalled his first terms at Harvard with some discomfort, where he had been one of an under-privileged group, living in a rooming house near Central Square and being only tolerated by those who came from fashionable schools.

Now, almost as if Lee were ill, Jessie Hayward virtually took over the running of the house, frightening Della and irritating Hannah in the process. In fact Lee did not find the extra company unwelcome at this time. He had a rooted objection to discussing his affairs with anyone outside, but this was family, and they could talk and talk and talk over and over the strange desertion that had taken place. Lee telephoned his office and told them he had flu and would not be in for a few days. For the moment his cases, those interesting cases, could go hang.

But being at home did not do much for him, and he mooned about the house, allowing Jessie free rein in everything she suggested. One day they drove to Dartmouth to see the old man, but very little came from it to shed light on what to Lee was still a complete mystery. The only irritating incident of the visit was over lunch, when Jessie asked her father-in-law whether he thought there was a man involved. Henry and his father both pooh-poohed the idea, and then, as it were, turned to Lee seeking confirmation.

Lee put down his knife and fork and said: 'After what has happened I guess anything is possible, but I'd say we lived in as near complete harmony, Ann and I, as you can get in this world. There's never been another man in her life – that I *would* have known – I mean in the years past – and there's never been another woman in mine.'

'It's the boats,' said Simon Hayward with conviction. 'When she used to come down here she would be busy as a bird dog, in and out and up and down the causeway. It's just the boats and the sea.'

Nevertheless, the suspicion, once put into words, did not altogether go away, and when they got home he began to search through his wife's papers and personal belongings. All he found was a very long letter from Althea, dated February, going into great detail as to what their life in New Zealand, in the Bay of Islands, in a boatyard, was really like, and making no attempt to glamorize it; though it was clear from some of the phrases that she by then knew what Ann was about. One of her sentences ran: 'I know you say Lee would loathe it all, but do you not think it worth giving him the choice?'

Other than this, the only contributory evidence was a drawer full of yachting magazines and brochures about life in New Zealand. As he closed the drawer he thought: 'I *would* have loathed it, every damned minute of it. I loathe the wet messiness of small boats, the fiddling with ropes, the scrape of sails, the smell of tar. And I'm easily seasick and I have a prosperous law business which I would not *dream* of leaving. So it would not have been much good her inviting me to throw everything up here and go with her! The option that Althea did not think it worth suggesting was that Ann should throw her silly romantic dreams into the discard and continue to live her life in Concord.'

A couple of days later he was in the garden and saw Letty Heinz leaving the house, about to mount her bicycle.

He called to her, and she turned eagerly, her face upturned, ready to smile at him if his expression permitted it. His expression did not permit it. He had a sneaking suspicion that she still knew more about the whole affair than she had so far told him. She might have encouraged Ann in her wild and scatter-brained scheme.

When he did not speak she said: 'I have called in to see Hannah to see if there is any word yet from Mrs Burford.'

'Have you had any?'

'Oh no. I do not expect any – not yet. She promises sometime she will write.'

'Do you know if she is travelling alone?'

'Oh yes, I think so. At least, she only bought but one ticket.'

'Which way was she travelling?'

'To Los Angeles, and then across the Pacific.'

'Perhaps she was joining someone – some other guy.'

Letty looked up at him quickly. 'She never mentioned anyone. I do not think that is to be considered possible, Mr Burford. That was not – never in her thoughts.'

Some birds were quarrelling in a nearby maple.

She said: 'You were very much in love with her.'

He fingered the Phi Beta Kappa ring on his left hand. 'We were deeply attached to each other.'

'Do you not have any sympathy for what she has done?'

'Perhaps I could find some sympathy if I could understand.'

'I assure you she was not happy to leave.'

'But she did leave.'

'She said before she left that she hoped you would understand – and accept. She said she thought you loved her enough for that.'

'Never mind love. It is a betrayal of our – our wonderful companionship.'

Letty was silent.

He wondered why he so disliked her.

'Your family are staying long, Mr Burford?'

'No, leaving tomorrow.'

'I'm sure you will have made all – all arrangements?'

'Some, yes. Not all.'

'I do not know if I can help any more.'

'In what way?'

'If later on you wanted to play bridge. It was just a thought. I would arrange it, the way I did for your wife.' When he did not answer she went on: 'I simply mean, I know the house and could make sandwiches or bake a cake or whatever . . .'

She knew the house.

He said: 'I can manage.' And then, aware of his brusqueness and his own reputation for good manners, 'But thank you. If I think more of it I'll let you know.'

V

BEFORE HENRY and Jessie left Jessie said: 'It'll be too early for you to make any plans, Lee, but I suppose you won't go on living in this big house alone.'

'I've decided nothing yet.'

'Naturally. Shall you keep both the maids on, d'you think?'

'Probably. Hannah's a good worker. And Della is always willing and helps with the garden when she hasn't anything else to do.'

'There are one or two very nice apartments for sale in Boston itself,' said Henry. 'There's a duplex just come on the market – near the Esplanade, overlooking the river. In time you might find that more convenient. You've always been a bit far out.'

'I shan't do anything in a hurry,' Lee said.

'Naturally,' said Jessie again.

By now of course everyone in the neighbourhood knew of Ann's going. Their reaction varied from the quietly sympathetic to the boisterously cheerful 'well, I'm sure you'll soon snap out of it' brigade. It wasn't, as some of them said between themselves, as if she'd *died*. She would come back; almost certainly she would come back. And if not, well, that was it. Maybe, they whispered, she'd found, or would find, a young lover. Fifty-eight was a funny age for a woman: past child-bearing but not, oh not, past wanting a bit of action. Sometimes at that age you couldn't keep them away from it. Lee was a good-looking, good-tempered man, but lawyers tended to get dried up, prosy. Who would blame her if she found she could do better? There was also a little wry amusement among those who did not like the Burfords so well, that their formal marriage had at last fallen apart.

Lee went to San Francisco for a few days' vacation. He had many good friends there but none of them had had any recent letters from Ann. Yet the friendship he was offered had the effect of making him feel more alone. He and Ann had been constant travellers, and he suspected it would be quite hard to discover some corner of the world where her shadow did not fall. The one place he was certain he would not visit was New Zealand.

He was almost relieved to get home. It was absurd to feel the break, the desertion, less among the most familiar of surroundings; but at home his work took up the days and often the evenings. He brought more work home with him. He thought of resuming the bridge evenings, which he had enjoyed, but could not summon up the enterprise. Letty Heinz had offered to help him, but Letty had dropped out of his life and he had no wish to bring her back into it again.

A few weeks later, a letter from Ann.

Darling Lee,

The longer I am away from you the greater the feeling of enormity oppresses me at what I have done. Yet I hope and pray that once the terrible feeling of the first break has passed you will be finding life comfortable and easy without me. I have now reached Auckland and Althea has met me, and we are staying a night at this hotel in Queen Street before embarking on the last stage of my journey tomorrow. The weather is lovely, the people are lovely and everyone most welcoming.

The trip has been tiring, constantly bumpy, and we had to spend an extra day on Fiji because an engine was malfunctioning. So we arrived a day late, but with the constant time changes I honestly cannot tell whether it is Wednesday or Thursday! There's a lovely bridge across the harbour here, just opened, which is as handsome as Sydney's. It is a fine city, with sea on almost all sides, and I bought some postcards of it, but then it seemed too trivial to send them.

We leave for Kerikeri on the Bay of Islands tomorrow, and I am eagerly anticipating what I shall find there. Forgive me for my eagerness, which is certainly not motivated by any eagerness to leave *you*. But it is a strange and wonderfully exciting world! We shall be at the extreme northernmost tip of New Zealand, with 700 miles of water between us and the next substantial piece of land,

which is New Caledonia. (Or maybe only 500 to Sydney.
I will learn more in due course.)

Dearest love,

Ann

Their next-door neighbours, if you could call them that,
were the Carters, who lived on flatter ground about a
hundred yards up the road. Bel Carter, who did not play
bridge, took to walking over on a Sunday evening to see him
and take a coffee or a highball. She seemed concerned for his
future and obviously wished to share his thoughts more
personally than he wished to share them with her. Bel Canto,
as Ann always called her because she had a fair voice and
aired it frequently at local concerts, was fortyish, a tall, dark
woman with the dignity which came of the long possession
of private money. Her dignity did not prevent her from
having an eye for an eligible man, but Lee hoped her interest
in him was only that of a friendly neighbour. Her husband,
who was as old as Lee, was attached to Boston University
and wrote books on maritime history. Bel was very relieved,
she said, that Lee had no immediate intention of altering his
lifestyle. The usual questions about Ann and the prospects
of her possible return had already been exhaustively
discussed.

Bel said: 'Is that Mrs Heinz in your employment still?'

'She never was – except for a while in '56 when Ann was
convalescing. Why?'

'I've seen her about the house once or twice.'

'When?'

'Oh, last week. Thursday, I think it was. And the week
before. Pretty woman, isn't she.'

'She was Ann's friend – I hardly know her.'

Later he asked Hannah, who said, 'Oh yes, sor. She

brought the kitchen curtains back. Mrs Burford had asked her to repair them. Then she came back this week to bring a cake she had baked, and just to see how we was managing.'

Weekends were hardest to fill. With the summery weather he was able to play golf most of the two days, only stopping when he was too tired to go on and therefore almost too tired to feel lonely. On wet days he drank rather a lot and played bridge at the Club. In lonely moments he tried to concentrate on his practice, and on a paper he was going to read at Boston University advocating a change in the law which would permit lawyers to practise beyond their own state frontiers.

The two maids took it in turns to cook his evening meal, but then Della fell ill so he started eating out three evenings a week. It wasn't an unwelcome change, because Della's Puerto Rican cooking was oily for his taste. One night he went to the Paul Revere on Gray Street and found Letty waiting at the next table. She half smiled at him and he nodded, but after the meal he stopped her when she was disengaged and said: 'I didn't know you worked here.'

'Well, I am sort of temporary while the other girls take their holidays; but I am hoping it will become permanent.'

'I have heard from Mrs Burford.'

'Oh, have you? How is she?'

'Well enough, it seems. She hadn't then reached wherever she is going, so it was just a letter to say she had arrived in New Zealand.'

'Oh . . . Oh, I see.'

There seemed nothing more to add. Then she said: 'Have you been playing bridge, Mr Burford?'

'Quite a lot. But not at the house.'

Letty Heinz said: 'I am glad you are playing – even if not at home.'

He hesitated. 'Perhaps one ought to begin again.'

She did not reply.

He said: 'You offered to come if I was arranging bridge at home.'

'Of course. I would be very pleased.'

'What about Wednesday next?'

'I am sorry, I am on duty here. I could come Thursday.'

'Make it Thursday then.'

They were about to separate when she said: 'How are Hannah and Della?'

'Della is off sick. That is why I am eating out.'

'I am sorry Della is sick.'

'Not that I enjoy Della's cooking very much, so it makes a change.'

'Can Hannah not come all the time?'

'I believe not. She has a family of her own—'

'Mr Burford.' As he was turning away. 'Saturdays I work here and Sundays at the church, but I am free on Thursday. Would you like it if I came early and prepared a meal?'

He turned the ring on his finger. 'Certainly. It would be a change.'

'I will try to be there about six thirty.'

'Make it dinner for four,' he said. 'I will ask the Macphersons.'

Her meal on Thursday reminded him of those she had cooked while she was staying at the house during Ann's convalescence. He had forgotten what a good bridge player she was – they won – and the Macphersons – a fellow lawyer and his wife – seemed to find her acceptable. Sitting watching her play a hand he thought her looks were more Germanic than Scandinavian, and wondered if that had subliminally prejudiced him against her. He always tried to be rational and tolerant about these things, but it was only fifteen years since he had been fighting Hitler and he couldn't yet quite forget it.

She was attractive tonight, her hair pulled back in a pony tail, a striped blue and white blouse with high white collar and turned-up cuffs, and a navy blue embroidered bolero.

He ought to let bridge take up more of his time, he thought. It was a preoccupation, a relaxation, a way of exercising his brain in a different, entirely unlegal but largely mathematical way. His sense of loss, of angry, hurt bereavement could be kept more at arm's length by the stimulation and the challenge.

When the evening was over the Macphersons offered Letty a lift home; she said she must stay to clear away but he said no, go, Hannah will do it in the morning. As he shook hands with her he said: 'I'll be in touch with you again. Thank you.'

'Thank you, Mr Burford.'

That night in bed he looked at the empty bed beside his and thought of his wife. To begin to do so at this stage of an evening was a sure recipe for insomnia for he could not stop dwelling on the happy times they had had together. To counteract it tonight he tried to think of the bridge hands he had just held and played – and won. It had been perhaps the most acceptable evening he had spent since Ann left. He wondered if he had misjudged Letty Heinz.

VI

USUALLY HE had his first round of golf on Sunday mornings with three medics: they started very early before most people had finished their pancakes and cereals. But one Sunday one doctor was on holiday and another couldn't make it, so Lee played alone with his own doctor, James Amis.

It was a pleasant day and Lee played well. He ventured a joke. He had a dry sense of humour and a fair sense of fun, but he had not been in a joking mood for the last few weeks.

James Amis cocked a professional eyebrow at him. 'You're looking better today, Lee. Are things beginning to sort themselves out a bit?'

'No,' said Lee emphatically. 'But I guess it's six weeks after the operation.'

'That's another way of putting it. I'm sure Ann will want you to go on enjoying life without her. And she may yet choose to return, although—'

'I suppose,' Lee said. 'Apart from the loss of my partner, who has been, who *was* such a good partner for so long – apart from that it has, all this has been a blow to my pride – ego if you like. I think of what I must in some way have desperately lacked that a woman should suddenly, after all those years, should suddenly decide she couldn't live with me any longer, so she up-sticks and goes small-boat-sailing on the other side of the world!'

'I don't think it was quite like that.'

'You tell me what it has been like, then!'

They played another hole. James Amis felt it would be better for their golf if he allowed the subject to lapse there. And yet, perhaps it was his duty . . .

'Lee.'

'Yes?'

'I was going to add that she may come back but that I don't *think* she will.'

'I'm not sure that I would want her now.'

'Oh, come. It's a pity if there is this – this feeling of rancour. I wish I could mend it. Perhaps I ought to try.'

'Did you know anything about this beforehand? Did you know she was going?'

'Not at all. I was only aware of her unrest.'

Lee hesitated between a three and a four iron, then put them both back.

'Unrest with me. Maybe I took her too much for granted.'

'I don't think it was that. As she no doubt told you, she wanted, she wants to try another life while there is still time.'

Lee made his stroke. The ball pitched short but it was a good lie.

'So. She was sick of her life here. The fact that we had been happy together for so long didn't count a button.'

'It counted a *lot*. Believe me, it counted a lot.' James Amis went in search of his ball, which had landed in the rough. When they eventually finished the hole and had come together again, he said: 'One thing I should tell you. It may not be vital but it may help to explain ... You remember that operation she had for a cyst on the womb?'

'Of course.'

'It was cancerous.'

Lee stared. 'I'd no idea. My God, I'd no idea. Why didn't you tell me?'

'She said I must not. She swore me to absolute secrecy.'

Lee followed the other man along the narrow path that led to the fourteenth tee.

'And it has recurred?' He bit his lip. 'No, of course, that

couldn't be the case. One doesn't rush off to New Zealand if . . .' He stopped.

'It hadn't recurred. It hasn't recurred. She came into hospital for a check-up for a couple of days in February while you were on that consultation in Denver. She was absolutely clear. A clean bill. It couldn't have been better. I told her to go home and forget it.'

'Then why . . . ?'

Amis frowned at the fairway. It was three hundred yards before one got to the bumpy ground before the hole.

'Her mother died of cancer, you know. And her grandmother.'

'Ah . . . I'd forgotten. So there's a greater risk of its recurrence.'

The doctor took out a two wood. 'Marginally . . . I suppose she looked on life slightly differently after 1957. She was fifty-six then . . . Of course anybody of fifty-six must be aware of the loss of youth, of the prospect of old age. But most people carry on without doing anything about it. I guess she felt she should do something about it.'

'By getting away? Escaping?'

Amis drove off. It was a hooked shot and landed again in the rough. Lee followed, and sliced his so that it went into the rough on the other side of the fairway. Lee said again, 'She felt she was escaping?'

'Not sure. But in a sense, yes.'

'But she can't escape that.'

Amis slid his club back into his bag. 'Nor can anyone else if their number comes up. But I reckon for age fifty-eight she's as healthy a woman as I've examined in ten years. Believe me. As I told her, there's no reason whatever to think of anything else. But all the same I guess she feels her life is

under a minimal threat. It probably provided the spring-
board to set things off. So she's jumped, and good luck to
her, however it turns out. I'm only sorry it's snarled up your
life.'

'It certainly has done that.'

The result of their last shots separated them again for a
considerable time. On the green Amis said: 'I hope you'll
think about rebuilding it.'

'Rebuilding what?'

'Your life.'

'I haven't even begun to think of that.'

'Well, you should. You should get things squared away
and run before the wind for a bit. See how things go.'

'I'd be glad, in the circumstances,' Lee said, 'if you could
avoid nautical terms.'

'Sorry. But how long before you retire?'

'Oh . . . three years, eight years, it's very much for me to
choose – so long as I don't lose my faculties.'

'You're very fit, you know. A bit overweight. But no age
really. You might even remarry.'

'I don't think that's on. Anyway, I'm past all that.'

'It would surprise me if you were. Did it not still go on
between you and Ann?'

'Oh, more or less. Not this last three or four years
much. It tailed off. These things do. It made no difference –
no apparent difference – to the feelings we had for each
other.'

'Did you and Ann never have a falling out?'

'I don't remember one.'

'I thought not. You were freaks.'

'Thanks a lot.'

'It's not an insult. Everybody said that about you. "Look
at Lee and Ann." It was almost too good to be true.'

'Well, it's proved too good to be true, hasn't it. Everyone must be congratulating themselves on the downfall.'

'No, they're not. Not except a few bitches. Most people I've talked to have been genuinely sympathetic. And if Ann *doesn't* come back, well, there'll be plenty of unattached women quite willing to take on a model husband.'

VII

DELLA'S ILLNESS proved to be pregnancy, and in July she left to get married. Letty offered to come a couple of evenings a week to cook his supper; this was on the evenings when she was not at the restaurant. He accepted the offer, but reluctantly, for he was still slightly suspicious of her. He still felt she might have had some hand in Ann's leaving; but in late July Letty brought up a letter that she had just received from Ann. It contained little that he did not know, but though couched in affectionate terms it said nothing to justify his suspicions.

Quite often now they arranged bridge for one or both of her evenings, and it worked pretty well. For bridge, he had to admit, she had a talent.

He gradually settled into a more comfortable routine: Hannah looked after most things, and Letty was a backup who did not intrude unless invited. When he happened to think about it he reckoned that Letty Heinz too would probably remarry soon. Personable, separated from her husband whom she never saw, her son a drop-out whom she never saw, she was ripe to be snapped up by any spare man that came along. Although, for all he knew, she might already be living with some layout in her flat in Gray Street.

Anyway, none of it was any concern of his.

He knew the white Episcopalian church she attended. It was on the edge of town and looked as if it had been put up with a child's building blocks. It was surrounded by small white houses which matched, each with its yard inside a paling fence.

He wondered where she had gotten her looks – from her Norwegian father? His legal brain, which still functioned efficiently, told him that Letty Heinz might have other ideas, might instead just possibly be negotiating herself into a position of indispensability in *his* household. She might even have ambitions for something more than merely becoming his housekeeper. He dismissed this as ridiculous. Certainly she never made the slightest move to suggest she had anything else in mind. Whatever else he liked or disliked about her he had to acknowledge that she kept her distance and treated him with respect. There was never a hint of challenge in her look, or a coy glance.

He had to go away to a case in Springfield. It was a difficult, exacting legal battle – one of those in which points of law seemed to become more important than points of justice – and when it was over, and successfully over, he travelled home with two of his partners who had been involved also. They talked and joked a lot, for it had been a famous victory. Sometimes Lee joined in, but mostly it was the other two, discussing the legal niceties; and they discreetly observed that the senior partner was still feeling his loss.

The case had been late ending, and now there was a delay on the line. Presently Sam McDonald said, as they'd been held up so much, how would it be if Lee came and had a meal with him and Maudie, and he could drive home afterwards.

Lee blinked and came out of his preoccupation and said thanks all the same, Sam, but no, there'd be food waiting for him. He did not know, in fact, whether anything would be waiting for him. He was expected home today but earlier. He should have rung but hadn't. It was one of Letty's evenings – but a non-bridge one – and he supposed she might wait a bit. Somehow, phoning to say he was delayed was too reminiscent of things past.

Yet just at the moment when Sam spoke he had been thinking of Letty Heinz. This was all pretty stupid. He didn't know if he even liked the woman, yet here he was day-dreaming about her. He came to the conclusion that he was the victim of a mass psychological conspiracy. The con-clusion of his friends was: 'Look at poor Lee Burford, all on his *own*, he ought to have somebody living in, *ministering* properly to his needs.' No less than three times in the last six weeks he had been invited out and found that at the dinner table he was seated next to some eligible widow or divorcee whom he hardly knew. They were all kind, attentive, well-dressed, mid-fifties or younger. Nice enough. But who wanted them? Not he. He wanted Ann's companionship, and since he couldn't have that he would do without. (Sometimes still when he lay in bed at night he fancied he could hear her breathing in the bed next to him.)

Both his companions on the train, as it happened, were divorced and remarried – and there were stories that Fitz-patrick's second marriage was already showing signs of wear and tear. His marriage to Ann had been something special, not to be repeated, not to be followed, not to be betrayed – however she had betrayed it – by some flippant affair or remarriage with the first woman who appeared in his sights.

When they arrived at the station they picked up their cars and made their individual ways home. Lee had much the farthest to drive, and it was nine by the time he turned into his garage, and he was pleased to see there was a light in the house. His mouth a little dry, he went up to the front door, put in his key and went in. As he put his case down in the hall Letty came out of the kitchen, wiping her hands and half smiling at him.

'You waited,' he said.

'Yes ... You said you'd be back but they reported fog on the news. I was not sure.'

'Thank you for waiting.'

He went across and kissed her. She accepted it as if it was the most natural thing in the world, and then went up the stairs ahead of him to pour him a drink and to listen to what he had to say.

VIII

SHE STAYED the night, but not of course with him. She continued just as usual, cycling up from Concord two evenings a week, and in the light evenings cycling back again. Life continued on its course.

But it was not *quite* the same. He had never kissed Hannah, nor ever would. He often wondered why he had done it on this occasion. Had he intended it as a gesture of appreciation because she had waited for him to come back? It was not unpleasant. She was a pretty woman. He hadn't kissed many women apart from Ann in the last thirty-odd years, except for the society kiss when you met someone at a party. To be truthful, it hadn't been very much more he had given Letty, just that it seemed to have a greater significance. If he had kissed Hannah she would have thought he'd gone out of his mind. Letty certainly hadn't seemed to think that. He almost got the impression that she had tried to return the kiss.

Talk between them became a little more personal after this. She explained that her own marriage had broken up when Carl Heinz's firm had promoted him and moved him to Virginia. She hadn't wanted to leave, so he had gone alone. It clearly hadn't been much of a marriage by then. He was now living in Parkersbury and had set up house with another woman. It occurred to Lee that Carl probably wasn't paying Letty enough for an allowance, but it was not his business to interfere.

Letty had not seen her son Leon for some time. Neither had his father. The boy was now almost eighteen and living off welfare. His mother assured Lee there was no real badness in the boy, he was just easily led and influenced. He'd always been affectionate towards her but he wanted to live with his friends, not his parents.

She herself, she told him, had been born in Brixton, England, where her father Christian Larsen had been employed in a wood-pulp and cellulose factory. When the factory closed the family went back to Norway, where her father worked as a railway clerk; and she had finished her schooling in Norway.

. . . Well, here he was, Lee Pemberton Burford, head of one of the most successful law practices in New England, recently deserted by his wife, and already feeling something – a little of something – only a little of something, but it was there – for a woman whom he still wasn't quite sure he even liked. He, in his seventh decade, grey-haired, with a lined face and an overweight body, who had spent all his adult life among talk of depositions, interrogatories, subpoenas and federal indictments, having thoughts and feelings about a young married woman out of his class and with an unknown background, and with not the slightest interest in him or his affairs.

Did she anyway consider him impossibly old to have any feelings at all? Nearly twenty-five years – more than twenty anyway – was an enormous gap. If she was looking for somebody to replace Carl Heinz, she no doubt had no interest at all in anyone over fifty.

But of course to someone in Letty Heinz's position he might be looked on as a social and financial catch. To hell with it. It was absurd, unimportant and unworthy of consideration.

A few weeks later another letter from Ann.

Darling, darling,

This may be the last letter for some time as we are going on a pretty prolonged trip: just three of us, Althea and I and a woman called Josie, who's over sixty but as tough as old boots. Between us our ages add up to almost 150, and our boat, a 30-foot clinker-built yawl, is about forty years old, so we are a geriatric quartet! We plan to sail across the Tasman Sea and I am fantastically looking forward to it.

I have bought a small cottage, just two up and two down with a splendid view over the little harbour and bay, and one sees wonderful sunsets. You would be welcome to come.

Of course you will know what the legal position is – afraid I don't – but as a deserting wife I do not feel entitled to any allowance from you *at all*. Nor do I *want* one, for it is cheap living here, and the little legacy my mother left me just covers things nicely.

I very much hope you are settling down by now. Your letter sounded sad, and I do not want you to be sad on my account. Nor hurt. Nor deprived. I am finding a new life which at present is a constant challenge in a way that living at Concord was not. Once again, I swear to you that I remember our marriage as a period of great happiness. Please be happy again – as I am.

Ann

P.S. Arum lilies grow here like weeds, and geraniums bloom all the year round.

IX

ANN'S PERSONALITY was still strong in the house. Most of her clothes were in the wardrobe still, her shoes in drawers, on stands, under her bed. Cosmetics and perfumes dotted her dressing table. After another couple of months Lee asked Hannah if she would tidy them up: throw nothing away but put things in boxes and label them, move most of her clothes on hangers into one of the spare rooms. Hanna said could she invite Mrs Heinz to help. Lee said yes. He omitted to say what he should have said, which was, please do it all before I get home. As it was, he found them in the last stages, and was a little surprised to find them both in tears.

Hannah said: 'Ooh, sor, she was a good lady. I wish her well, but she should not have gone.' Hannah went out of the room, leaving Lee staring awkwardly at Letty, who was by the window blowing her nose.

She looked up. 'I knew her so short a time but she has been my best friend. I do not think she should have gone neither.'

Lee looked round the room. It smelt of Ann's scent.

Letty said: 'Do not suppose we have been doing not anything but snuffle and weep. We have been working hard. It is difficult sorting out what should go where. But just before you came in Hannah picked up her scent atomizer and sprayed it across the room, and that gave us a sentimental turn thinking we shall not perhaps see her again.'

He stared at her. 'She has chosen a more exciting life than I could give her. That may be a justification.'

She put away her handkerchief and picked up a couple of nightdresses.

'I suppose it was her dream.'

After a moment he said: 'Do you have dreams? Like that, I mean.'

'Not like that, Mr Burford. I dislike being on the sea.'

He stared at a faded photograph on the wall. It was of Boston after the great fire of 1872. He felt more sympathetic towards Letty than he had ever done before, because of her obvious affection for his lost wife.

He said: 'Is your life dull?'

She sounded surprised. 'Dull? Mine? Why do you ask?'

'I don't know what you do with it – in the daytime, that is.'

'I work at one or two things. And for the Church.'

'Are you religious?'

'It is not very strong, Mr Burford. But perhaps more than most people these days.'

'You never speak of your life in Norway. How long were you there?'

'Ten years.'

'Were there any other children?'

'One brother, Magnus. He was five years older than me.'

'Was?'

'Yes. He died.' After a pause she added: 'I was – very fond of Magnus. I – loved him. My son is like him. Not small like me, but tall and broad-shouldered and blond—'

'A Norseman?'

She smiled. 'Perhaps that is how you would say it.'

He hesitated again, aware of a rare, very unlegal impulse. Hesitated, fingered his ring, then went on.

'Would it give you pleasure to come to Boston sometime and take lunch with me?'

They could hear Hannah banging about downstairs. She had got the vacuum out. 'Hoeing', as Della chose to call it.

'I should greatly enjoy it, Mr Burford. But I do not think it would be quite correct, would it?'

'Why not?'

'I am paid by you for work I do for you. Gentlemen do not take their employees out to lunch.'

'And if this gentleman chose to?'

'I am – not sure. The talk would get around.'

He grunted, aggrieved at her reply; aware that she might have strict convention on her side but irritated by her small-town attitude.

'It is very kind of you,' she said.

'No matter. No doubt you have better things to do.'

'Far from it. I should like to – perhaps later in the year? If you will ask me again. We can talk about Ann.'

'Of course,' he said stiffly.

'I must help Hannah.' She moved to leave the bedroom, then stopped. 'If you will permit it, I should like very much next week to visit my son. I have not seen him since

75

February. I am not sure of his address, but I think I can find him. It may take a day or so.'

'Of course. I shall probably eat at one of my clubs in Boston before coming home.'

'Hannah perhaps could come more often next week.'

'No. Keep the rota as it is. And tell Hannah not to bother with dinner. I shall be eating out tonight.'

She said: 'At the Paul Revere?'

'No. Not at the Paul Revere.'

CHAPTER FOUR

I

RAMADAN HAD just begun, and although Agadir was a sophisticated modern port and holiday resort, the Muslims in the four-hundred-year-old Kasbah on the hill were preparing for their long fast. They listened also to soothsayers, for it was a tradition that tomorrow was the night of destiny on which the fates of men should be foretold and decided for the year ahead. Some of the soothsayers, particularly El Ufrani, foresaw a forbidding future. Ufrani, who was reputed to be a hundred years old, saw calamity before him, a judgement on the godless population for not adhering more closely to the laws of the Prophet. He disapproved of the development of the town as a seaside resort to which infidels flocked in their hundreds – soon to be thousands. He disagreed vehemently with M. Bouamrani, the Governor, who welcomed the mushroom growth and pronounced that Agadir should soon become another San Francisco. He disapproved of the Casino, where Moroccan women, their faces uncovered, gambled with the French, the English, the Germans. He disapproved of the naked flesh on the beaches. Most of all he disapproved of the frivolity and godlessness of his own flock who observed Ramadan reluctantly and, he suspected, sometimes only in part, but feasted noisily as soon as dark fell and stayed so feasting and drinking into the small hours.

77

He said ill things would come, and instanced as a warning a couple of earth tremors which had occurred earlier in the month. The rest of the population treated them as nothing important. The last really serious upset had happened more than two hundred years ago: these latest rumblings, like the rumblings of thunder, raised no more than a lifted eyebrow and a philosophical shrug.

II

LAURA LEGRAND woke at seven on this first morning of her holiday, and saw the sun shining through the slats of the venetian blind. She rolled over, looked at a pink pouting face beside her and remembered that she had taken Françoise into her bed last night.

There was often competition among the 'girls' for the other woman's loving attentions, and while Laura generally preferred Vicky it was necessary to spread her favours. Vicky was the youngest of the three, and she was more or less responsible for this holiday, having had a stroke of luck with one of her clients. A rich property owner had stayed long enough to be confidential and Vicky had learned of a new development that was planned near the Quai de Varennes in Bordeaux. She had consulted her old friend Laura who only two years ago had come from Paris, in despair at being hounded by the police, and opened a Maison de Passes, quite near where Vicky operated. Unlike Vicky, Laura was a businesswoman, and she at once consulted a lawyer, and found a small *épicerie* for sale in the centre of the proposed development area. Having ascertained that it was a *propriété foncière libre de toute obligation*, she had then approached

Françoise, another refugee, and together they had persuaded
Vicky to buy the shop; the three of them had pooled their
limited resources to pay for it. It didn't matter, Laura argued,
if they must temporarily carry a large mortgage. She could
put her cousin in to run the *épicerie*, and they would hardly
lose in the long term even if the development didn't come
off.

But the development did come off, and the powerful
property company found itself thwarted by a solitary shop
whose freehold it could not buy and which held up the
project. Having carried the mortgage and the responsibility
for nearly a year, the three ladies were in no mood to be
hustled, or even intimidated, and negotiations had gone on
for a further six months before a bargain was struck. As a
result, and even after paying off the cousin and the bank and
all the legal fees, they were richer than they had ever been in
their lives, better off probably than they had ever dared to
hope, and were now determined to celebrate and to spend
money while the sun shone.

The sun was certainly shining this morning; a shaft of it
fell directly on Françoise's snub nose, but it did not wake
her. Laura regarded her friend dispassionately. She was the
least attractive and the least successful of the three; she had
a thick Burgundian accent, which she had never tried to
amend, and broadening hips which her clients did not seem
to mind. She was a good-natured young woman and not
choosy about whom she took in. But she had never run a
house, like Laura, nor had private clients, like Vicky. For a
while, when she first worked in Paris, she had been a battery
tart, getting through as many as a hundred clients daily.

Like Laura, she had been driven out of Paris by the over-
zealous attentions of the police. Laura had known with a
sense of foreboding, when votes were given to women, that

they would exert pressure on their menfolk to close the high-class Maisons Closes, where you could put on a show of elegance and it was not just bang, bang, bang all day long. Girls were expected to *talk* to their men in such superior places, if the men so wished. Great elegance and the strictest cleanliness prevailed. No girls ever went outside touting for custom. And when he left, a man must agree that he had been satisfied before he was expected to pay.

Both the younger women had worked at Laura's house in the early days, when times were still good. Françoise, having had a child, which died, had been down on her luck, and Laura had taken pity on her, invited her to come for a trial period to see if she could adjust to their more cultured ways. In those days Françoise had a rural charm and prettiness, looked like a Dutch milkmaid, Laura always said; and there were men who fancied that type – even liked her to dress up in clogs and the rest, though minus some normally essential garments. So Françoise had adapted her style, though without ever quite losing the bad habits learned in the Rue de Courcey. But when she had another child, which lived this time, she had said she wanted to return and work in Dijon, and Laura had not tried to stop her.

Vicky was a different sort altogether. Though brought up by a drunken mother and a succession of noisy extrovert stepfathers, she had wanted to be the lady right from the start. She had a splendid figure: wasp waist, long slim legs, perfect bust, could have been the Number One in the Maison Laura. But her choosiness had just been too much; she sometimes quarrelled with clients for not agreeing to their sexual whims; and often there was contention because she would not let her customers kiss her. 'Kissing is too intimate,' she would protest as she opened her legs. There had never been any doubt in her mind as to the profession she wanted to follow, but her schoolgirl reading had always been about the great kept ladies of the world, and it was her ambition to go private as soon as she could.

So Laura was not surprised when she had said she was going to marry a Bordelais doctor and had left the house. (Not that she ever did marry him in the end, but she stayed in Bordeaux and worked up a small clientele of her own.)

They had kept in touch over the last few years, chiefly by telephone on a Sunday morning since neither of them was really a letter writer; but their amiable friendship had been maintained. Both the younger women fancied themselves a bit in love with Laura, and their little amorous pranks made a refreshing change from normal professional work.

Françoise stirred and coughed but did not wake up. What a podge she was getting, Laura thought; she needed to go on a diet, a strict regime. Little chance there was on a holiday: she'd be into the ice cream and the chocolate cakes as soon as she stirred. Nor would she take advice. She must have put on three kilos this last year. If she became a great porker she'd lose her livelihood.

Not that any of them was exactly a Venus de Milo these days, Laura thought. Even Vicky was thickening and losing her complexion. Not so surprising with herself: fifty-five next birthday, and it had been a hard life after being turned out of Paris, but these two should still be in their prime. The total profit from the sale of the shop was still not completely assessed, but with luck they might not *have* to work again, or at least could take it more easily. Laura wanted to go back to Paris with her share. One did not need to go crashing back into the big time, with all the hazards and hassles of police raids and paying protection; there were a few lucrative little sidelines she thought she could build up. It would be a relief not to be on the go all hours God sent.

While she had been helping her cousin Étienne in Marseilles – where she had gone after being driven out of Paris – it really had been that: open from eleven in the morning till two the following morning. A lot of housework thrown in, cooking and cleaning; no proper wages, only so much a customer and relying on tips. And in Marseilles particularly there had been the business of 'foreigners'. Sometimes Algerians would flood in, and some of the girls, not fancying them, would lock themselves in the lavatory. Then the men would turn nasty and threaten to break the place up. It was best not to call the police, even in Marseilles, because that way you drew attention to your calling. Not that the police were above dropping in for a quick one when they felt like it.

Anyway, good riddance to all that. It was a sunny morning and they were on their holidays – real holidays this time – staying in a posh hotel; none of them had had anything like it before. Laura eased herself out of bed, stared disgustedly at her bloated face in the mirror; *mon Dieu*, that needed attention before any other inhabitant of the hotel saw it. Particularly that tall thin man whose knee joints cracked, the one she had sat next to on the plane. He'd looked a bit oncoming, that fellow. Not that she wanted any action of that sort, but vanity told her that she preferred to reject him, not be rejected by his indifference.

She went to the telephone and ordered breakfast for three. What luxury! This really was a smart hotel, and a white-coated waiter would come in with an overflowing tray. Then they could all sit out on the latticed balcony on canvas chairs and sip coffee and bite croissants and chatter together and view the scene and make plans for the day.

She waddled over to the bed and pulled the thin sheet

back, exposing the fact that Françoise had been sleeping naked. Laura gave the big round bottom a hearty smack, and went across to wake Vicky. Then she pulled up the blinds with a vigorous rattle.

The sun streamed out of a cloudless but hot and sultry sky, the swimming-pool glimmered among the palms and the ferns; beyond was the sea, well out at the moment, glassy and colourless like a giant jellyfish with a white lip. A few people already sat by the pool under striped umbrellas. The beach was dotted too, and near the sea a football match was in progress.

III

THE HOTEL Saada was six storeys high, square but elegant, with white stone balconies and red-striped sunblinds to every window. It was the design of one of the new young architects who were springing up in Morocco and putting up fine, elegant buildings, as aesthetically pleasing as any in the world. It had been open only five years and at this stage was full.

Matthew Morris was among the first up. Always an early, optimistic riser, even though his industry had never quite matched his enterprise.

In a blue linen shirt and white shorts he breakfasted off orange juice and apricot jam with croissants and lovely strong coffee. Then he strolled out into the sun. It was pretty hot – hotter than he had ever expected in February. The temperature on the thermometer by the pool registered 30° C in the shade. That must be about 86° F by his reckoning. One would have to look out for sunburn on the first day.

But the sun was hazy and the sea looked only moderately inviting. A howling dog had disturbed him in the night.

He wasn't fond of pools so he strolled down to the beach with bathing trunks and a towel. Here a few umbrellas sprouted, centred round a kiosk that served drinks and snacks. He chose an umbrella as far away from the rest as possible, and threw his book down. While he was changing he stared back the way he had come, looked out at the growing ring of hotels, realized the potential of such a scene. The beach was enormous, not only in breadth but in depth. Two full-size football games were being played, yet they were dwarfed in the expanse of fine sand. With the aeroplane opening up every likely sunspot, Agadir was set for a blossoming future. There were great areas of land adjoining the beach as yet undeveloped. With a little money to invest, who knew what the profit might be?

Unfortunately he had no money. (Couldn't really afford this holiday.) The idea of making a big profit by investing in something at the right moment and selling at the right moment strongly appealed to him. Writing novels, whatever the ignorant might think, was grinding hard work. If it paid off, maybe that was an acceptable position. When it didn't pay off, or paid so poorly relative to the amount of work put in, it was hardly a tolerable way of life.

He walked and walked, first over soft sand, then over firm sand, and stepped through the little lip of white into the sea. It was not as warm as he had expected. This after all was the Atlantic. But it was the contrast with the exceptional temperature of the air. He swam along towards some rocks, then lay floating for a time just enjoying himself. It was worth coming, just for this.

He wondered when he should ring Edouard de Blaye. Without any particular effort on his part, he had come to know a number of influential people. A Wykehamist, single, in his twenties, good-mannered, with a keen sense of humour and enjoyment, able to play the piano and the guitar, fluent in three languages, fond of the arts, he was a natural for the invitation to dinner or a weekend. This had been even more so in Paris than in London; and among his acquaintances, or friends, was a slim blond Norman Frenchman whose father was the very rich Baron de Blaye.

They hadn't seen each other for more than a year, but Edouard had told Matthew that his father had built a luxury winter house in Morocco – at Taroudant, only fifty miles from Agadir – and Edouard had issued a vague but warmly meant invitation to come and see them if he were in the vicinity and would like to spend a few days there. It had been one of the reasons why Matthew had chosen Agadir over other possibilities; it would be agreeable to accept the invitation at the end of his holiday, or earlier if it suited. He had only booked for one week at the Saada. It would be agreeable to spend a few days in luxury – and free luxury – before returning to England and life entirely on his own again, in genteel poverty.

Matthew had never been one of these angry young men – he was too easygoing – but once, when a schoolboy of fifteen, he had run away from home. He got on quite well with his stepfather, who was a successful stockbroker, but he felt he had nothing much in common with him – nor really with his mother either – and did not want to go to Scotland with them. When he was eventually found and brought back he was decidedly unpopular as his disappearance had wrecked their holiday.

He had called himself Matthew Arkell, which was a name he picked out of the obituaries in *The Times*, and had wandered cheerfully with his guitar almost as far west as he could go. Working a day here and there, playing in a pub at nights, he had finished up at a farm at St Just in Penwith, where they had eventually found him. He had good-temperedly explained his case, his reasons for going, his experiences on the road, clearly and without rancour or regret. All very simple, yet all very complex. John Morris had taken him to a psychiatrist, who had told them not to worry, the boy was passing through an identity crisis. 'What rot,' Matthew said when his mother incautiously told him the verdict. 'It isn't that at all. I know damn well who I am, but I also know that who I am is not who I want to be!'

In the end he had written it up in a humorous way after his return to school; and putting it on paper had helped him to sort out his feelings. He won a prize for this effort and it was printed in the school magazine – presumably being thought acceptable because it was home he had run away from, not school.

It was time to go inshore, but his body had grown accustomed to the water, and it no longer felt cold. Rona, he knew, would have loved this, and he felt briefly a heel for not having told her where he was going and invited her to come, possibly, just possibly, with the idea . . .

But it couldn't ever be. She had made her feelings explicit, and she wasn't one to change her mind like a weathercock. There *had* been a girl like that once in Venice, but not Rona. Her mind was too logical; too cool; it had command of her feelings. And to tell the truth, if he could make enough to live on without her, he would be quite content.

If he faced up to the facts, looked at himself in the mirror, weighed life up, he was quite relieved to be out of the married state for a while. He was gregarious, didn't like to be alone, but it was good to have no ties. After all he was not leaving a little wife who depended upon him for support – the very reverse! Rona might miss his lively company, but she would enjoy not having to spend half her salary on him.

He wondered what sort of a temperament Mlle Deschamps possessed. (A glance at the register had told him her name. Nadine Deschamps – some address in Paris.) She was very beautiful. He thought it likely she was connected with the stage or high-class modelling. But alone? She surely had no need to be. Between engagements? Between lovers? Would she have any feelings to spare for him? Perhaps today or tomorrow some dark-chinned young Frenchman would turn up and claim her.

His feet touched sand, and he ploughed out of the water, shaking his head like a dog to rid himself of surplus moisture.

The current and his own energy had taken him well north towards the port. Some Moroccan boys were heading and dribbling a ball. It came towards him and he dribbled it back, tricking a couple of the boys before falling in a heap just short of their improvised goalposts. They giggled and he had another go, forcing it past the grinning lad in goal. Dusting sand as he got up, he waved to them and went on. Some older lads, fishing, eyed him speculatively but clearly concluded that in his bathing trunks he would not have a cigarette to give them. The old town clustered in the shelter of the hill with the Kasbah like a fort on the summit. A dark cloud haze obscured the sky behind; it might have been smog except that there was no industry to create it.

A yellow dog was rolling in the sand, perhaps to rid itself of fleas. When it saw Matthew it stood up and came towards him, tail wagging. He had seen two other dogs of similar size and colour playing around in the sand. They seemed to have no owners but they looked neither ill-fed nor ill-treated.

Being welcomed and patted, this one decided to follow Matthew for about half a mile before finding some other interest and trotting off towards the sea.

Then Matthew saw the girl. She had just come onto the beach and was spreading her towel under an umbrella. She also had chosen an umbrella as far away from the rest as possible, but in a different direction from his own. She was wearing a white bikini, and her slender limbs were already lightly tanned as if not unaccustomed to the sun. He picked up his own towel and, since there were still umbrellas to spare, walked over and chose one about twenty yards from her. His intention had been to go in and ring Edouard de Blaye, but that could wait.

The heat was so considerable that his body had dried completely on the way back; his hair was only just damp at the base of the neck. He clasped his knees and watched the French girl go in to swim. What a walk! One supposed she had been taught, but it simply looked elegant and wonderfully assured. His mind drifted off to imagine some emergency in which he could be of incalculable service to her and so begin a friendship in which she was eagerly grateful to him and anxious to be his friend. But could you, dare you try something on with a woman with a walk like that?

A shadow moved across his sunbed. 'Hi, Matt, enjoying the view? Nice bit of stuff over there, isn't she. Gor, makes you feel you've been wasting your life!'

Jack Frazier. In white slacks which looked as if they'd never been on before, short-sleeved scarlet shirt, floppy sunhat. Matthew had noticed earlier that they were in adjoining bedrooms on the second floor. Frazier's thin brown aquiline face looked darker under the hat: he would have passed for a Moroccan. The inevitable damp cigarette end smouldered at the corner of his mouth, and the small suitcase was tucked under his arm.

'Never known it like this before. Least, not in February. I reckon it's the Chergui.'

'The what?'

'The Chergui. Usually we get sea breezes here, but this is the hot wind from the Sahara. Phew! What time is it?'

'Ten thirty.'

Frazier fiddled with his watch. 'Always forget to change it.'

'You not swimming?' Matthew asked.

'Maybe. Not yet, though. Waiting for my car. I ordered it while I was in Casablanca. Said nine thirty. But everything's late now, since the French left. Slack, y'know. You mark my words. All these wonderful roads the French built: they're all going to pot. Give 'em a few years to slip back. The Arabs are all the same.'

'Are you French?' Matthew asked.

Frazier looked at him sharply. 'Why d'you ask?'

'I just thought you might be. I know enough French to know that you speak it without an English accent.'

'Ah, hum, yes, well.' Frazier kicked at the sand. 'Haven't lived in France for donkey's years.' He looked at his watch to make sure he had got it right. 'Wonder if those bastards have brought the car yet.'

Frazier was off. As he moved away he said: 'I got some business this morning. Maybe I'll swim this afternoon. See you.'

After he had gone Matthew closed his eyes. The sultry day had given him a headache. He must have dozed off, because he opened his eyes and the sea was empty. He screwed up his eyes to look for a bobbing head: none there.

He half started up in alarm, then saw the French girl had returned to her sunbed. She was just lying down and rubbing her legs with a sun cream.

Being olive-skinned, Matthew browned easily without burning, and usually he didn't bother with cream – it messed up one's clothes – but this sun, though a bit hazy, might be fairly lethal.

He dozed again – very strange to be so sleepy and lethargic. Must ring Edouard. Elevenish was a suitable time. He woke to see the stray yellow dog inching its way into the shadow of Mlle Deschamps's umbrella. In spite of indolent attempts on her part to wave it away it crept, belly on sand, a little bit closer.

Matthew got up, walked across to the other umbrella and tried to pick up the dog and carry it away. Not a success; the dog weighed a ton and soon wriggled away from him and squatted down a few yards off.

'Thank you,' she said in English.

'Not a success, I'm afraid.'

'You should not have tried to pick him up. They seem gentle animals, but it is better to be careful.'

He dusted his hands and made to scare the dog away. It shrank back another six feet, hesitated, looked at him with a bloodshot eye and loped off.

'It is not so much that I mind his company,' she said, 'but I do not fancy the possibility of – of the *morsure de puce.*'

Matthew smiled at her. She was sitting up clasping her knees.

'You knew I was English?'

She nodded. 'I supposed so. Though I heard you speak fluent French last night.'

'I spent two years in Paris.'

'Ah.'

'You are from Paris, mademoiselle?'

'Yes.'

There was a pause.

He said: 'I am grateful to the dog.'

'Why?'

'Because I was trying to think of some excuse to come over and speak to you.' He laughed infectiously.

He could not see her eyes for the dark glasses, but the frank approach didn't seem to have offended her.

She said: 'It is so hot. Usually there is a breeze from the sea.'

'My friend Frazier tells me this is from the Sahara. I've forgotten the name he gave it. He says it's very unusual for this time of year ... You have been here before, mademoiselle?'

'Once, yes.'

She had not invited him to sit down.

'This is my first visit to Morocco,' he said. 'I hope to hire a car. Do you have one?'

'No.'

'I have a friend in Taroudant. I intend to see him. You have friends here?'

'I am simply taking a break. And looking for the sun.'

'I hope there's not going to be a storm.'

'If there is it will soon be over.'

They watched the three Frenchwomen who had wended their way through the gardens and were now ploughing through the soft sand of the beach towards the sea. Their beach attire was no smarter than their travel costumes last night. The youngest wore a bikini, the others were in one-piece suits, but they all looked as if the swimgear had been borrowed from someone else. They bulged in the expected places and some unexpected places besides. Breasts were reluctant to remain covered, thighs wobbled, hair escaped from under fussy caps. But any thoughts that they might be regarded as amusing or even ludicrous never occurred to them. They talked in loud voices and laughed and puffed out cheeks at the heat, and the youngest one tripped on ahead while they called comic remarks to her. Presently they were in the sea with squeals and squawks and waving arms. Only one, the oldest one, it seemed, could swim, and they stayed bobbing about and splashing the water at shoulder level.

Matthew looked at Nadine, and they exchanged smiles.

'I don't see any life-saving equipment,' he said.

'There's a belt and rope by the pool . . . At least these ladies are enjoying themselves.'

'Are you not?'

She shrugged. 'I did not mean that.'

'I'm glad you didn't mean that.'

There was another silence, then he excused himself, saying he had a telephone call to make.

III

'THIS IS THE Baron de Blaye's residence.'

Matthew pressed in the *jeton*. 'May I speak to M. Edouard de Blaye.'

'Who may I ask is calling?'

'Matthew Morris.'

'A moment, sir.'

Matthew fingered another *jeton*.

A heavier voice. 'This is de Blaye. Who is speaking?'

'Oh, I'm sorry, sir, it was your son I was calling. He will know my name. Matthew Morris.'

'Unfortunately my son is not here. He is in St Moritz, skiing.'

Matthew swore under his breath. Of course he should have made sure before he left England. But it had all been decided in such a hurry . . .

'I'm sorry. I shouldn't have troubled you. I knew Edouard, your son, when I was living in Paris, and he pressed me to come and stay with him in Taroudant if I were ever in this country.'

'Where are you speaking from?'

'Agadir. The Hotel Saada.'

'Oh. Unfortunate. He will be here I expect next month. Will you still be here then?'

'I can't manage more than two weeks. How is Edouard? Please give him my regards. We were great friends in Paris and he told me about the lovely house you have here.'

They talked for a few moments, and Matthew put in another *jeton*. Then the Baron said: 'Do you have a car?'

'Er – yes.'

'It's only an hour's drive from Agadir. My wife is in Normandy, so I am almost alone at present. Perhaps you would care to have lunch with me one day?'

'I shall be delighted. And honoured.'

'Good. When would suit you?'

'Almost any day.'

'Let me see, I have business in Rabat on Friday. Tomorrow? Is that too soon?'

'Not at all.'

'Good. Come about twelve. In time for a swim before lunch.'

'Thank you. You're very kind.'

They were about to ring off when Matthew said: 'Baron.'

'Yes?'

'Might I bring a lady?'

'Naturally. It will be my pleasure.'

As soon as he had hung up Matthew went to the concierge and obtained the name and number of the car company. There was only one, it seemed. And when he rang them they said most of their cars were already rented out but he could have a Renault Four. He settled for that.

IV

AFTER ABOUT an hour he went down to the beach again. The three Frenchwomen were lying in the garden in the shade of a great palm tree, gasping like newly landed fish. They had not changed, and dark patches marked the canvas chairs they sat in. On the beach Mlle Deschamps had not moved. Her book lay face down in the sand. The yellow dog had returned.

He carefully pushed the dog away. She lifted her glasses to see who it was.

'Sorry. I disturb you.'

'It's not important.'

He squatted down in the sand beside her.

'D'you mind if I stay?'

'Not at all. But I am going in in a moment.'

He ran the fine sand through his fingers. 'I have hired a car. It will be delivered tomorrow morning at nine.'

'Ah.'

'One of the problems of air travel,' he said, 'is that one is more or less lifted up and deposited from place to place and sees nothing of the country in between. You say you have been here once before. Did you come to know much of it then?'

'No. A lot of it was in – a lot of my time was in the desert.'

'Are you an actress?'

'Yes.'

'I think I have seen you in some film.'

She smiled. 'Possible. But I do not think it likely. And you, monsieur?'

'I? Oh, by profession I'm a writer. An author, you know.'

There were few advantages, Matthew found, to the trade he had worked at, but it did sometimes impress people. Much depended on the people: booksellers and booksellers' assistants, for instance, almost always assumed an expression of frozen contempt – partly defensive, no doubt, because they had never heard his name and partly because they knew instantly that they had no copies of his books in their shops. But some ordinary people took note, especially if they were Celts or French or German.

Difficult to say what impression if any the information had made on Mlle Nadine Deschamps.

'Only three published yet,' he added, the hint of apology in his tone being totally assumed, since at his age even two was a good track record, especially if one didn't know the sales figures.

'My compliments. Are any of them in French?'

'Not yet.'

'It will come,' she said.

There was a pause.

He said: 'I mentioned Taroudant. Have you been?'

'No.'

'I am going tomorrow. My friend's father, the Baron de

Blaye, has a winter house there. It's no distance. Perhaps sixty kilometres. I shall be going for lunch. I'm told they have a pool.'

Nadine took her book up and shook the sand off it. Then she put it, together with her sun cream and a pochette, into a larger beach bag. It was a fine green canvas bag decorated with red poppies.

He said: 'Would you come with me?'

CHAPTER FIVE

I

JEAN TOURNELLE, also known as Johnny Carpenter, also known as John Frazier, also known as Frère Jacques, parked in the shade of a date palm, then walked the few yards down the Rue Beni Mellal to the home of his father. This street, round-cobbled and not easy for motor cars, was just on the edge of the French Quarter, the line here being not so distinctly drawn as in Fez or Marrakech. The sun glared down on the white walls. In an hour the narrow street would be mainly in shadow: this was midday. Canned Arab music came in a mournful monotone from the café on the corner. In the carpet shop next door two men crouched under an awning stitching slippers. A yellow mongrel dog, apparent brother of the one on the beach, scratched in the dust.

Colonel Tournelle, as he was universally known, lived in a pleasant villa at the end of the street where it turned into the Rue Cambon. The villa was square and white with a barely cambered French tile roof, and the entrance hall looked through into a small palm-treed garden with a lily-pond and a fountain. Ever since he left the Army Gaston Tournelle had done well for himself.

In 1923 he had married Fiona Carpenter in Paris, where she had found herself stranded when the dancing company she was with folded up. Tournelle was then in the Army, a good-looking corporal, who shortly after his marriage was sent to Morocco with his regiment to garrison the area round Rabat and Casablanca. A few years later he was seriously wounded in a skirmish with the Riffs, and in 1938 applied for his discharge. During the war he was in the Army commissariat in Casablanca, but at the end of it had never returned to France. Settled in Agadir, he contrived to make a handsome living in the black market. As a quartermaster sergeant, which he had been for the later part of his military life, he knew all the problems of supply and demand, had excellent contacts, and knew how to negotiate his way round the law. He had never been in trouble with the authorities and had never been so greedy as to involve himself in organized crime. (It was rumoured that he had recently made a fat profit from the devaluation of the dirham.)

Johnny had been born in Casablanca in 1924, and had spent his first ten formative years in barracks and then on the streets of Agadir. In 1934 his mother, tired finally beyond endurance by her husband's string of girlfriends, had returned to her parents in Wolverhampton, taking her only child with her, and Johnny had changed his name and become a British subject.

But he had never lost touch with his father.

He was in trouble in England in his late teens, put on probation for stealing a motor bike, given a day's imprisonment for breaking into a shop, then four months for a repeat offence. His mother blamed it all on Gaston's influence.

But that was the lot. After that he turned over a new leaf, or became cleverer. The police had interviewed him repeatedly whenever a break-in occurred in the neighbourhood, but he had always had a cast-iron alibi. For years he had worked as a motor mechanic in one of the big firms, but had lived at home, never married.

He knocked on the white-painted Moorish door, and it

was answered, as he had half-expected, by Maria Jerval. Unlike the rest of his women, Maria had stuck and refused to be discouraged, and made herself useful to Gaston and finally indispensable. She was a squat woman in her late thirties, the nubile figure which had first attracted Gaston long since gone, but still with good eyes and a fair skin for one with such lank boot-black hair. A half-caste, she refused to speak any English, but now had a firm grasp of the household, not to mention the two girls she had borne him. Gaston should have married her – and now could – but he and Johnny conspired to silence in the matter of Fiona's death six years ago.

'Oh, it is you,' she said.

She did not like Johnny. She did not like it that he was Gaston's only son. She resented his visits, which she felt were a reminder to Gaston of her own inadequacies in presenting him only with girl children.

'Maria,' Johnny said with false heartiness. 'How are you?'

He stooped to kiss her, but she turned her cheek.

They went into the dark little vestibule that led through to the garden and the pool and a mass of nasturtiums. One of her daughters put her head round a door and then was gone.

'You have lost weight,' he exclaimed, knowing it would please her. 'Is my father here?'

Her eyes strayed to the case he carried. 'No.'

'He will be back soon?'

'I have just been to visit him,' she said. The wide sleeve fell back from her arm as she brushed her hair back. Eight bracelets jangled. 'He is in hospital.'

Johnny felt a lurch of apprehension. 'When? What is wrong? My father never ailed nothing!'

'His heart. He was taken ill on Wednesday. He is in a unit. What do they call it? Cardiac.'

They went through to a larger room beyond, which had a floor of olive-green herringbone tiles and soft woven rugs on the walls. One of the daughters brought in mint tea in an ornate Moorish silver teapot. Johnny felt he could have done with something stronger.

Maria became slightly less hostile as she poured the tea and they talked. The absence of Gaston made it easier between them. Gaston, she said, had been taken with acute pain on Friday night; the doctor had diagnosed a coronary; Gaston had been taken away and was recovering slowly but was still on the danger list.

'I'll go see him,' Johnny said.

'Not yet. The doctors said he must not be disturbed. I was allowed only to sit five minutes . . .'

'His only son.'

'Tomorrow or the day after, perhaps. You are here for some time?'

' A week maybe.'

'You gave us no warning.'

'I made up my mind quite sudden. I thought: I'll surprise them.'

Maria's eyes strayed again to the suitcase at Johnny's feet. 'He will be in no fit state to transact business, if that was your thought.'

'Business? Who says business? I'm just here for a holiday, like. But I always want to see the old man. Always ask his advice about things.'

'You are not to worry him . . . Where are you staying?'

'The Saada.'

'Expensive.' Maria pursed her lips. 'So you are doing well?'

'Well enough.' Johnny had no intention of confiding in

his common-law stepmother. He was shaken up, thrown right off balance by the news. He had reckoned confidently on his father's help; it had been a part of his scheme all along; Gaston would have known exactly the safest way to launder the money. Also, Johnny needed a new passport. He had two with him, but both of them had little trailing connections with the past. He needed something absolutely new. He had no intention whatever of staying in Morocco longer than absolutely necessary. Morocco was too near London. And, who knew which of his pertinacious friends, particularly Mr Artemis, might not sniff out the French link, and bribe a sight of the lists of air passengers leaving for France yesterday? Even the police might sus him out. The sooner he left for somewhere like South America the safer he would feel.

But now . . .

After a few minutes he made an excuse and left, walked back over the cobbles, squeezed past a donkey whose panniers were so stuffed with sisal hemp that it almost filled the street, reached his car, put his suitcase carefully on the passenger's seat and drove off, scattering a group of Arab children who were playing with a rag ball.

What now? Go back to the hotel and ring the hospital from there? Maybe tomorrow the old man would be sitting up and speaking, able at least to give advice, names to look up who would help in this emergency. Johnny had not kept up with his schoolfriends. With his confidence in his father it had not entered his head that he would need to. How old was his father? About seventy? But he had looked so tough, as if his years in the Army had pickled him into an enduring mahogany. Black, close-growing hair, hardly tinged with grey, coarse, weathered skin, thin, hooked nose, black, wary eyes: the eternal corporal. Johnny could not imagine him between white sheets, a drip feed or whatever, dials attached to wires on his chest.

Johnny remembered the secret safe behind the panel in the wall of his father's bathroom. Doubtful if Maria knew of its existence; if she did she certainly never saw it opened. It would have taken comfortably the contents of the little suitcase. Twenty per cent for Gaston; that would have been expected; a fair deal. But now where was the safest hiding place for the next two or three days? Nothing in the bedroom of his hotel. No doubt the hotel had a safe for 'valuables'. But the case was a bit too large not to invite curiosity. Or he could carry it around with him wherever he went. This too would be conspicuous; but if the case never left his side there could be no opportunity for prying servants to pick the flimsy locks. Moroccan servants, he knew, were not all that reliable.

He wished now that he had taken the other course of flying first to Switzerland and banking it there. The strictest secrecy, he knew, was preserved. But in his career Johnny had never even met a Swiss banker. You couldn't just go into a bank without an introduction and ask them to take care of hot money for you for an indefinite period.

As he turned into the Boulevard Mohammed V the sun went in, and he saw that the haze had turned into dark opaque cloud. A storm perhaps. It would help to clear the air. The sea, glimpsed between the hotels and the other buildings, was the colour of a soup tureen. Half a dozen yachts seemed planted immovably, immobilized like boats in a Dufy painting. Only a tanker, sending out a little black dribble of smoke, was perceptibly stealing towards the harbour.

The gates of the hotel; drive up between the praetorian guard of umbrella pines. A taxi was at the door, two people getting out. He parked his little Renault under the trees and followed the porter, who was carrying in luggage. The new arrivals were at the reception desk, as clearly American as their luggage. The man, much the older, was tall and good-looking and well-dressed, but unsuitably for a holiday town. Grizzled grey hair, clean skin, good-toned voice as if he were used to employing it in public. The woman was about thirty, small and slim, in a thin, long, flowered frock that disguised her figure. She was pretty, good eyes, good fair-browny hair, and spoke in an undertone as if the last thing she would have thought of was employing her voice in public.

'Burford,' he was saying. 'And Mrs Heinz. It was two single rooms with a sea view.'

'Of course, monsieur,' said the receptionist. 'Rooms thirty-four and thirty-five. Ahmed will show you. Your luggage will follow. May I please have your passports.'

II

THEY HAD spent three nights in Paris. They were to have three nights in Agadir, three in Cairo and three in London on the way home.

The last few months had seen a slow process of affiliation. Early on in those months he had acknowledged to himself that he no longer disliked her; but it was long after that before he admitted that she attracted him physically. Of course there'd been the 'feeling', the sensation that she was provocatively female, but he had half resented its effect on him. In the end he came no longer to resent it. He thought about her a lot when she was absent, and found himself watching her when she was present.

Not that she came more often – it was two evenings only a week, with bridge sometimes to follow. And she would cycle home, or be given a lift and walk up for her cycle next day. He kissed her goodnight frequently now, but more often than not she turned her cheek. It was all very friendly but very impersonal. She kept at a distance and kept him at a distance. She did in the end accept his invitation to lunch in Boston at Locke-Ober's, and that was a great success. Her voice, with its foreign undertones, was rather husky, and when she laughed it was not a musical sound. But she had a quick brain – not at all like Ann's, but acute and sometimes humorous.

Another letter from Ann confirmed her contentment in her new life and showed no hint that she might return. Indeed, he had raised it in a previous letter but she had not replied to that at all.

He suggested to Letty that she should give up her work in the restaurant and cook for him six evenings a week, but she made excuses about having committed herself to the proprietress and not wanting to let her down.

He still missed Ann very much, but he was growing accustomed to becoming more his own man. As a single man, he was invited to make up the numbers at several places where they had not been accustomed to go. He began to enjoy women's company more for itself. But warily. The only woman with whom it seemed safe not to be wary was Letty Heinz. She was easy-natured, good-tempered, willing to be a friend, but not much more.

He began to cut his lunch in the city each day, and took to walking distances instead of taking a cab. He felt he could lose ten or twelve pounds, get rid of some of the flabbiness of middle age. He began monthly visits to the dentist, having his teeth, which weren't in bad condition, cleaned up and renovated. He ordered two new suits. He left the barber who had cut his hair for twenty years and went to a fashionable one who let it grow a bit longer and made something of it without getting too way out.

As he had said once to James Amis, he was still living with a sort of emotional trellis behind him. If he looked back and through it he looked at the ruins of a life; he looked back at all the comradeship and kindness of his departed wife; he remembered the early days, so many happy moments, so many vacations together, so much experience shared.

But as time passed he found he *could* look a little more forward – perhaps to nothing more than a shallow flirtation with a pretty woman who meant nothing to him, could mean nothing compared to what was gone. Perversely he was not interested in any of the other opportunities that had so far come his way. Just as perversely, he was interested in Letty Heinz. She might not come of his social group, but she was appealing, pretty and she did play such good bridge.

The slow progress of their friendship seemed sometimes to come to a complete halt. Then it would move on again, and usually with a little move forward from what it had been before.

He had told her in November that he was planning one of his holidays, to take time off from his office and make a trip to Europe and Africa early in the New Year. He had shown her the brochures, the maps of the itinerary, photographs of the places he wished to visit. Since leaving Norway she had never been back to Europe, and she showed interest in his plans. Christmas he had spent with his brother-in-law, but the next time he saw Letty he suggested she might like to go with him.

She had shied away at first, and he had not pressed her –

just left the suggestion to soak in. Then the next time he mentioned it he pointed out that he needed companionship, no more, that they would travel as a businessman and his secretary that if she didn't accept he would take his own secretary from the office, though he would much prefer it if he took a friend of Ann's, and that they would be away scarcely more than two weeks. Had she ever flown in a jet? He was looking forward to it. It turned out that she had never flown at all.

The first sign that she was weakening was a remark that if they did go together, she would tell people in the neighbourhood that she would be visiting her uncle in Baltimore. In the end they left on separate days and joined forces at Idlewild. This subterfuge irritated him; he had a reputation to consider and this clandestine way of travelling suggested he had something to hide. Whereas he had nothing to hide. But if Mrs Heinz thought differently, so be it. The main thing was she had agreed to come.

The first time he and Ann had crossed the Atlantic by air, five years ago, they had had to put down to refuel at Gander and Shannon. Now, with these new engines, in a new Boeing 707, they flew non-stop to Paris, leaving New York at seven o'clock in the evening and arriving in Orly next morning at eight.

After they had slept for a few hours, trying to shake off the jet-lag, they walked about Paris in fine grey mild weather. They went first to the Louvre, but he saw at once Letty was not interested in pictures, as Ann had been, and they did not stay long. With his new companion in mind he had booked in at the Hôtel de la Paix, in the very heart of the city, and on the first afternoon they spent a couple of hours sitting at a table watching people pass by. She was fascinated, her eyes glinted with excitement, and he was pleased to watch her. They walked again as darkness fell, had a quiet dinner in the hotel and went to bed early to try to pick up more of the lost sleep. He kissed her goodnight at the bedroom door.

'Thank you, Mr Burford. It is so good here. This was a beautiful dinner, better than I can ever cook for you. I am sure I am going to enjoy it all.'

He said: 'OK. OK. But let's just make one move forward, can't we? Could you after all this time come to call me Lee?'

She looked up almost in relief, as if she had been afraid the move forward he was going to suggest was something more physical. 'Of course . . . Lee. Thank you. What time do you wish in the morning?'

'I'll ring you. Breakfast in bed, of course. If you like you can tell me what you want and I'll order it for you.'

'Thank you, Mr . . . Thank you, Lee. You have been very good to me.'

'Not perhaps as good as I'd wish to be.'

This was more than he had ever said before. He blamed the wine.

Perhaps it was the familiarity about travel which had brought them literally closer together. Heads bent over passports, food on trays on the plane and her difficulty in getting the knives and forks out of their plastic wrappings. Trying to sleep, hands and knees almost touching. Her luggage coming first off the carousel and their amusement and speculation because his was the last. Sitting together in a taxi, she dropping her handbag and spilling tweezers and nail varnish and some coins, and their groping together on the floor to retrieve them, signing in at the hotel, and shall we have coffee now or go straight to our rooms? Translating dollars into francs and changing money.

Before they left – two weeks before they left – Lee had had another letter from Ann. He carried it with him but had not shown it to Letty.

Darling, darling,

I am writing this from a yacht called *Nimrod* and we are off the coast of North Borneo. We're at anchor, having taken refuge from the high winds that have blown up. There is a heavy swell, so do not take my erratic hand-writing for some sign of deterioration!

I love New Zealand, and have crewed for many people who have come out here to escape the pressures of civilization. Normally I go out just for the day, or maybe two days, but this time I was invited by the Parfitts (whom I mentioned in my last letter) to go off for a long cruise round Papua New Guinea, and thence on to Borneo. There are three of the Parfitts, English and very charming, and I simply could not bring myself to refuse!

There are pirates, we're told, in these waters, appar- ently Filipinos, but it is really the weather that is holding us up, and I don't think we shall get home for Christmas. There's a hurricane somewhere in the vicinity and John Parfitt is taking no chances. In the meantime I could write you ten pages describing all the remarkable things I have seen. I hope sometime next year to sail up to Cairns in Queensland and travel back overland by bus, south, probably to Sydney and then get a crewing lift home to N.Z. I want to see much more of Australia.

Darling, something frightful has turned up. The N.Z. Immigration Authorities are prepared to accept my appli- cation for Residency only if I have no dependants who might come over and apply later! I have told them I have no children and that I am amicably separated from my husband, but this does not satisfy them. You are of almost pensionable age and they are anxious that you shall not arrive, say, next year, take a job and presently expect to be supported by them! Isn't it pathetic?

Forgive me, all this seems terrible, and it is all my fault, I know. Would it be possible that we could be divorced?

Of course this would not prevent your coming out to see me – as I *truly* hope you will. Perhaps next spring? When I left N.Z. the bottle-brush trees were just coming out, a glorious crimson. I hope they will not be over too soon.

How is everybody in Oakbridge? Please give my love or regards to anyone you meet and who asks about me. Father writes to say he is well and I know he would like to come over. But he does not want to leave his cats. *Nous verrons!*

Dearest love,
Ann

On the second day in Paris they walked for miles; Lee reckoned it was the equivalent of thirty-six holes of golf. They lunched at the Jules Verne in the Eiffel Tower. They ate *pigeonneau rôti aux bolets* and drank a good white wine. She obviously liked wine and as yet she lacked his or Ann's fastidious tastes.

As did all her experience. In spite of being thirty-eight she had seen so little and done so little. She had married Carl Heinz nineteen years ago. Leon had been born the next year. She had had a bad time, had had a bit of a breakdown. Heinz had been able to provide an apartment for his family but had necessarily been away a lot. What interested Lee to speculate was what happened when he came home.

In mid-February, after she had agreed to come away with him, she had taken another week off to visit her son in New York. When she came back she said that this time he had been difficult to find but she had eventually seen him three times. He seemed, she said, contented enough in his new life – if content was a word that could be properly used in this respect. He belonged to a youth cult, advocating peace and love. She thought there were drugs involved but hoped they were the innocuous ones. At least he had made clear that, while acknowledging her concern for him, he did not want to come back to Concord.

That second night they dined at L'Arpège. As they were drinking coffee at the end of a wonderful meal Lee showed her Ann's letter. She read it slowly, then again.

'Ah, so. That is unfortunate. And shall you agree?'

'Agree to what?'

'A divorce.'

'I haven't decided. But yes, I suppose I shall. She has chosen that life, and I don't want to put obstacles in her way.'

'You must try not to be bitter, Lee.'

'No,' Lee agreed. 'No. I am trying not to be.'

There was a long silence. The extra wine he had drunk had given him broadening thoughts.

'Did your husband beat you?' he asked eventually.

'Did he what?' Her eyes widened in surprise. 'Beat me? Ah, no. He is not that type.'

'Never even hit you?'

'Of course not!'

'Sometimes I fancy I could hit you.'

She stared at him, half laughing at the outrageousness of this statement from such a restrained man. 'I don't believe that! Why should you?'

'Why should I not? You are so damned – reasonable. So detached.'

'Oh.' She was scandalized. 'You have been very kind to me. I hoped I had been of help to you. And I have come away, and it is lovely.'

'Do you love your husband?'

'. . . No.'

'Whom have you loved, then?'

'Loved?'

'Yes, loved properly.'

'Oh . . . my brother. My son . . .'

'That's a different sort of love.'

'And in a way . . . Mrs Burford. I care so much about her happiness. And I care for yours. She asked me . . .'

'What?'

'She asked me to look after you when she was gone. I – have been trying to do that.'

Quicksands moved.

'Is that all you have been trying to do?'

'Yes . . . mainly.'

'She asked you . . .'

'One day she made me promise. She said: "After I have left he will need all the company and help he can get. He won't *seem* to. He looks very composed, very self-sufficient, but really he'll need kindness and thoughtfulness and friendship, and I want you to promise me . . ." So I promised.'

'That's what she said?'

'More or less.'

'And I guess that's what you've done.'

'It's what I have tried to do. I do not know if it has been successful. At first I did not like to intrude on you. I thought you might feel I was interfering. But gradually it came to something more. You began to ask me to do things, and I did them gladly. For me – I have enjoyed it.'

'Because you were obliging Ann?'

'That, yes. But not just that.'

A lady in an extraordinary hat, conceived as a jockey cap out of the light dragoon guards, was entering the restaurant. At any other time Letty would have been hypnotized by the sight, but now she scarcely saw it.

Lee said, choosing his words carefully: 'How I regarded you when you were first a friend of Ann's I'll not bother to go into. But over the months I have come to regard you a little differently. Life has changed very much since Ann left. And it has changed me. I confess I have found you – attractive and good company. Other thoughts and expectations have flowed from that. I hoped that this holiday would be a mutual pleasure for us both. But . . . but if you have only come away with me because of a promise you made her – and if you feel – feel some sense of disloyalty to her in – in being anything more than a companion to me . . . then I am defeated . . . Completely defeated.'

She didn't reply, and presently he called for *l'addition* and they left.

III

THEY SAW much in the afternoon, but later he could not remember what he had seen.

Whether he liked it or not, on this trip his blood had begun to carry an extra charge. What was happening or had happened in the world around him seemed to have less importance. Waves of pleasure made him even forget his work, the briefs and the cases he had left behind him – and nearly forget the disaster of Ann's desertion and the contents of her latest letter. He was truly alone, and yet there was excitement in being alone – and a new excitement in this new companionship.

But now he had a feeling that he had come up suddenly, horribly against a brick wall. If Letty was only companioning him because she had promised Ann ... his hopes and pleasures and emotions of yesterday were in the trash can.

Was there, he wondered, a hint of lesbianism in the situation? It had never crossed his mind in Ann's case, in spite of the odd women friends she had sometimes picked up. But if Letty were a full-blown lesbian it might have touched some responding spark in the other woman. But *was* Letty that? Did that explain the breakup of her marriage, the absence of men friends, her withdrawn attitude to him, finally her confession that she had never ever been in love?

In the evening they dined at Le Dôme. At the end of the meal he could contain himself no longer.

'Are you in love with Ann?'

'What?' She blinked. 'What is that?'

'I said are you in love with Ann – my wife?'

She hesitated. 'In love with her? I do not know. I am not sure how you mean it. I think I love her, yes. She is perhaps the most lovable woman I ever met.'

'If she had stayed, could it have become a relationship?'

'You mean women together? Butch women and dykes – is that what you call it?'

'That is what people call it, yes.'

'Well, the answer is no.'

'No?'

'No.'

'So your marriage with Carl was for real?'

113

'Of *course* it was for real! But it was not a *happy* one!'
He blew out a slow breath. 'Oh, my God! Take another
glass of wine!'
'Thank you,' she said stiffly, 'I do not wish more wine.'
In enormous relief he put his hand on hers. 'Forgive me.
I've been getting my wires crossed. But can you blame me?'
'Of course I can blame you!'
'Look,' he said. 'Look. There's a lot I don't understand,
but thank Christ one cloud has been cleared away. Look...'
'Why should I look any more?'
'Letty,' he said. 'I am not a conceited man. I am *years*
older than you, and it is not difficult to appreciate that you
may like me but not come on for me in other ways. Also that
you feel a loyalty towards my wife. What I can't quite figure
out is why you have allowed me to kiss you over the last
months and have apparently shown no aversion – and
seemed to welcome my company – yet it has apparently
meant nothing to you at all.'
'Of course it has meant something!' she said. 'It is – it
brings the pleasure! I enjoy it. I am also ... still flattered by
it.'
'But you want nothing more.'
She frowned as if in slight perplexity, but did not speak.
'You dislike what is called the sexual act?'
'Yes, I think that may be so.'
'You see ...' He ran his hand through his hair. 'Of
course I understand your feeling about Ann. And in no time,
it must seem to you I have thrown off my love for her and
am looking elsewhere! It isn't natural, you think. Or if it is
natural it is not admirable. Well, that may be so. But
humanity is often not very admirable – as I have spent
a professional life discovering. And since Ann left I have
been – lonely.'

'Ah, lonely. That is a different thing.'

He said suddenly: 'Did you often make love with Carl?'

'What? Oh ... I do not know. What is often? He is – was away so much.'

'And when he did make love to you – was it pleasurable?'

She hesitated. 'I do not wish to talk about it.'

He refilled her wineglass and moved it a few inches nearer to her. 'I want you to tell me about it.'

She looked at him with a flicker of anger in her eyes. 'Why should I? It is no business of yours.'

'Forgive me but I consider it to be so.'

'I am not in your court to be cross-examined in front of a judge!'

'Certainly not. But I want to understand – to help.'

'You will help by not asking such things.'

'So it wasn't pleasurable.'

'Probably that is something wrong with me.'

'I doubt it.'

'I think we should go home.'

'Cab tonight? I think I've walked enough.' He motioned for the bill.

She nodded, and they waited in silence. Then he said: 'So he was brutal . . .'

She carefully folded her napkin and stood up. 'Shall we go?'

'And be arrested for leaving without settling the check? Sit down, Letty. Please, dear Letty, sit down.'

She sat down and he saw she was close to tears. He said nothing more. Money passed, compliments were exchanged, he took her thin arm; a taxi was summoned, and they were driven back to their hotel.

The Café de la Paix was ablaze with lights and pulsating with people. He did not suggest a further drink in the café, but steered her upstairs, and at her door gave her a chaste kiss that no one could take exception to.

But he fancied that her lips were warmer and a little more vulnerable.

IV

THEY WERE leaving for Agadir on Saturday morning. There was one more complete day in Paris, and they made the most of it. They talked little of personal things while walking and sightseeing; but at lunch they were seated next to a group of noisy Germans, and she was obviously put off by them. They moved tables. She said: 'Sorry.'

'No matter . . . Every nation has its share of people who should be marked "Not for Export".'

After a pause she said suddenly: 'My father died in a concentration camp.'

'Letty, I'd no idea!'

'Why should you? I do not talk of it.'

'Perhaps it would help if you did talk of it.'

She did not reply.

'Was he in the Resistance?'

'No. But he had an English wife and was known for his English sympathies.'

'What happened?'

'He was arrested twice on suspicion, taken to a place in Oslo called Victoria Terrace. The third time he was sent to Oranienburg, near Berlin. Six months after that they told us he is dead, has died – they say of "pneumonia".'

'I'm very, very sorry. You should have said something to me.'

'Would it have made any difference? It is something I prefer to forget.'

'Which, of course, you could never do.'

'No. I have it in my heart.'

When they got up to go she patted his arm and said: 'Can we walk again? It is so good, this walking.'

When they were outside he said: 'When did you quit Norway?'

'In the spring of 1941.'

'You and your brother and your mother?'

'My mother and I only. After my father died my brother went into hiding, joined the Resistance.'

'Was it not difficult for you to leave?'

'Oh, yes. But we were being – persecuted. It was decided we must leave while we were still free. One night in the spring of '41 we both stepped out of our flat, closed and locked the door and never saw it again. We took cover in a safe house for a week, then left in the back of a lorry for the Swedish frontier. It took a long time, for we had to lie up every day, and the days were getting longer. We hid in carpenters' shops, bakeries, caves. Then we had word from my brother that we were to take the train for Trondheim. We were given new papers. That too was a nightmare.'

'And?'

She shrugged. 'We got out of the train at a country station. It was dark. We walked in the dark for miles – often through snow. We hid next day. The second night we came to a lake. On the other side was Sweden. The lake was frozen but was beginning to thaw. There was broken ice everywhere. Our guide was an old man. He said we must risk it. There was a half moon and we could see the ice floes, some of them standing up, and black patches between which we were afraid was open water. We stumbled in up to our knees

117

near the shore, but underneath there seemed to be another layer, and we slowly made it across, until we could see the lights of Sweden. Dawn was breaking as we got over. Someone greeted us, two men. They had seen us coming. They helped us – to safety . . .'

It was a silent walk for the rest of the way home. As a young lawyer Lee had taken a course in psychology, but it was instinct rather than timing that persuaded him to avoid more pressure on her now. He sensed that this vacation was make or break for them. If her feelings were not involved, his were. It had happened uninvited, pretty well against his better judgement. If she cared next to nothing for him it would have been much to be preferred if he had brought Carita, his part-Spanish secretary, who was pretty enough and just divorced and no doubt would have allowed him some discretionary latitude if he had wanted it. But instead it had become this woman and no other.

Tonight he suggested they should take another drink in the Café de la Paix before going upstairs, and she agreed. They sat indoors because a chill wind had risen to spoil the exceptional mildness of the evening. She had allowed him to buy her a fox fur, and she wore this tonight over an off-the-shoulder frock of black velvet. He noticed two Frenchmen eyeing her with interest, as he had seen other glances yesterday. He was not the only man who found her attractive. Her clothes would not set Paris alight; but she had carriage and good looks.

He said something and she laughed at it. She so seldom laughed, and as he had noticed before it was not a particularly musical sound, but he was glad to hear it. The defensive mood was passing.

They sat a long time. Then they collected their keys and went up to bed.

She opened her bedroom door, and he pushed the door open and he went in.

'Lee . . .'

He kissed her rather sensuously, as he had kissed no other woman except Ann for a quarter of a century. It pleased him (almost) that he knew how. The fox fur slipped to the floor. He put his hands on her bare shoulders. Some might have thought them bony, but they were warm and fine-skinned, and for some reason inexplicable to science had come to mean more to him then than all the other warm shoulders in the world.

The door, being swayed against, gradually shut, cutting off the light from the corridor; but the bedroom was partly lit by reflections coming through the windows from the café two floors below.

After a little while she gently pushed him away.

He said: 'Letty, you have come to mean a lot to me.' He kissed her on the forehead and went out.

V

NEWCOMERS WHO arrived at Agadir by the same plane as Lee and Letty had been a little later reaching the Saada because M. Henri Thibault had ordered a hire car to meet them at the airport, and had specified a Citroën DS saloon. Instead he was offered a Renault Four. M. Thibault was an important man. Director of the Banque de Crédit Générale, governor of the St Sulpice Hospital, chairman of the Seine et Oise Charity Schools, possessor of the Légion d'Honneur, he was not tall but impressive in breadth, a man of substance in every sense of the word. His wife, though not of such breadth, was of similar build. They were not used to being cramped together in a small car, which was why they had ordered the Citroën, a car very much like the one he drove in Paris. Even to attempt to get into the small car was an affront to their dignity.

They railed against the man from the hire car agency, who spread his hands in a show of helpless incompetence: the company no longer had a Citroën DS, he said, a former customer had wrecked it by driving off the road into a ravine. At the moment, alas, the only car available was the one they were being offered. In a day or two a Peugeot would become available – *not* what they wanted, but roomy and almost new. He would go back and tell the office of M. Thibault's complaint; perhaps something could be done even tomorrow. Today, alas, there was nothing else to offer.

In the meantime the porters had packed their considerable luggage into the boot, with the overflow on the two back seats, and were waiting impatiently for their tips.

Grunting in annoyance the two stout middle-aged people allowed themselves to be edged – or wedged – into the car, the tinny door slammed and presently they drove off down the long, featureless road to the town.

M. Thibaut had been to Agadir twice before on business, so he knew his way to the hotel. His humour was not improved when he reached the Saada to find five similar Renault Fours parked in the drive. They were no doubt hire cars like his own, and it crossed his mind to suspect that the hire company, which was the only one in Agadir, just didn't have any other make or type to rent. As a man of superior station and achievement he was irritated that there would be no difference between him and other guests.

They climbed out of the car and having been shown to their room, which was on the second floor and the best in the hotel, they decided to go straight down to lunch. Mme Thibault had been in a very nervous, tetchy mood since her daughter's wedding, and they both felt they deserved a quiet, restful, expensive holiday.

The day was so hot that everyone was using the outside dining-room by the pool. The Thibaults were shown to a table shaded by a big umbrella. M. Thibault, imperialed but not moustached, wore a white suit with white doeskin boots and a black bow tie. He was sweating and irritable and immediately ordered something off the menu that sent the waiters scurrying. Estrella Thibault had once been a very attractive woman and had taken reluctantly to age and fat. Her hair was done in grey-pink curls, and the pink silk dress with its three rows of valuable pearls was too tight for her high-sitting bosom.

At the next table were an American couple they had seen on the plane; he, much the older, wore a cream linen jacket and dark slacks; she had changed into a flimsy yellow dress that made her look sallow. Beyond them, and eating alone, was a thin, hawk-nosed, nervously active man who chain-smoked through his meal. A small suitcase on the next chair was his only companion.

A few empty tables further on was a dark-eyed beautiful girl in her twenties, in a pale beige sleeveless linen blouse and short beige shorts and red sandals. Sharing the table with her was a good-looking cheerful man of about the same age. He was paying her a great deal of attention, and she was not resenting it.

'You must tell me again,' Letty said, fingering the menu. 'I know *potage* is soup, but what is *potage de Crécy?*'

'Watercress soup.'

'Ah . . . And *dindon?*'

'Turkey. I'd think the fish would be a better bet here.'

Estrella Thibault said distastefully: 'Is this the hotel you stayed at before?'

'It's the best in Agadir. Of course this is very much a seaside resort.'

'Perhaps we should have gone to Marrakech. These are – very much – what you might call holiday-makers.'

'Of course. I brought you here because of the wonderful air. There's none better in the world.'

'You sound like your friend, the Governor.'

'Well . . . we both need a rest. And M. Bouamrani is giving lunch for us tomorrow. We shall meet such notables as there are.'

'Few French, I would suppose.'

'Oh, do not be so sure. Information has been sent ahead as to who I am – who we are.'

Mme Thibault wrinkled her nose. 'M. Boum – whatever his name is – is, I suppose, is . . .'

'A Moroccan, yes. But of course educated in French ways.'

'It's the women so often who let them down. D'you remember the Minister from Senegal who brought his black wife?'

'Too well. Too well.'

The *specialité* was brought and served: jellied eel in Chablis. Thibault complained to the waiter because he suspected they had been fobbed off with a Moroccan white wine. After some expostulations and reassurance the couple decided reluctantly to eat their hors-d'œuvre; and at this moment three middle-aged women came into the restaurant. They were common-looking. However they dressed they would have been common-looking, but their dresses did not help. One was in a violet trouser suit, one in an ebulliently low-cut blouse and shorts of shocking pink and the youngest and best-looking of the three wore a black flowered house-coat over a loose bathing costume.

The waiter was about to show them to a table near the pool, but the eldest and stoutest in the violet trouser suit halted suddenly as they passed the table where the Thibaults were lunching.

'Tibby!' she exclaimed. 'Well, my faith! *Regardez!* I have not seen you for *years*. Not since the good old days after the war. What goes? What have you been up to?'

The Frenchman had not risen. He gazed at the speaker, first in alarm, then with extreme hostility.

'Good day to you, madame,' he said, and then half rose. 'Good day!'

The last sentence was dismissive but Laura refused to be dismissed.

'Let's see. D'you know Françoise? No, you wouldn't: she was after your day. Nor Vicky? Françoise, this is M. Thibault, my old friend and buddy. Let's see, how long is it, Tibby?'

M. Thibault said: 'Good day, madame,' and sat down again and turned to his wife, whom he had made no attempt to introduce.

Laura seemed settled, standing firmly on her thick legs, but Vicky pulled at her arm. 'Come on, my cabbage, let's have lunch. I'm starving.'

So they moved on.

Lee's French, which was serviceable if not fluent, had been able to pick up the interchange. He passed it on in an undertone to Letty. Though they were careful not to look too obviously, it was clear that Mme Thibault and her husband were having words. Thibault's nostrils were white against his flushed face and little black beard; his wife's mouth was like a purse from which abuse – or something like it – dripped in muttered monosyllables.

As they sat down four tables away Françoise exploded with laughter. Her full breasts shook inside the low-cut blouse. 'Dear, dear, Laura, you surely collect 'em! *Alors!* Who is he? Customer of yours?'

'Of course. Naturally. That is to be assumed.' Laura tidied her hair, which was always falling about. 'Tibby. Years ago. Of course. He was a regular, used to come in once a week, matter of routine, like. What was he? I think a bank manager or something from Crédit Lyonnais. Right little devil he was. Well, well, just imagine meeting him!'

The waiter came to take their order. Laura was feeling peevish, not liking the way M. Thibault had brushed her off. When she was a madame discretion was part of her stock in trade, but she'd been out of Paris for years and now she couldn't care less. Anyway meeting Tibby like this had been a big surprise. She was on holiday, for God's sake, and maybe now had enough money not to need to live on men's appetites ever again, and she was feeling, for God's sake, lively.

'Right little devil,' she said, crumbling and buttering a bread roll. 'You can't imagine what his little trick was. Pretending to lose his watch and have six of my girls kneeling down looking under chairs and tables, their bare butts sticking out for him to look at. Then after some minutes he'd choose the one he fancied and take her upstairs ... We all knew it was a game, but we all played along and it was harmless enough.'

Vicky giggled, but Françoise laughed out loud.

She said: 'In the Maison Lapin where I worked for a short while before I came to you, *mon chou*, there was a man like that only worse, much worse. *Mon Dieu!* He would hire six girls to lock him in chains, and then they all had to take it in turns to pee on him! Ho! ha! ho!'

'Please,' said Vicky, fanning herself. 'If you will. Let us not have such talk. I wish to retain my appetite!'

'*Merde*,' said Laura, glaring across at M. Thibault, which seemed to close the conversation.

VI

'LEAVE IT BE,' snapped Thibault. 'Allow it to be forgotten. She was just a common woman I had to meet in the course of my business and charitable affairs.'

'Business and charitable affairs!' snapped his wife. 'I did not know your charity was extended to trollops like those three. Regard them! What dress! What vulgarity! One comes to Agadir to escape the winter and stays at the best hotel! One does not expect one's husband to be accosted by the street sweepings of Paris!'

'Conceive of the fact,' Thibault said bitterly, 'that in the course of a wide commercial and public-spirited involvement in all – *all* – strata of society, one cannot pick or choose everyone one meets. I certainly cannot be certain but I suppose it was when I was with Crédit Lyonnais – ten or fifteen years ago. A bank, you will perhaps be aware, must be prepared to accept custom, deposits from all conditions of persons and to transact business with and for them. It would be a sorry world if every client who entered the door of a bank was compelled to bring a certificate of moral character! Good God, not all *your* relations are above reproach. Think of Cousine Adèle! Think of—'

'Ten years ago,' said Mme Thibault, 'a likely story. Even fifteen years ago you were an *inspector* of banks. An inspector of banks! Not an inspector of whore houses!'

A waiter came to take away their plates, and another to lay fresh places for their second course. After they had gone Mme Thibault said: 'Where *did* you meet her if it was not in a *maison de passes?*'

'I cannot in the least remember. I have told you so! I recall her only very vaguely.'

'She seems to know *you* well. *Tibby* indeed!'

'No doubt when the weather cools,' said Thibault, 'you will permit your choler to abate. You are here for a holiday to recuperate from the stresses of the wedding of our youngest daughter, if you remember—'

'Of course I remember! How can you speak Catherine's name after you admitted friendship with an obvious prostitute—'

'I admit *nothing*! And kindly keep your voice down if you do not wish to make us the laughing stock of the hotel . . .'

The bickering went on for a while, observed among others by Matthew and Nadine, who had decided to share a table for lunch.

'Do *you* think they are *poules?*' Matthew said, with a nod towards Laura and her friends.

'Don't you?'

'Appearances can deceive but – well, it's hard to see them as anything else!'

Nadine sipped her wine.

Matthew thought it over, then glanced back at the bickering Thibaults. 'Hell hath no fury,' he said, 'like a woman who has got her husband in a corner . . . D'you know, I've never been in a brothel, either English or French. And it's not because I don't like women.'

'So I observe. But then perhaps you have never had the need . . .'

'Need? Oh, I—'

'I mean because of your looks.'

He half rose to make her a bow. 'May I quote you?'

'I mean I do not suppose you have had to run after women, have you? Brothels surely are for men who for one reason or another are deprived. Is that not so? Unattractive men, undiscriminating men, married men who cannot afford a regular mistress, men with kinky tastes, men with uncontrollable appetites, young men who are too timid to develop a proper relationship . . .'

'Just men.'

The sky was still heavy, low-lying, dense, the sun hazy, the heat cloying.

He said: 'Do you have a special boyfriend?'

'Not at the moment.'

'Have you been married?'

'You tell me *you* have. But in England it is all so serious. In Paris . . .'

'Yes?'

'When two people live together they are often known as married. When they go through a civil or religious ceremony, they are known as married-married.'

'And you?'

She smiled gently, lashes on cheeks. 'I have been married.'

'And are no longer?'

Still smiling she shook her head.

He said: 'My horoscope told me I was going to be lucky.'

'Aren't you assuming a lot?'

'What? Well, yes, I suppose so. That may be so . . . But we have known each other at least the best part of a day.'

'Now you are teasing.'

'Well, yes, if you take it that way.'

'How else am I to take it?'

'That we have formed an *amitié*.'

'You use the French word.'

'Because it can mean whatever you may want it to mean.'

They went on with their lunch.

He said: 'We shall meet tomorrow morning, then, if not before. It should be a pleasant drive.'

'I did not think I had actually said yes.'

'Then please say it now.'

'I am not known to your friends.'

'Please say yes. Please, please, please.'

'They will not expect me.'

'I told them I hoped . . .'

'What?'

'I hoped to bring a lady.'

'You were presuming on a beach acquaintance of about ten minutes' duration?'

'I was hoping that my dearest wish would be granted.'

'Oh, come, M. Morris, too much flattery . . .'

'Not flattery. Oh no, not flattery! It would give me outrageous pleasure.'

'You do not speak quite like an Englishman.'

'They vary, you know. Little ones, big ones, fat ones, thin ones, cold ones, passionate ones. You'd be surprised.'

They said no more until they had finished lunch. Then he said: 'Well?'

She smiled. '*Je le veux bien.*'

CHAPTER SIX

I

JOHNNY FRAZIER, alias Carpenter, alias Tournelle, goes into the telephone booth to call his father.

He has had a restless night. First because of the news of the old man's illness, which effectively scuttles all his plans. And second, no doubt prompted by the first, has come a succession of nightmares. It is curious that scarcely any of them involves the police.

He dreams of his bedroom door being quietly opened and Big Smith stepping in, with a grim smile. Greg Garrett follows him. Joe Rooney carries a rubber truncheon.

'Well, Johnny,' Big Smith says, 'so we've found you at last. You *have* been a trouble to us. All those false scents. But we *knew* we'd catch up with you in the end. You must have known too, didn't you? Or did you take us for right suckers? Eh? Tell us just what you thought. There's plenty of time.'

'Time?' Rooney says. 'Why wait? Let me just knock his teeth out first. Then maybe he'll be able to explain just what he had in mind.'

Johnny dreams he pushes himself up the bed until he is in a sitting position, and begins.

'Difficulty is, it's *hard* to explain. In fact there is *no* excuse possible, *no* explanation of *any* sort, however far-fetched, but the plain truth. I tried to double-cross you. We

129

went through this robbery as partners; and I decided to let you all down and pinch the lot! Or all the best part. All the most negotiable part. The rest is in my flat. You'll have found it by now. Maybe there's quite a nice little haul left there. I only took the cream. And after all I haven't spent much. It's all under my bed in this case. You're welcome to take it back.'

'That's what we intend to do,' Big Smith smiles. 'After we've dealt with you. After we've really finished with you.'

But in a later dream of the night it is Mr Artemis who comes in with his tinted glasses and the blood blister on his lip and his fat white hands: he leads the way followed by the other three. They are standing by the side of the bed: Smith and Garrett and Rooney, all waiting for the word to start on him. And he is trying once again to stumble through his explanations, his excuses. And Mr Artemis rubs his nose and says: 'Let's see, how thick are these walls? Will they hear his screams? That wouldn't really do, would it? Perhaps we'd better carry him out on to the beach. There's *lots* of room there. And it's dark and it's lonely: no one will dare to interfere with us there.'

So it is while they are seizing him and gagging him and tying his hands that he finally wakes up, to stare in a steamy sweat out of a window where dawn is still no more than a smear in the east. No stars visible: land and sea drowse in an ominous haze.

He gets up and gulps some soda water and tries to clear his head of the miasmas of the night. He is, he knows, in danger. They *may* trace him. They will certainly do their damnedest. If they do so while he is still in Agadir he is as certainly doomed to a nasty end as his nightmares have foretold. Two or three days. He feels sure that, barring some extraordinary twist of fate, he will be safe for another two or three days. In that time he can do – could have done – all that is necessary. This is Sunday. By Tuesday he could have been away – on a ship leaving Casablanca for Buenos Aires, Baltimore, Brisbane, he is not all that particular. It is just essential to keep moving until the trail is lost. For a reasonable commission his father could have arranged it all.

But his father is in hospital. Every plan is awry. He had thought in his mind that he would maybe leave half the money in the old man's keeping, in the safe in the wall. Now he can no longer trust the old man to stay *alive*. So what is the answer? Even if the passport is contrived, do you take all the money with you? Carry the case around with you, with the intimacy of guilt, for the duration of at least one long sea voyage?

Johnny has always had the ultimate hope of settling somewhere French or French-speaking. Maybe Martinique, or Montreal or Mauritius, or one of the South Sea islands. Though English was his mother's tongue, he has always felt drawn to the speech and the food and the culture of France. He would like to marry a French girl, settle down comfortably to the retired life of a man with an adequate bank balance. The dream, it seemed to him, was within reach. (As well as the nightmares.) His father's illness makes the pleasurable dream more remote, the horror more probable.

'I wish to speak to Colonel Gaston Tournelle.'

He has said this some minutes ago, and now, just after he has inserted a second *jeton*, comes the reply. 'Colonel Tournelle's condition is serious but stable. He is still in special care. Perhaps if you rang tomorrow . . .'

'I'm his son. His only son. I've come a long distance special to see him. I'm not able to stay long in Agadir. Could I please speak to the doctor in charge.'

Another wait. He pushes open the door to get some air.

131

In the foyer of the hotel, where he is speaking from, he sees the mismatched American couple get out of the lift and go through to the garden. She is wearing cream shorts which show off her slender pale legs, a navy blue halter top and a flowered sunhat. Johnny's male mind, while concentrating passionately on the business in hand, registers that she is attractive rather than pretty.

'M. Frazier.'

'Yes?'

'Dr Eyme says if you come about eleven you can see your father for five minutes.'

'Thanks. Thanks a lot.'

He is there by ten thirty. The hospital, a white, square, functional building, is on rising ground between the main town and the Kasbah on the hill. Johnny parks and smokes a cigarette and then goes in. It is a similar day to yesterday, the sun part hidden between rafts of cloud which have drifted up since dawn. The light breeze seems hotter than the air.

He gives his name and is shown into a waiting-room where all the patients are Arabs. This is a change Independence has wrought. It used to be a hospital for Europeans only.

After twenty minutes his name is called and he follows a nurse down a long corridor and into a crowded ward, at the near end of which, behind protective screens, a man lies in a bed in rather the condition that Johnny has pictured yesterday. There is a large moving graph which pulsates in jagged lines, presumably monitoring the heartbeat of the patient. A black nurse is standing by the bed. Johnny steals over and peers down. Gaston Tournelle has a tanned leathery complexion that could never look pallid, but Johnny notices how

132

bloodless the lips are and the nostrils of the prominent nose. His eyes are half open.

'*Mon père*,' whispers Johnny.

'Ah,' says Tournelle, in a voice surprisingly powerful for one so ill. 'Jacques . . .'

For a few moments they make polite conversation – or Johnny makes the conversation, the replies come in monosyllables. He is aware that time is passing, but he has to go through the motions of being a sympathetic son. In the meantime the nurse in attendance, who from the shape of her nose looks as if she comes from the far south, remains in attendance, standing by the edge of the screen, watching the heartbeats, no doubt, but clearly hearing everything that is being said.

Johnny explains that he is in Agadir only for a few days, that he is staying at the Saada, that he came to his father's house yesterday, anxious to discuss some urgent business with him, only to learn the sad news of his illness . . .

As he is speaking he fancies he detects a renewed interest in his father's black eyes; even severe illness cannot destroy the acquisitive instincts. Eventually Johnny says: 'Nurse, could I maybe have a word in private, like, with my father?'

She looks ungracious. 'You have been here already four minutes. Dr Eyme said you should not stay more than five.'

'Give us a minute or two longer, eh? It's very urgent.'

She transfers her weight from one heavy leg to the other. Then she shrugs and says: 'Do not excite him.'

Johnny watches her waddle off down the length of the ward. Then, speaking in a half whisper, he tells his father something of what has happened, muttering half truths, part in his haste, part from habit.

He does not notice, but the heartbeat on the screen slightly quickens. His father says: 'How long can you stay?'

'Not long. It wouldn't be safe.'

'It depends who wants you.'

'I'd best go soon. What I need most is a new passport.'

His father sighs. It is his body rather than himself that is making an admission of fatigue and distress. 'I cannot move as yet. I shall be lucky – out in a week. It is more likely to be two. Can you wait that long?'

'No.'

There is a long silence. The eyes close. Johnny has a fearful apprehension that his father has gone to sleep. A quick anxious glance at the dials, in case . . . Then Tournelle utters one word.

'Ardrossi.'

'What?'

'Ardrossi. Benjamin Ardrossi.'

'Who's he?'

'Someone who – might help you. I have known him – thirty years.'

'Can you trust him?'

'No.'

'. . . Then . . .'

'He will do what I ask – if he is well paid. He will do what you ask – if I ask him.'

'Why?'

'Because I know – about him – what he would not wish – to be publicly known.'

'Time is up,' says the nurse, flexing her broad nostrils. She has marched up and down the ward three times, and is now back.

'How can I find him?' Johnny asks, ignoring her.

But she squeezes past him and puts a hand on his father's forehead, dabs at his face. 'It is time.'

Tournelle waves her away with a tired hand, as if she is a troublesome fly. 'Casino. He is a *tailleur*. Say I sent you . . .' His eyes flicker.

'Could you trust him right down the line?' Johnny demands.

'No, not everything. But see him for yourself. Judge. Get what is most urgent. Then see.'

There is nothing more to do, nothing more to say. Johnny stands up. 'I'll come again.'

'Yes.'

'Tomorrow. I may stay three or four days. It depends how things turn out.'

'Yes,' says his father, and closes his eyes again.

Johnny goes out on tiptoe, out of the hospital to his boiling hot car.

II

THE ROAD from Agadir to Taroudant is not picturesque. It runs through the outskirts of the port, where encampments of gypsies and Berbers exist and shanty towns half grown mask the spread of the new settlers; then across a desolate plain dotted with argan trees which yield an oil from their seeds and so induce goats to climb them in search of food. When Nadine first saw a group of them up what looked like a desiccated olive tree, ten and twenty feet from the ground, she refused to believe they were goats, and presently she persuaded Matthew to stop and got out with a camera to photograph them. But the goats were camera-shy, and as she came near them they slipped and slithered down the tree as if pretending they had never been up in the first place. Laughing, Matthew drove on a bit further and they stopped again some distance away. Nadine's telephoto lens did the rest.

Matthew said: 'They call the goats here black grasshoppers.'

'I do not believe it! You are teasing again.'

'And those little trees provide all sorts of things: wood, coal, fruit. You see them nowhere except Morocco.'

'How do you know all this?'

'I've been reading it up. I'm telling you this while it is fresh in my mind. I'll have forgotten it tomorrow.'

'You have a poor memory, then?'

'Not for faces. Some faces.'

'You'll still remember me after a week?'

'Ten years hence I shall be saying: "That was the day I first met her."'

'Second. You've already forgotten yesterday.' She glanced at him. 'You do not look like a Baedeker reader. I always picture Baedeker readers as people with little round spectacles and pebble lenses, stooping and rather stout and very intense.'

'That's what I am,' he agreed. 'Very intense.'

As they neared Taroudant, bumping along in their box-like car, the countryside softened and they came upon olive groves and fields of maize and orange trees in verdant elegant ranks.

Matthew had been instructed to fork left before they reached the town, but he missed the turning and they found themselves facing the great ochre walls of the city. They did not go in through the big wooden gates but asked a policeman who had decided to spend a happy hour directing the non-existent traffic, and he sent them back on their tracks to a turning which was hardly observable for mimosa and lilac trees. They drove along a three-mile track until the smallest of signs pointed left.

Iron gates, which were closed. A tall servant came out in a white jellaba with a ceremonial dagger at his hip, and was told their business. The gates were opened and they went on.

A sandy drive between hibiscus and jasmine bushes. A low-lying pillared house flanked by palms and oleanders. All the land around was green.

A white-jacketed footman, dark-skinned but with the light eyes and high cheek-bones of a Berber, let them into a circular hall and through into a spacious ornate room in which stood a stocky middle-aged man who came towards them with outstretched hand.

The Baron de Blaye was in his fifties, brown hair greying and worn long at the back in a succession of handsome coiffured curls. Not a good-looking man, but his expression was ironical, sophisticated and pleasantly welcoming. He was wearing white Moroccan slippers, beige linen trousers and a white silk shirt open at the neck. A cream cravat tied at his throat did not hide the crucifix nor the string of crystal beads round his neck. His skin was fair, his eyes blue, and Matthew remembered that the family came from Normandy.

By now it was nearly twelve; de Blaye said they must have a drink at once and then, if they cared to, could swim before lunch. He seemed to take to both of them instantly and there was no lack of conversation, about Edouard with Matthew, and about the Paris stage with Nadine.

The house was designed like a Moorish palace. High-domed ceilings, arched windows with leaded lights, tall bronze lamps, mantelpieces and doors decorated with intricate arabesques, antique carpets on marble floors.

All swam in the pool, which was surrounded by orange and lemon trees. Pierre de Blaye said the oranges grown in Taroudant were the finest in Morocco.

After they had swum de Blaye excused himself and the other two were left in deck-chairs drying off in the brilliant sun.

Driving the car he had had little opportunity to look at her; now as they sipped at a vodka and orange a waiter had brought he stared at her candidly and decided she was the best thing he had ever seen. His blood ran thickly. She turned and met his gaze, did not lower her eyes but looked as candidly back at him.

'What are you thinking?' she asked.

He let out a breath. 'Oh, just how lucky I am.'

'Yes,' she agreed. 'You have lovely friends.'

'I meant lucky to have found you.'

'*Found* me,' she said. 'Am I a stray cat to be picked up and fed a saucer of milk?'

'Picked up, gladly. We can leave the milk till later.'

She studied him, decided to put into words what she was thinking.

'I know very little about you, Matthew. Some small, *small* amount of your history – oh yes, whatever you think suitable for a press release, but not more. You think me good-looking?'

'Wonderful!'

'Ah yes. Well, I think you good-looking. We are much of an age; we have no ties – except that you have a wife you have just left. But there must be more than that before . . .'

'Before?'

She shrugged. 'From your look, that was what you were thinking.'

'That was what I was thinking.'

'A little holiday *affaire*? A trifle sordid, isn't it?'

'Not if we don't make it so.'

'How can it be lifted out of the rut?'

'With passion,' he said.

She took in a slow breath, looked across the pool. 'The air is light here, hot and yet fresh. That is the way I remember it in Agadir.'

'Perhaps we shouldn't go back.'

'Now you're being romantic.'

'Is there anything wrong with that?'

'You must always be practical with a Frenchwoman. Didn't you know?'

They drank for a few moments in silence.

She said: 'He is a nice man. And very rich. I wonder if he is faithful to his wife.'

'Hi, wait. None of that!'

'I was only thinking.'

'Teasing maybe.'

The servant came to refill their drinks, but both refused. Matthew rose.

'It's nearly one. I think we should go and dress.'

III

THEY LUNCHED in another circular room with alcoved lamps and an oval dining table with a pink damask cloth shading to pale blue as it reached the floor. The curtains at the two high windows were of finest lace, outlined in yellow

139

satin. They ate lamb and rice, and chicken breasts in pimento gravy, then the lightest of pastry pies containing minced pigeon with tomatoes and hard-boiled eggs. Pouligny Montrachet to drink. Silent servants, white-coated, glittering poignards at waist.

'I have little liking for Agadir,' said Pierre de Blaye. 'Its name you know is Igoudar, meaning a hill fort. In that area there used to be warring tribes, each within its small enclave, Berbers mainly, who would often quarrel with another group, raid them with bitter enmity. Some of these groups still exist, and have become restive since the French left. But the town itself has a wonderful beach and little else. It will develop, but in doing so will become less and less like the rest of Morocco. Why did you both come there? I take it you came individually?'

They smiled and each gave an explanation, Nadine telling of the film she had been in and her decision, between parts, to revisit the town and find some winter sun; Matthew making up a story on the spur of the moment about his novels and coming away, seeking stimulus and inspiration.

'So you have no commitments drawing you back this afternoon. Why do you not stay the night here?'

Some bird was screeching outside.

'Well,' Matthew said, 'it's more than kind of you. For my part I'd be delighted.'

De Blaye said: 'We have guest bungalows; I have built four. They are just down the path over there. My servants have too little to do, and I am alone here at present. It would give me pleasure.'

Nadine smiled. 'I have no night things, and of course—'

'My mistress, who is coming next week, is about your build, I would think. There are a number of her belongings which she has left here and I know would make available to you.'

Nadine hesitated and sipped her wine. 'You are too kind, monsieur.'

De Blaye laughed. 'What does that mean?'

'It means I shall be happy to stay.'

IV

IN THE AFTERNOON, following a siesta, they walked around the grounds, among the red and yellow pomegranates, the bougainvillaea, the geraniums, the green lawns. Behind a hedge of climbing begonias they found a donkey, blindfold, turning round and round an old waterwheel, whose buckets of water were being routinely up-ended into a succession of trenches so that the garden was being irrigated.

'It is a sort of oasis. We have three such wells. It was because of them that I built here.'

As darkness fell de Blaye drove them into Taroudant and they walked through the souks, buying a few trinkets here and there.

They stopped to watch a man marvellously carving chessmen with his chisel, and working a lathe with one bare foot. The Baron said: 'It is a pity you have to return to Agadir at all. You have a car? Why do you not tomorrow drive over the High Atlas to Marrakech, spend a day there and then go on to Fez? The old town of Fez has not been touched for two hundred years. Not a European building of any sort. Lyautey built the new town outside. If you wish to see Morocco as it used to be, go to Fez.'

Matthew glanced at Nadine. He said: 'It's a tempting thought.'

They had been given two bungalows side by side, with a dividing rail on the balcony and a communicating door inside. De Blaye had made no attempt to assess their relationship: they were probably lovers – or why come together? – but the two entirely separate accommodations, individual entrance hall, bedroom, bathroom, kitchen, left the choice open.

She had come in a sleeveless silk dress, he in a check shirt and flannel slacks. Pierre de Blaye had found a cream haik of fine wool for Nadine, silk-lined, beaded and caught at the waist. He offered Matthew a handsome jellaba, but Matthew refused it in favour of black trousers belonging to de Blaye's brother, who was tall, and a silk shirt and a crimson smoking jacket.

As he settled the coat as comfortably as he could – it was made for someone with broader shoulders – he looked at himself in the full-length gilt-framed mirror and decided he would do. The bedroom was warm, for in an eccentric corner fireplace a wood fire burned, giving off odours of cedar and eucalyptus. He went through the passageway to the door dividing the two bungalows and tapped. The door, which was of studded leather, absorbed his summons, and it took three louder knocks before Nadine opened it.

'By God,' he said, 'you look – ambrosial.'

The cream cloak with its glittering ornaments set off her beauty. He bent and kissed her. She responded coolly, with a smiling detachment that did not rebuff but promised no immediate intimacy.

'What strange words you use sometimes,' she said. 'Ambrosial? Does that not mean . . .'

'If you pressed me I'd say it meant food of the gods.'

'Just now you were thinking in terms of saucers of milk.'

'It was you mentioned milk. Anyway . . . my evening has begun.'

He took her hand and they went out of his front door and walked through the jasmine-scented darkness towards the main house.

'Are you an impatient man?' she asked.

'Yes, in some things. Very.'

'I was afraid so.'

'And impulsive.'

'Impulses,' she said, 'which you must sometimes regret.'

'Oh, I don't think so. Impulses are meant to be followed.' He laughed. As usual it was an infectious sound.

She said: 'My father was a doctor. A specialist in liver complaints. If you have lived in France you will know how important the liver is to most of us! He made money. He had many mistresses. My mother had frequent lovers. They did not break up: they just went their own ways. For their only daughter you might think it would be natural, easy to live a – a – what do you call it in old England? – a profligate life. But that has not been so. There have been many flirtations but I have only had two men. Both were serious. Both *affaires* ended. It was not without distress. I don't like what is now called casual sex.'

They were on the steps to the house. Discreet lights gleamed. He said: 'When I married I was pretty much in love – at least I think I was – and so was she. We both put up a fair attempt to make a go of it. But when it came unstuck I don't think either of us was desperately hurt. I still like her. She still likes me – though she doesn't approve of my indolent life—'

'Indolent!'

143

'Well, to her it seemed so,' he said, remembering that he had claimed three novels published. 'So we agreed to part. There's no man on her side nor woman on mine. Perhaps we didn't feel deeply enough for each other. Perhaps I have never felt deeply enough for anyone.'

'Do you think that a good recommend?'

'How can I recommend myself?' Again that infectious laugh. 'But I love beauty. I love your beauty.'

Nadine said: 'But you have never been serious about a woman. Is that so?'

'Well, I wouldn't really—'

'What *do* you feel deeply about? Anything? Your books? Writing? Literature?'

'Oh, no. I like books but not enough. Music is what fascinates me.'

'Music? Ah . . .'

'I told you. That was why I went to Paris. I hoped to do something with it. I play the piano. I play the guitar. I sing. But none of them well enough. I'm doomed to be the eternal amateur.'

'What sort of music? Jazz?'

'Everything that comes out of a musical instrument. Bach, Stockhausen, Haydn, Gershwin, Fats Waller, Puccini, Sullivan, Berlin . . .'

'And you sing?'

'More or less, yes. And you?'

'Me? I don't understand music like that. But yes, I can sing a little. And dance.'

'Tonight,' he said, 'we'll both try.'

V

THE THREE French ladies had had a good morning. They had bathed and tramped along the beach in the heat and found a kiosk where they sat and drank Pernod and ate *pastillas*, which were fluffy pastries stuffed with crushed almonds and honey. They had all enjoyed a good breakfast, but the sea air had given them raging appetites which they saw no reason to resist. As the third Pernod was going down an Arab appeared leading a camel and offering them a ride.

They all saw the funny side of this. They thought the Arab, who was called Jusef, very funny because he had no top teeth at all except a solitary gold one right in the front, and when he smiled, which he did frequently, this gleamed through his beard and set them off into peals of laughter. Vicky said she had always wanted to ride on a camel, so after a good deal of haggling over price she mounted two steps, cocked her leg over and slumped into the saddle with a cry of triumph which turned into a squeal as the camel got up.

They proceeded along the beach, the older women laughing and shouting lewd advice to Vicky, who lurched and shrieked and hung on while the tall, elderly camel was led by its owner mooching on its bony, ramshackle legs and stopping now and then to champ its jaws and shake its head from side to side.

They described a circle, so that at the end of the ride the steps would be conveniently near. Eventually amid whoops and yells, Vicky lowered herself to safety. Françoise said her skirt had ridden up so high she thought Vicky usually got paid extra for showing that much.

They had two more drinks, a chocolate ice each and then began to weave their way back across the beach in search of lunch. The sun had come out from behind its clouds and the day was sweltering. The hotel seemed far away, and Vicky said she felt like she'd joined the Foreign Legion and was staggering over the desert towards an oasis, just like in a movie show.

The last quarter-mile was covered with many pauses for rest and argument. There was a stage at which Françoise's laughter always turned to belligerence; but Laura slapped her down and led the way until, oh, bliss, hard ground was under their feet and they were home. They had been out so long that time had gone ahead of them and early lunchers were already eating round the pool.

'Let's leave our things and go right in,' Laura said.

So they hobbled round through the palm trees and sat in the open door of their car, rubbing sand out of toes and combing sandy hair. Laura draped her swimming costume over the steering-wheel and the other two left theirs hanging from the windows and seat backs where they could dry in the sun. Then, glassily but hungrily, they stumbled back from the front drive and weaved a way among the tables for lunch.

M. and Mme Thibault were not at their table today. Nor were Mr Burford and Mrs Heinz. Nor Matthew Morris and Nadine Deschamps.

VI

THE THIBAULTS were about to leave for lunch with the Governor, M. Bouamrani. Henri Thibault had made certain that his arrival in Agadir should not go unnoticed. Although convinced that his own eminence was not likely to be overlooked in France, there was just the risk that in the less civilized parts of the old empire there might be a slip-up. So his secretary had written to the Governor's secretary. And the newly elected senator for the department of Nievre, a M. François Mitterrand, had been prevailed upon to drop an enlightened line, which would ensure he, Thibault, was accorded proper deference and hospitality. Indeed M. Mitterrand had suggested to Thibault that before he left Morocco he would do well to seek an audience of the King, who naturally would want to meet one of France's leading bankers and philanthropists.

Thus it had been arranged, though Estrella did not know. Thibault had been saving it as a pleasant surprise; but this disagreeable contretemps with the egregious Laura had soured the situation. Estrella, herself the daughter of a banker, whose benevolent intervention had contributed to Henri's rise, had once been a very pretty girl. As a rich man's youngest daughter, she had been quite the catch of the season, vivacious, sexy and playful. Lucien Costals had not thought much of the young man she finally took up with – pompous little fellow with shifty eyes – but Henri had turned out fairly well, had fathered three girls, taken advantage of every business opportunity offered him; had known how to cultivate people in high places and altogether had carved a career for himself.

So far as one could tell, he had also made a good husband. The trouble at quite an early stage was that Estrella had not adjusted her attitude to her loss of looks. At fifty she still wore the clothes of a thirty-year-old. She continued to treat men coquettishly and to expect them to respond. In the best society in Paris much older women than she could still dominate their circle, but she had neither the personality nor the intellect.

She was showing, in her husband's eyes, neither personality nor intellect in her attitude towards his encounter with Laura Legrand. She had blown the whole thing up into a great balloon of indignation and contempt. He was disgusted with his ill-luck and disgusted with his wife. Every woman knew that men sometimes had little affairs on the side: from the interchange she knew absolutely nothing of the details (fortunately).

Yet he had no wish to make this a serious quarrel between them: the old father, Lucien Costals, still existed at eighty-seven, and though no doubt he would have laughed aloud if told the whole truth, he still doted on his daughter. And with his banking holdings he still controlled some of the purse strings. There were two brothers-in-law.

They had been invited for one o'clock at the Governor's House, and it was now after twelve thirty. Estrella, provokingly, was taking an age to make up her face. As always she was doing too much, laying on the mascara and the rouge. The very look of her over-curled and pinkish hair irritated him. He paced up and down, pausing now and then to glance out over the smiling scene. The sun had at last come out and the hot land breeze had strengthened. Flags and the frills on umbrellas fluttered. From here you could see a corner of the angular swimming-pool and a couple of empty tables. He looked at his watch. Estrella took no notice. She was now putting little points of rouge on her ear lobes.

'Hrrhm!' said Thibault. 'It is now twelve thirty-eight. I should not wish to be late.'

Estrella did not reply. With the handle of a comb she was tidying her curls, twisting them more perfectly into place.

'I have left the car near the front door,' said Thibault. 'You have only a few steps to walk.'

'You can go without me if you wish,' Mme Thibault said.

Her husband greeted this remark with the contempt it deserved. As if she would make all these preparations for nothing!

Presently, with agonizing concern for every small detail, she made herself ready, picked up her Venetian bag, made sure her Ghent handkerchief and other items were safely stowed away, gave a hitch to the shoulder of her ivory lace dress and stood up. He went to the door and opened it for her. Without acknowledging this, she stalked out.

Of course the lift was engaged. It was only two floors to walk down, but she made no move to do so, while he pressed and pressed at the button. Eventually it came and they descended in slow motion until the lobby was reached.

Thibault made an effort. 'Our car is just on the left. Shall I bring it round for you?'

'Please.'

The sun struck him as he went out, putting on his panama. Most of the Renault Fours were out. Only one other stood a few paces away. Same colour, same hire company. They were scoundrels and rogues, Thibault thought. They had not even been to see him this morning with an upgraded car. They had never had any intention of attempting to satisfy him. He might, he thought, refuse to pay. Certainly he would make a strong complaint to the Directeur. (He might even mention the matter this afternoon. Perhaps the Governor would put a car at their disposal.)

You could never trust the Arabs, he thought, as he opened the car door.

He stepped back. A vivid yellow bathing costume was draped over the steering-wheel. Another one – a two-piece suit of an eye-catching green – lay on the passenger's seat. Shoes were in the back of the car, and a bunch of striped towels; and still one more costume hung out of the back window on the opposite side. There were dark patches in the car where things had *dripped*. And there was *sand* . . .

Estrella Thibault, standing stiffly beside an indoor palmetto palm, was surprised to see her husband stride angrily in and, taking no notice of her at all, march across to the reception desk.

'Someone has been tampering with my car!'

'Sir?'

'Someone has been using it, utilizing it. This is outrageous!'

'Sir?' The concierge was coming out from behind the desk.

Thibault looked at his watch.

'No.'

The concierge stopped.

'Order me a taxi!'

'Yes, sir.'

'At once. We shall be late! Our appointment is with the Governor!'

'Very good, sir.' The man picked up the telephone. 'A *petit taxi*?'

'No!' shouted Thibault. 'A car! A proper car! A limousine! At *once*!'

'Very good, sir. Right away.'

CHAPTER SEVEN

I

EARLIER IN THE day one of the little Renaults had been driven far south along the coast and had passed Tiznit before it was time for lunch.

Lee was accustoming himself to the gear change, which operated from the steering-wheel, and Letty was the map reader. Not that there was much chance of going astray; once you were out of Agadir it was a flat, featureless drive with few side roads or opportunities to take the wrong turning. Before they left Agadir Letty had bought a tin of cooked ham, a knife, some paper plates, two bottles of beer, two glasses, French bread, French mustard, butter and tomatoes, so when they stopped some miles short of Goulimine under the shade of a group of date palms, they were self-sufficient. They finished up with oranges.

'I don't think,' Lee said, 'there's *anything* more enjoyable than a picnic. Not the most original thought in the world, but I'm prepared to stand by it.'

'And without beggar boys,' said Letty. 'I do not think they are ever as hungry as they look, but I do not enjoy eating and being watched.'

There was a flush of pleasure in her cheeks. She liked Morocco, its strangeness, its remoteness from anything she had ever known before.

After lunch they drove through Goulimine until the

metalled road ended and there was only a camel trail. Lee said they could now claim to have eaten at least one orange in the Sahara, but Letty was nervous lest the car should get stuck in the sand, so they drove back to the little fortified town and wandered round among the camels and the donkeys and the mules, amid a smell of spices and dung and leather and rancid oil. Men of all ages were squatting against the ochre walls in their white, brown and blue robes, and there were stalls selling honey and molasses and almonds and fried fish and sheep's kidneys. Black-capped Jews strolled by, and a student or two carrying books and prayer mats. Overhead the storks were making a great noise as they nested in the ruined walls of the fort.

They took a few photographs and bought some sweets and a metal teapot for making mint tea, and a fistful of bananas, and got into the car to leave, when they were accosted by two 'Blue Men' seeking a lift. Lee smiled a question at Letty and then nodded to the men. They grinned and climbed enormously into the back and sat there, formidable-looking but polite, and smelling of goat. The Blue Men spoke no French, so conversation was confined to nods and grunts. They were driven for about ten miles, to a hamlet under some palm trees, then they climbed hairily out with large white grins and taps of thanks on the side windows.

Letty said: 'When I heard first about Blue Men I thought it was their skins that were blue, not just their robes!'

'Sometimes the dye does get onto their faces and hands,' Lee said.

They stayed a moment or two watching the two men walk towards the shacks, which in fact were hardly more than roofs of branches and boards covered by earth and supported by thin tree stumps with a few stone and mud walls.

They turned and waved. Lee and Letty waved back and then drove on.

Letty said: 'Carl is always so very careful about who he gives a lift to. He never picks up women because they may try to blackmail him and claim he has assaulted them. I wonder what he would think about us picking up two Blue Men!'

She had said little more about herself since she told him about their escape from Norway, except that when she reached America she had worked as a Red Cross nurse in New Jersey for the rest of the war. She had met Carl Heinz early on when he was brought to her hospital for treatment after a plane crash, and they had married soon after.

Her brother had been killed in 1943, and her mother had also died, though only two years ago.

So she was almost as much alone in the world as Lee. Soon after Ann became friendly with her, Lee had caught sight of her in Concord in company with a big, fair, lumbering boy with a mane of Nordic hair. It had meant nothing to Lee then but he supposed now it was Leon, the errant son. According to Letty there had frequently been noisy, even violent, rows. Yet Carl had left his wife more than a year before their son. It was not he who had driven the boy away.

They stopped at Tiznit for tea on the way back.

'There's not much to buy,' Lee said as they walked into the souk. 'I might get a cover for a hassock – an ottoman. This white one – is it elephant hide? It would look well in our drawing-room.'

She said nothing.

He said: 'Are you hoping your husband will come back?'

'No! Oh, no.'

'Then why don't you divorce him?'

'It does not seem to matter. I receive an allowance.'

'How much does he send you?'

She named a monthly sum which, as he had suspected, was paltry. He knew roughly what long-distance truck-drivers earned.

'That is not enough. I can get more for you.'

'I do not think I need it.'

'You might not have to work at the Paul Revere. In any case it would be better if you divorced him.'

'I do not expect ever to marry again. I do not know . . . Sometimes I think I am not capable of loving anyone with the whole of my heart. Perhaps I did my brother – but then he went . . .'

'Your son?'

'Leon? Yes, of course. Deeply at times. But he wished to go away. From home. Maybe I failed him in those early years. The war was on. I was nursing. I think maybe I failed to give him the sort of love he needed when he was a baby. And as he began to grow up the marriage began to go wrong.'

Lee said: 'It's not uncommon for the young to want to get away from their home, from the influence of their parents. And, I assure you, that doesn't always depend on the amount of love and loving care they get at home!'

They drove on for a few miles.

Lee said: 'I should like you to give up the restaurant work and come to me whole time. I think what with your bridge and your cooking you have made yourself – indispensable.'

She half smiled, for he was smiling. 'It is kind of you to suggest it. I could not ever take Mrs Burford's place.'

'Nobody's asking you to. But I take it that in spite of your – your detachment you have some care for my welfare?'

'Of course I care for your welfare! I – I'd care for anyone who has been hurt, badly hurt, badly let down, when it is not a fault of their own!'

'Rather the same as you'd care for a mongrel dog with a broken leg?'

She patted his arm. 'Please. You know I did not mean that. You always shoot too many guns for me in argument.'

'But you always have the last gun.'

It was a straight, empty road, which was lined with tall palm trees, with the sea glimmering in the distance.

He said awkwardly: 'I told you that you have come to mean a lot to me. That is something over which I have little control. I'm not exaggerating my feelings when I tell you this. Whatever you feel or don't feel, I guess it's a fact of life between us from now on. I'm not sure we can carry on in just that same casual way when we get home.'

'I should not wish to lose your friendship. I value that . . .'

Changing down in this little car was not too easy until you had mastered it, and there was a grunt as he did so now. Perhaps emotion played its part in his lack of timing. They overtook a convoy of donkeys carrying panniers overflowing with heavy grasses, then a solitary camel, distinctive with its swinging walk, and a baby donkey trotting at its side. They all seemed to belong to two Arab urchins who looked hardly big enough to wield a stick.

She said: 'You have been so very good to me. Thank you.'

'But the point is I presume that you don't have any such feelings for me.'

There was a long silence. Then as Agadir came in sight she said: 'I have a great feeling of warmth and liking for you, Lee. I do really have. But . . . perhaps that is not quite what you meant.'

'No,' he said, 'that is not quite what I meant.'

II

DINNER WAS over at the Gazelle d'Or. Sumptuous was a word Matthew would have avoided as an author – it was over the top, too often used by tabloid journalists – but there was not another one he could quite think of which so properly defined the feast they'd had. It was a mixture of the best of French and Moroccan cooking, though they drank only French wines. After dinner they went into the circular drawing-room and sipped mint tea freshly brewed by an elderly Arab who squatted on the floor by a window and carried the cups around and refilled them if required. In one corner was an old spinet, and Matthew went across and tried it. The sound was tinny and sharp.

'It is a seventeenth-century *épinette*,' said de Blaye, 'and in poor condition. I intend often to have it restored, but there is no one in my family who plays, so I keep it as a beautiful piece of furniture.'

Matthew tried 'Jesu, Joy of Man's Desiring', and then for a change a bit of Dave Brubeck; but neither was satisfactory. As he was getting up de Blaye said: 'Try that other thing. You may find it more interesting.'

Matthew picked up an instrument from a side table. It had the look of a guitar but clearly was not. He plucked at it and it made a promising sound.

156

'A *vihuela*,' said de Blaye. 'Spanish, you know. It is even older than the *épinette* but in much better condition. You play it like a lute.'

It was about the size of a guitar but it had ten strings. Its body was delicately veneered.

'I found it in Chouan last year,' de Blaye said. 'Do play it if you can, as I have not heard it properly used.'

'Doubt if I can do that,' Matthew said, but quite challenged. He plucked a few melodious noises from it and grinned at Nadine. She smiled back. He tried 'Smoke Gets In Your Eyes', which didn't come out too badly. Then he tried Brubeck again but it was a dismal failure. He began to tune the instrument, but lacked a middle C. He played '*Torno a Sorrento*', broke off halfway because he had forgotten how it went. Nadine hummed a few bars and enabled him to finish it.

He played for half an hour. This included part of a Sonata in E minor by Scarlatti, 'Tea for Two' and 'I'll See You Again'.

Both listeners applauded when he got up. In fact he was delighted with himself that it was so good, knowing how awful it might have been. Well-fed and wined but ever susceptible to atmosphere, he had risen to the occasion.

'Why do you not now sing some duets?' Pierre de Blaye suggested. 'You have a good voice, Nadine. Sing with Matthew or sing alone?'

It was another hour before they finished. They ranged from 'O Sole Mio' to '*Carmen*', from '*Je ne regrette rien*' to 'Some Enchanted Evening', which only Matthew knew and had to sing himself.

'*Mon Dieu!*' said Pierre de Blaye. 'This is good. You must stay. I have business in Rabat tomorrow, but it will be done in half a day. Stay a week until my Alessandra comes. She sings a little. We could form the Taroudant Quartet!'

It all broke up with laughter and joking. Matthew was in his element and at his best. Nadine, laughing, said she *must* return to Agadir tomorrow as she was expecting calls from her agent. But in a few days, if Matthew was willing to drive her ... Matthew was very willing. They were all flushed with wine, and flushed too with making music and sparking each other off.

As he steered her from the main house towards their bungalows he said: 'Why don't we go on as the Baron suggests? Drive over the Atlas tomorrow to Marrakech, a couple of days there, then Fez, then return here Thursday, back to Agadir about next Saturday.'

(Disagreeable thoughts in the back of his mind that he hadn't enough money to do this; but the night was too good to be spoiled by financial considerations. He could borrow from de Blaye.)

They were linking arms, and her hair brushed his as she shook it. 'Daumier is ringing me tomorrow. It was an arrangement.'

'Telephone him from here in the morning. That shouldn't be a difficulty.'

They took a few more steps. She settled her hand more firmly into his. 'I haven't enough money on me. Nor have I clothes. Virtually no make-up, certainly no personal things. Let's do the other thing he suggests – go back and come again about Thursday. I'd love to meet his mistress. Then – if we really feel like it, we could go to Marrakech about Saturday, then Fez, if you wanted to, maybe fly home from there, or Casablanca or somewhere.'

'You think we might do that?' he said gratefully.

'I think we might do that.'

'Hurray!' he said, giving a skip.

There was companionable silence then until they reached the bungalows. It's always easy to con yourself, but Matthew knew he had never felt like this for any woman before. She was cultured, elegant, sophisticated, yet fresh and simple; direct, uncomplicated. And he thought her loving would be the same.

'Nadine.'

'Yes, Matthew?'

'You know what I want.'

'Yes, I know what you want.'

'Of course one can trot out the hoary old siege guns. What's two days to get to know someone? And you don't want a sordid sorry little holiday affair. Well, neither do I. But it won't be that way.'

'Won't it?'

'Well you have to agree, this evening has been rather special, hasn't it?'

'Oh, yes.'

'So I don't suppose the night would be anything less special – if you'd allow me to sleep with you.'

Nadine paused to pull at a piece of jasmine and to sniff it. She said: 'Will you promise not to make me laugh?'

III

THEY MADE love in her bed under an ornate circular medallion of carved cedar and gilded cornices, while the aromatic fire smouldered in the corner grate. The flickering of this fire and an oblique slit from the hall was all the light they had, but it was enough.

They came together with hunger and anticipation – and indeed laughter – wine and music and the sexual urge blending in a discerning passion. She was a new experience to him. A frustrated romantic, he had always sought more in women than they were able to give him. Now he took it all and was lost in it all. Nor did she withhold herself in any aspect or degree.

At times they lay together breathing in each other's breath, short of their own. They spoke now and then in monosyllables, exhaustion bringing renewal and renewal exhaustion.

As the fire burned down and its flames flickered to a glow they presently lay side by side and presently slept. The whole day had had a sort of laughing magic, and this was its consummation.

CHAPTER EIGHT

I

THE CASINO, a square building, largely timber-built, with a low central dome, was set back from the sea front but only five minutes' walk from the Saada.

Johnny Frazier went by car.

It was nine o'clock. He had walked in at the Casino at five and been told that Benjamin Ardrossi did not come on duty until eight, so Johnny had had his dinner first.

He would dearly have liked to leave his suitcase behind in some safe place but didn't dare.

The Casino was all a-glitter and quite busy. This was high season, and the hotels were full. The first people he spotted were Laura and Françoise and Vicky. They had been noisy at dinner, and Laura had made things worse by stopping at the Thibault table and apologizing to M. Thibault for using his car as a clothes horse by mistake. Thibault had sat there with a would-be-executioner's expression while Mme Legrand explained for the second time in tedious detail how it came about that one Renault Four looked very much like another.

Johnny had seen them leave before him, and he was not surprised where they had been off to. He hoped they had used their own car this time. They were seated at one of the two roulette tables and intent on play. All along, Johnny speculated, they seemed to have money to splash about.

Maybe they were not whores but widows of rich fairground proprietors or owners of bowling alleys. Money came in all guises.

He enquired of an attendant, and M. Benjamin Ardrossi was pointed out. A thin dark man with an apron-string of black beard running thinly from ear to chin, a narrow hooked nose and some gold teeth which showed when he spoke. He was operating at the table where the three women played.

People were standing around watching the circulation of the little ball. He edged his way nearer until he was behind the croupier.

In the brief pause after the winnings had been distributed, the losings raked in, and the new bets were being laid, Johnny Frazier said: 'M. Ardrossi?'

The croupier glanced round, then back at the table. 'Yes?'

'Colonel Tournelle gave me your name. I'm his son.'

'*Faîtes vos jeux,*' Ardrossi called. '*Mesdames et messieurs, faîtes vos jeux, s'il vous plaît.*'

More quietly. 'So?'

'My father's in hospital. Did you know?'

'Yes.'

'I came wanting a bit of help. He couldn't oblige. He suggested you might.'

'Might what?'

'Be able to help me.'

'In what respect?'

'I would like a quiet word with you.'

'*Faîtes vos jeux,*' called Ardrossi. '*Faîtes vos jeux. Rien ne va plus . . .*' And then, 'I break for coffee in half an hour. Wait by the cash desk.'

'*Ça va,*' said Johnny, and moved away.

But Laura had spotted him.

'Johnny! Come and join us! We need a morsel of help. Lady Luck's been no good for us, so maybe a touch of Gentleman's Luck will roll the ball right. Didn't know there were so many damned ways of losing.'

She had him by the arm. The heavily made-up face was flushed; but the blue eyes, though bleary, were shrewd enough. With her free hand she kept twitching up the shoulder of her dress where it wanted to fall off.

He allowed himself to be led to the table, and Françoise was yanked out of her chair to make room for him. Oh well . . . Gambling was a weakness of his.

He began cautiously, changing only a few hundred dirhams and using them for the shorter odds on *impair* and *manque*. He lost them all, bought some more chips, took larger risks, and began to win. He concentrated on 2 and 8, only because it happened to be the 28th of the month. Half an hour passed quickly, and he became so absorbed that he only just raised his eyes in time to see Ardrossi slipping out of his seat to be replaced by another croupier. He was nine hundred dirhams up, and the three girls were noisy with praise, as they had profited too.

'Coming back,' he promised, as he got up. 'Just off for a few minutes, see? I'll be back.'

'What's in that case?' Vicky asked playfully, tapping it. 'Been robbing a bank? Never seen you without it. D'you take it to the john, eh?'

'That's where I'm going now,' said Johnny, withdrawing it from her touch and tucking it under his arm. 'Didn't know I was a tax collector, did you? I'm here on business. Catching dodgers. *And* young women who take other people's cars for their drying rooms!'

Shrill laughter followed him as he made for the cash

desk. Ardrossi was leaning against a pillar, with a freshly lighted cigarette in his hand. Standing up, he was a much shorter man than the impression given in the croupier's chair.

He made a movement of his head, and Johnny followed him into a darker corner of the room. Ardrossi went off, and came back with coffee.

'Tournelle is still sick? I heard it was his heart.'

Johnny nodded. He was summing the other man up, deciding how far he could trust him. It had been left to him to decide.

'He's better. But it'll be days before he can be moved, maybe a week.'

'Your name is Tournelle?'

'Well ... it was. I'm half-English. When the marriage broke up my mother took me to England and I took her name.'

'Which is?'

'Carpenter.'

'Ah.' The croupier put brown sugar in his coffee. 'And ...?'

'I came from England on Friday. I wanted something from the old man. I saw him this morning, and ...'

'Yes. I understand. And what do you want from me?'

Johnny said: 'Another passport.'

It looked from a distance as if Françoise had fallen out of the chair he had recently vacated. There was quite a noise and a commotion, but other people blocked the view.

'Friends of yours?' asked Ardrossi.

'What? No. Women staying at my hotel.'

'Are you wanted by the police?' Ardrossi asked suddenly.

'Nothing like that,' said Johnny. 'But would it matter?'

'It might add to the urgency.'

'I wouldn't want to wait long.'

'Speed always costs more.'

'Of course. But by that do you mean you can fix this?'

Ardrossi tapped at his cigarette, and some fine ash drifted onto the parquet floor. A small twisted smile.

'Most things can be arranged, with adequate time and adequate funds.'

Something in Ardrossi's smile decided Johnny not to trust him with the contents of the suitcase.

'I'd want to have it at the earliest.'

'And therefore the most expensive.'

'If you say so.'

There was a pause. The commotion round the roulette table had died down.

'When?'

'When can you do it?'

'Do you have spare passport photographs?'

'No.' Johnny had thought of this but decided against it, thinking he would probably grow a beard. But, he had realized too late, beards take a long time to grow.

Ardrossi was pained by this lack of foresight. He pinched the bridge of his narrow nose between thumb and forefinger.

'It *can* be done, of course, but ... Tomorrow morning first thing, I would suggest for the photographs. Seven o'clock. Then it will have to go to Casa. There are no facilities here. This will cost you a thousand dollars.'

'Too much,' said Johnny automatically. One bargained for everything in Morocco. 'Five hundred.'

'You can have it complete by Tuesday morning. But it will be not less than a thousand.'

The essence of bargaining is that the buyer must pretend he is not keen to buy. No such leeway here. One could only approach it another way.

'A thousand if you have it ready tomorrow night.'

Ardrossi lit a cigarette from the butt of the old, then stubbed the old one out. His glance strayed to the case Johnny carried. 'I will have to telephone my friends in Casa. It will be necessary to fly the photographs – and your present passport, please – as soon as they have been taken. Whether it can all be done in time to catch the evening plane back I do not know. But in that case it would be another two hundred dollars. I assure you, that is very cheap. Your father, I am certain, could not arrange it for less.'

Johnny was suddenly angry. This little Jew had him over a barrel. Bargaining be damned. He could do nothing but agree. That glance at the suitcase. People did. If you carried a suitcase on a beach or into dinner or at a casino people stared. And speculated.

'I'll pay a thousand,' he said.

Ardrossi put down his cup. 'I must go in a moment. Twelve hundred it has to be, if you want it tomorrow night. I come off duty at eleven tonight. Think about it until then.'

Johnny realized that twelve hundred dollars would hardly disturb the packages in the case under his arm.

'OK,' he said. 'If you can guarantee.'

'Six hundred now. Six hundred on completion.'

'Can you guarantee it?'

'If the plane runs. It usually does. But it will be late when it arrives.'

'Do we meet here?'

'No, better at your hotel. I must go.'

'Where tomorrow morning?'

'Rue Moulay Ismail. A shop on the corner. A photographer's shop. It is near the port.'

'I'll find it. Seven a.m.?'

'Seven a.m. The shop will be closed but will open if you knock.' Ardrossi stubbed out his second cigarette. 'And the money. Six hundred tonight.'

It was all there. But not to be taken out publicly. 'I'll meet you at eleven.'

'Very good.' Benjamin Ardrossi bowed courteously to the other man and walked back to the roulette table.

Johnny followed him and rejoined the three women; he set about losing the nine hundred dirhams he had won.

II

LEE AND LETTY ate early, then strolled along the boulevard in the direction of the Casino. But they did not go in. He linked her arm. The movement was his but she made no attempt to withdraw.

Suddenly aware that things were not going to work out on this trip as when he left America he had subconsciously hoped, knowing now that his life was washed up and this vacation was a mess, and Ann's desertion was just as dire now as he had hoped it never would be again, he began to talk about Ann to this other woman who cared nothing for him at all. He told her of the vacations they had had together while they were still young, of their honeymoon in Mussolini's Venice, when the mosquitoes were still rampant, of rain in St Mark's Square and duckboards needed to cross it, lovemaking and eating grapes on a wet afternoon. Of Ann, ever adventurous, during the early fifties on a visit to Vienna, getting caught up in a political march, unaware and uncaring of the issues involved – this on the fringe of the Russian sector – and of her being arrested and Lee having to take along an attaché from the US Embassy to apologize and explain.

The First World War, he told Letty, had ended just in time not to interfere with his Law School; but he had seen a year of the Second as an ambulance driver in Italy before being blown up and invalided out. Ann, too, by flagrantly lying about her age and pulling strings not unconnected with her father's position in Congress, had contrived to enlist, and had traded on her knowledge of French (she had been at school in Paris) to be taken on as an interpreter with the First Army, where she had caught the eye of General Bradley and become his platonic friend.

He went on and on, telling Letty details of his married life that he had almost forgotten. Sometimes a trace of emotion came into his voice in spite of himself; but on the whole he took care not to seem to be evoking sympathy, not to be asking even for understanding. Sometimes the lightness of the stories lifted him so that they could both smile at the misadventures and the misunderstandings.

When they got back the night was still hot and overcast, so they had a drink on the terrace, and went up to bed soon after ten. They kissed outside the bedroom doors. There was a glint in her eyes as she smiled at him and slid out of his arms.

When she had gone he stared bleakly at the closed door. He knocked.

She opened it immediately, looking startled.

'Your cape,' he said. 'You forgot it.'

'Oh, thank you.' She took it from him. It was the cape he had bought her in Paris. She looked down at it. She fingered the cape as if she had not seen it before.

He said: 'Goodbye, Letty.'

She said: 'I wish I could make you happy.'

He said: 'You can.'

'Yes, but only in a way. It is the most unimportant part of love.'

'For me,' he said, 'it is the most important right now.'

'Yes, but in the morning . . .'

'I would be glad to let the morning take care of itself.'

III

SO IT HAPPENED. In a half light, not so tastefully arranged as in the bedroom in Taroudant, they lay quietly on the bed together, and when they were naked he stroked her gently for quite a while. Presently he parted her thighs and entered her – not like a commanding hero but like a snake in the grass. He then did absolutely nothing more, propping himself up on his elbows, partly to take his weight off her and partly to look at her face.

She said: 'Lee, I . . .'

'Ssh. Say nothing, Letty.'

He did no more while the seconds ticked away. Silence in the room except for their breathing. There was music tinkling outside.

Her eyes were half-closed, her expression strained. And a long minute went by, and another minute began.

Then he leaned forward and began to kiss her mouth, using each of her lips individually like new senses to be explored. And he began to grow again within her. The second minute was near its end before he began to move his loins, and then very gently. Her eyes had been open for some little while now, clear and hurt and staring; then they slowly glazed over and tears started on the bottom lids and as quickly dried. She gave the deepest sigh: he watched her breasts rise and fall.

He was losing himself, and he knew she was. And with a rising sense of elation he arrived at the certain belief that she had not experienced this before.

He edged and manoeuvred and gently moved her whole body, timing his own senses, holding them back until he knew she was coming. Then together they climbed to the peak.

CHAPTER NINE

I

MONDAY, THE 29th of February, 1960. Leap Year. The third day of the Fast of Ramadan.

The day broke heavy and sunless. Gulls were noisy, circling and screaming over the sullen sea. Dogs had howled again in the night, and animals were generally restless. In the early morning there was what many people took for a heavy rumble of thunder but others recognized as an earth tremor. When it was over pictures were here and there aslant on walls. Cups had rattled. Cutlery had tittered together on newly laid breakfast tables.

But nobody took alarm. The occasional tremor was something one was used to, living here. It was part of the general order of things, part of the climate. There had been something rather bad once upon a time, but that was over two centuries ago . . .

On the Saturday and the Sunday Johnny Frazier had occupied some of his time in the little travel shop, which had its main office in Casablanca. In there he had examined the options open to him to leave Morocco by sea, and had whittled these down to two vessels, one to leave on the Tuesday forenoon, the other on Friday evening. The first was an American tramp steamer called the *Merrimac*, out of Baltimore, and loading a cargo of canned sardines for Rio de Janeiro. She was licensed to carry six passengers, and a berth was available. The second was a Norwegian cruise ship, the *Vesteraaven*, which would put in for two nights before leaving for the Canary Isles and thence to Cape Town. Again there were cabins available.

Johnny preferred the *Merrimac*, whose destination was a better one for him, but he could not book a cabin, except provisionally, without an available passport, and the *Vesteraaven* gave him an extra day's grace if the passport was delayed.

He had chosen the name Henri Delaware. He had decided to become a French Canadian, a vague nationality which, so long as he wasn't in Canada, would give him a wider scope for invention. When this was known to Ardrossi he demanded an extra five hundred dollars, but in this at least he had resorted to bargaining and they had settled on an overall total of 1,450 dollars.

It was worth it to Johnny because of the speed promised. After the *Vesteraaven* there was no really suitable ship leaving Casablanca for nearly three weeks.

Johnny was up at six on the Monday. He looked at the case. His whole life centred on that case. Everything he had done, all the risks he had taken, was still taking, all the plans ... What the hell if people stared? They would not knock him down, run off with it.

He took it with him.

A stout elderly photographer in a blue skull cap let him in and the job was done in no time. Ardrossi hovered in the background. Handing over his own passport was worrying to Johnny, but they insisted it was necessary in order to make an exact copy. Anyway he had another with him, though it was too hot for safe use. He returned to the hotel for breakfast. He would go and see his father later in the day but not tell him he was leaving on the Tuesday morning. He would just pay his bill early that day and slip away to join the ship. Her approximate departure time was ten a.m. It was going to be tight for time, but if he caught the eight thirty plane it would give him just long enough in Casablanca to confirm the booking and pay for the voyage. Then away.

He had had no nightmares last night. He had stayed gambling until the Casino closed at two, had lost money but not heavily, and had drunk much more than usual. He had helped Mme Legrand and Mlle Reynard to hoist the somnolent figure of Mlle Grasset out of her chair at the roulette table, and resuscitate her with playful slaps into a state at which she could stagger out of the Casino and be squeezed into the Renault. He might have gone back with them to the hotel to help them in, for Françoise in her cups became as lumpy and cumbersome as a flock mattress, but it was just nearing eleven, and it had been necessary to catch Ardrossi.

He spent the morning lying sweating on a chaise-longue by the swimming-pool, counting the minutes as they crawled past. Laura, Vicky and Françoise appeared about eleven and crowded round him, full of last night and the fact that Vicky at least had come out a winner. Françoise was no worse for the drink she had had yesterday. Hangover did not exist in her vocabulary; and it seemed fairly clear that all three of them intended to spend today in an alcoholic haze. They insisted on buying Johnny a large Pernod, and he raised no objection; he found their conversation amusing and their company helped the time to pass.

By now they had confirmed his suspicions of what their profession was, and he listened cynically to reminiscences and anecdotes about their more peculiar clients.

During the morning M. and Mme Thibault put in a brief appearance at the corner of the swimming-pool but, seeing who was there, as quickly left.

At twelve Matthew and Nadine returned from Taroudant. Nadine was content but thoughtful, Matthew exuber-
ant. This association had started quite casually for him,
almost in a superficial way; she was very pretty and elegant,
with a rare quality of personality which captivated him. A
fillip for his holiday. But it had grown into something more
than that, reaching down into the unplumbed depths of his
being. For the first time in his life he knew himself to be
really in love.

For the first time he knew what head over heels meant.
The day had new and more brilliant colours. Sitting in the
car beside him she was beyond compare. The scent of her
silky skin had got itself into his bloodstream so that she was
within him, a part of him, to be remembered, savoured,
cherished and soon, soon, very soon to be renewed in all its
fullness and passion.

Pierre had again suggested either that they should go on
to Marrakech or stay here while he was away, swimming,
sunbathing, eating and drinking and being waited on by his
incomparable staff until he returned. But Nadine had tactfully said no. They had agreed to return on Thursday.

This also really suited Matthew. He had come with just
enough money in Agadir to get by, but in this company he
needed more: he was anxious not to allow Mlle Deschamps
out of his sight. As long as money could be found to allow
him to be with her, whether in Agadir or back in Paris, there
he wanted to be. Time today to cable his mother and get her
response before Thursday. Borrowing from your mother was
not a practice he approved of; he had done it only twice
before when in dire emergency; but this he felt was an
emergency, if sublime rather than dire.

Nadine's thoughtfulness was not because she had not
been stirred by the events of the night – rather the contrary.

Only once before in her life had she been affected to this degree by a man. She liked it. She liked it very much. But that time had led to disaster. She did not want the sort of trauma that had been hers when Jean-Paul had moved out of her life. Going along with the natural sexual instincts of a woman charmed by the passion of this good-looking young Englishman went a very French practicality and intuition; and she was not yet sure about Matthew.

She told herself it was perhaps just the burnt-child syndrome: I have been this way once before and how wonderful it was and then how unbearably awful; watch your step before you go and burn yourself again. Here was a young man of great personal quality. His knowledge of music and art – his obsession with them – his standing as an author with two or three novels to his name. Individual brilliance. But how stable was he emotionally? Capable of being carried away by the feelings of the moment. Capable of great charm – and sexual vitality – and the ability to convince that this was what he really meant and always would mean.

Twice she had picked out contradictions in his presentation of himself. Once it had been three novels he had written, once it had been two. How many, if any, had really been published? Was it unkind to care? Nadine cared. Not on the level of his personal achievement but on the level of his inner honesty and commitment.

In the meantime she was content enough to let his attentions wash over her like a warm sea. Nothing like this had been in her thoughts when she came to Agadir. It had happened within two days, like a flash of lightning, like an earth tremor.

II

THEY HAD stopped once on the way home. Just after they had left the orange plantations and the olive groves and come out upon the plain where the argan trees grew, Matthew braked because he saw a large obstacle in his path. At first he thought in the heat haze that it was an animal, then he saw it was a rock. If he had driven into it it would have wrecked his front wheels.

They both got out and looked around. They stood in a hot windless silence. At first Matthew was cautious, wondering if this were a booby trap, with a dozen wild beggars waiting to spring out and rob them and steal their car. But there was nobody. Nor was there much cover for anyone to hide. The only place of concealment was a craggy bluff about twenty yards from the road, red sandstone, with a few wispy clusters of vegetation clinging to its side. The boulder in the road was of red sandstone. Looking up, it was possible to imagine that it had been dislodged from somewhere near the top and had rolled down, shedding dust and bits of rock, until it came to a stop in the middle of the road. There it stood, uncompromising and very large and blocking their way. But who had dislodged it? There were no robbers; there were no tittering children.

Matthew went across and shoved at the rock. It was movable – with effort. In any case where it stood it was a hazard to traffic. Matthew looked up and down. There was no traffic. But sooner or later would come a bus. He heaved at the side of the rock and was able to topple it over. He heaved it again: this was more difficult for its largest side was now downwards. But he did it.

Now he could get past. But a bus could not. His sense of

civic responsibility was not normally great, but he heaved a couple more times and the boulder was no longer a menace to travellers. He dusted his hands, rubbing off the clinging, cloying reddish dust and looked round again. Nothing but the hot windless silence.

Nadine was standing a few yards from the car, hands behind back, staring across the plain. He came up with her.

'Thing must have just rolled down,' he said. 'Unless some wild kids did it for fun and ran away. Anyway, we can drive on now.'

She said: 'The goats have all gone.'

'Yes, I suppose they have. Maybe it's too hot for them in the mornings.'

'It was morning yesterday.'

He looked around. 'That's true.'

'No birds either. It's . . . lonely.'

He did not speak but put an arm lightly round her.

She said: 'Look over there – towards Agadir.'

The landscape was so level that it disappeared into the shimmering distance, but Matthew could see a dark cloud, covering a third of the sky, over towards the sea.

She shivered.

'You can't be cold,' he said.

She smiled. 'You have that old English saying: "Somebody must have stood on my grave."'

'You know English too well.'

'I lived there for two years when I was eighteen, nineteen. In Windsor.'

'As a guest of the Queen?'

'She was unaware of my existence.'

'She didn't know what she was missing.'

Nadine frowned at the sky. 'Do you think there will be a storm?'

'It was brooding like that when we left.'

'I know.'

He said: 'Are you psychic?'

She shook her head. 'I just feel an oppression which – which isn't at Taroudant.'

'Do you want to go back?'

'I certainly do. On Thursday.'

'Not now? Not reverse right round and go back?'

She looked at him. 'You know it wouldn't do, Matthew. It's only two more days there – three nights. Maybe a thunderstorm will clear the air.'

'So long as you don't change your mind.'

'No, I won't. Not over that.'

'Oh, well. It was worth a try. In we get.'

They returned to the car. He did not at once start the engine.

She said: 'What are you looking at?'

'You.'

'Well . . . I suppose I cannot complain.'

'Nor can I.'

After a few seconds she said: 'Drive on, Matthew.'

He put his hand to the key but did not turn it. 'Good moments in life are rare.'

'Yes . . . yes. Perhaps there will be others.'

'Many others,' he said.

There was not a sound outside. Only a total hot silence.

'Drive on, Matthew. Let's get in before the storm.'

III

LEE AND LETTY went on the beach quite early, bathed, walked, bathed again. They sat at one of the little kiosks sipping Campari sodas.

They had both slept restlessly after the events of the night. Just as day was breaking he heaved up on his elbow and looked for her, then realized that sometime afterwards he had gone back to his own room. He did not knock on her door until nearly nine, when he found her already dressed and eating breakfast on the veranda. They exchanged commonplace words, polite, casual, a little forced.

Just as they were leaving he said: 'Letty, about last night . . .' but she shook her head.

'Not now, Lee, please.'

He did not know whether he ought to feel pleased or remorseful about the outcome of the night, but he knew precisely what he did feel – which was damned triumphant. At Idlewild airport, while waiting to meet Letty, he had wandered into the airport bookshop and bought himself a sex manual. He had read it surreptitiously in quiet moments of their trip, and last night he had put into practice some of its advice. It had worked to such good effect that his own sensations had been heightened. His experience as a seducer was scanty, and he was massively elated that he had done so well. He felt thirty years younger.

On the beach they did not mention last night, nor at the café. Her face was composed, unresponsive, a little clouded. For the moment he was content. Often he felt people talked too much, analysed too much. It was one of his own failings.

The beach was busy this morning. Two football games were in progress, and more people than usual, it seemed, were walking and strolling about in the warm air. It was a pretty scene. The man with the camels came up, offering them a ride at a reduced rate, but they smilingly refused. Silk blouses, jewellery, daggers and rugs were also offered from time to time.

Because they were on the beach they hardly noticed the earth tremor, which took place at about midday. The table gave a shudder and someone shouted in the café behind, that was all. Lee remarked that he had read somewhere that Agadir had been built on a rock fault, so he supposed one had to suffer these little inconveniences. They got up together and walked unhurriedly in to lunch. Once or twice he took her hand, but there was no returning clasp so he allowed it to slip away.

Over lunch he asked her to marry him. She gently refused.

'May I ask why – after last night?'

'Because as I said at the time it was just something – separate.'

'To me it was very special.'

She sipped at her wine.

'. . . We are both married.'

He made a gesture. 'In the circumstances that can hardly be looked on as an obstacle.'

'It would not work out, Lee. We do not come of the same world. I . . . I am not at all ashamed of my family – indeed, I am proud of them – but among the – the old families of Boston and Massachusetts – and you belong to such a one – the standards are still quite rigid. Through you I have come to know many of your friends. They accept me as a bridge player but I would never be invited to join their Club. If you married me they would laugh.'

'You misunderstand them. As my wife you'd go anywhere. Anyway you're not marrying them.'

'I do not think I could ever take Ann's place. Although she has left her home – *and* you – it is her house. You must realize how much she made it her own. The rugs, the ornaments, the vases, the pictures. Every time I am in the house I see her – as I know you must.'

'So you would have me live alone for the rest of my life – or marry someone else.'

'That is something only you can decide.'

'Would it help,' he asked, 'if I moved house, if we went to live in some quite different part of the county? We might try Rhode Island. Maybe near Providence.'

He saw her hesitate and knew that she was not convinced.

'Don't answer now,' he said, knowing well enough that she had answered but that she had not explained. Unless the explanation was the one that he feared most of all, that she had no real, genuine feeling for him.

The three French ladies had heard even less of the earth tremor than the Americans, for they were in their car and Laura was driving, and that meant that ordinary noises, vibration and rattles were totally overborne by the noise she made. No one has ever driven a car as noisily as she did. She crashed the gears, she revved the engine to racing limits, she slipped the clutch, she lurched and braked and talked at the top of her voice all the time.

'*Tiens*, that *crétin* has left his car where there is no room for me – ah! just past – did I touch it? No matter, shut your mouth, Vicky – no one will know. Sacred name of a little blue man, why do they not observe the rules of the road! *Merde*, that cursed donkey – ha, ha, ha, that gave him a shock, I'll lay a curse; had he been a nick slower we would have left him with no arse! – where the hell is second gear? Do we turn right, Vicky, *do we turn right?* – Well, I've done

it now – we'll see where this avenue leads – *quelle pisser!*
The man does not look where he is walking! Ah, I have gone
back to first – a million curses on these gears; Françoise,
bestir yourself, I am not here to drive you about in your
sleep! *Sot! Bétise! Babouin!* I have forgotten, where are we
going?'

'To the port,' said Vicky.

'*Hélas!* Then we are going the wrong way.' Without
regard to other traffic Laura made a sharp U-turn. Something
rattled and fell off in the road, probably a casualty of the
early scrape, but none of the ladies bothered to look behind
to see what they had lost. They rejoined the main avenue at
a breakneck speed and zoomed off towards the port.

Eventually, with a jerk and a jolt Laura brought her car
to a stop nine inches from a fruit stall. They all piled out and
began to prowl and wobble around the market, which was
in essence more a point of assembly for all sorts of early
season delicacies about to be crated and shipped to Europe.

It seemed that some event had disturbed the stallholders,
for they stood in groups talking and glancing anxiously
about as if waiting for something more to happen. Laura,
Vicky and Françoise, having been insulated from the tremor
by reason of being in the car, strutted around unaffected,
buying an orange here, a banana there, until they reached a
kiosk serving mint tea and sweetmeats and caramel cakes
and roast chestnuts and fried eels.

Thy sat down gratefully, as the cobbles had been trying
their high heels, but the proprietor informed them that there
was no alcohol to be obtained in his shop. Disgruntled, they
sipped strong black coffee and listened to the monotonous
wail of the radio.

Back in the car, Laura drove suicidally up to the Kasbah
on the hill, but there was no alcohol here either, only narrow

cobbled streets, dark alleyways arched over by houses with trailing creepers, old men sitting knees up against walls, the radios again blaring Arab music, pottery shops with open fronts, gaudy scarf shops, dyers, wood carvers, blind beggars, mangy cats, the smell of the tanners and the smell of goat.

'*Alors!* Let's go back,' Françoise said. 'I'm thirsty.'

'And hungry,' said Vicky.

Laura turned the car noisily to head down the hill, and they lurched and slithered over the loose surface while the port and the town of Agadir and the great expanse of beach swung in front of the windscreen.

Halfway to the bottom there was a fork in the road, and Laura, whose sense of direction was not of the best, bumped off to the left. Vicky at once told her she had gone wrong, but Laura said: '*Tiens*, what matter? All the roads lead down.'

In fact they did not all lead down in quite the same way, and after half a minute they rounded a bend into a quarry which was full of camels.

They came round quickly, missing the rump of one and the nose of another by a nostril's breadth. Vicky gave a squeal of delight, Françoise one of apprehension as she thought they were about to have a smash. In fact Laura, driving like Fangio, swept and swirled among the tall brown animals and only had a slight accident when she was through the worst and out the other side. Her foot slipped off the brake and they thumped into a six-foot-high wall of camel dung which four boys had been compressing into bricks for use as fuel.

They were immediately surrounded by faces, some of them grinning, some curious, some wrathful, some with heavy nostrils breathing and snuffling, big liquid expressionless eyes and slow champing jaws. All forms of nature seemed to be instantly interested in the little cream car stuffed with women.

Laura got her window wound down and became instantly involved in an argument with two of the boys, which would have been more satisfactory if Laura had known Arabic or the boys French. Eventually a tall, bearded, distinguished-looking man with a wall eye intervened and communication was established.

This was the camel market, he explained, swirling his cream jellaba; this was held in Agadir on the fourth Monday in every month. Did they want to buy a camel? If so, he had two excellent beasts hardly yet grown – a four- and a five-year-old. He was in charge of the sale, he said, and would be honoured personally to conduct such distinguished ladies round the camels and enable them to pick the best beast and to obtain the best bargain. All three ladies said they did not want to buy a damned camel, but Vicky seemed half-hearted in her refusal, so the tall man and two other friends at once transferred their attention to her. She incautiously lowered her window, and at once was closely engaged.

A particularly large camel put its head against Françoise's window and rubbed it noisily.

'Oh, look!' screamed Françoise, with a crow of laughter. 'It's blowing bubbles!'

The man with the wall eye said: 'Nay, nay, Mrs, that is a big man camel and he shows he wishes woman camel; dangerous, he bite, whey-oh! take him away, Ibrahim ... Allow me, madame. Pray alight and I will personally escort you.'

To the shouted imprecations of the other two, Vicky allowed herself to be helped out, when Mustafa, as he was called, swept away the boys who were dancing around, first on one leg, then on the other, out of sheer interest, and escorted her away from the broken wall of dung towards two smaller camels tethered to a post. One of them, looking round with a reproachful eye, suddenly let out a dismal howl that had half the camp trumpeting in response. When the noise had died down Vicky had disappeared among a white-shouldered crowd of men.

'*Mon Dieu*,' said Laura, banging her fist on the steering-wheel. 'She'll be raped!'

This seemed greatly to amuse Françoise in the back. She tittered and tittered and tittered and tittered. Eventually between splutters she said: 'Charge 'em all extra if they're more than half an hour.'

Laura whirred the self-starter, but the engine did not fire. She glowered at the scene. 'Might be a lot of schoolboys after their first, eh? You remember I had that place opposite the technical college? No, you weren't there: you were still at the Rue de Courcey. Charging extra for over the half-hour, *mon Dieu*! It was half-price for the students! Holy Mary, they were a lively, eager lot. All pretending to be eighteen, borrowing the same identity card over and over. In and out, it doesn't take long when they're that age. Bang, bang and they've finished.'

Mustafa said: 'Now these two splendid beasts come of the finest Hageen stock, just suitable for a lady. Look at their slender legs, their sinewy frames. This one is my *prime* possession, Esu, just four years old. Admire him. Examine him. Look, put your hand on his muzzle, he is as tame as a bird. See his beautiful tender eyes.'

Considering this was the animal which had created all the racket, Vicky was cautious about approaching him too closely, but she was edged forward while Mustafa continued his sales talk.

Laura, having had no satisfaction from the starter button, tried the horn instead.

'Where're you going?' she demanded suddenly, as Françoise opened her door.

'Can't stand that noise!' said Françoise. 'Gives me the wobblies. I'll go find Vicky.'

To their surprise, at that moment the crowd of grinning men parted and Vicky appeared, unraped and unruffled, followed by Mustafa and Esu. Mustafa, having reluctantly named a price, was now following Vicky with an amended quotation.

'Can't do,' Vicky said, spreading her hands. 'Go by plane, understand? Can't get camel on plane. It would stick in the door.'

'Ah, madame, *you* do not understand. He can be shipped. He can go to Marseilles and you could meet him there . . .'

A bearded face, untoothed but smiling, appeared at Laura's window.

'Can no start? Eh? Car broke down? Eh? You want push? A hundred dirhams. Eh?'

Laura hesitated. It was a lot to ask for a push, but she needed a drink. And to get that little fool Vicky out of trouble . . .

'*Ça va*,' she said, and began to fumble in her handbag.

'*Et moi, mad'moiselle. Et moi!*' More voices and more beseeching hands.

'It will take three of us,' said the toothless one. 'I and my two boys. They shall come at a special rate. Specially for you. Thirty dirhams each! Eh, what? That is all.'

'Rubbish!' Laura snarled. '*Canaille!* One hundred dirhams is more than you deserve. Come along. Fifty now, and fifty when we start. *Vicky!*' she screamed. 'Get into the damned car! *Merde!* When will you learn?'

'I cannot buy it,' Vicky was saying. 'It is too dear. Yes, I know you will amend the price. You cannot amend it enough for me—'

'I swear on my mother's grave,' Mustafa said. 'Never will you have so splendid a chance again. Esu is a model beast, mild, well-bred, gentle, all that you could wish. Come now, make me an offer . . .'

Complicated negotiations on the other side of the car were near completion. Laura was prepared to pay sixty dirhams down, with another fifty-dirham note held delicately between finger and thumb by Françoise just out of reach of the grasping fingers. As soon as the car started she swore she would hand it over.

Laura reached over and opened the off-side front door. 'Come in, you little piece of dog shit, when will you ever learn to control your stupidity!'

Vicky gave Mustafa a fifty-dirham note which she had in her jacket pocket. 'That's all,' she cooed, 'that's all. Lovely camel, lovely camel, yes, yes. Maybe one day I'll come back.' She slid into the car. '*Adieu, adieu, adieu!*'

Mustafa's hand, clutching the note, was holding the door open, but the efforts of the toothless one and his two sons just then propelled the car forward with a jerk and he had to let go. The door slammed, the car engine fired, the car bucked into first gear, and Laura had the presence of mind to declutch. The engine roared. With tremendous presence of mind she found reverse gear, and the car lurched away from the pile of dung. Arabs scattered wildly. Françoise was about to pull her hand back, but Laura screamed at her: 'Give it them! Give it them!'

Then, lurching and jerking like an over-burdened mule, the little Renault began to thread its way through all the congregation of camels; once again Laura proved her mastery over fate by avoiding collision or assassination, and the car gathered speed towards what looked like, and in fact proved to be, the exit road.

They slithered and rattled down it towards Agadir.

'*Alors!*' said Françoise.

'*Tiens!*' said Vicky breathlessly.

'*Merde!*' said Laura.

IV

AMONG THOSE who felt the earth tremor M. and Mme Thibault showed the greatest alarm.

One of their suitcases had been carelessly replaced on the top of the wardrobe when they were changing yesterday to go out to lunch, and this toppled over and crumped by the dressing table to add to the general rattle and commotion.

Estrella flew to the window as the vibration stopped. She stared out over the gardens to the sultry sea. Nothing apparently had changed. Two small tramp steamers smoked gently at the entrance to the port. One or two people in the deck-chairs were sitting up looking around as if they had been disturbed. A waiter at the poolside picked up an overturned glass.

'*Mon Dieu,*' said Thibault behind her. 'What next? That is worse than a thunderstorm!'

'Of course it is worse than a thunderstorm!' she cried. 'What next indeed! This, this is more than I am prepared to stand! We shall leave at once!'

He picked up the suitcase and put it on the bed. 'Leave for where? We have made the reservation here for two weeks! No doubt they would release us, but we cannot just take up our bags and leave. This is Morocco, not France.'

'It is quite intolerable,' she exclaimed. 'From the moment we came here it has been frustration, annoyance, insult – what insult! – and now danger!'

Thibault said pettishly: 'If one comes to Africa one runs an additional risk of – inconvenience. The climate is clearly unsettled. I—'

'Those dreadful women,' Estrella said, changing tack. 'Everywhere I go, everywhere I look, they are *there*, a disgrace to the fair name of France. And how they have insulted us – hanging their frightful clothes in our car, giggling lecherously whenever we go past. And one or more of them conspicuously drunk. I don't know how the manager of the Saada – who, let us face it, is a *Frenchman* – can tolerate their odious presence in what is *supposed* to be the best hotel! I do not know how *you* can tolerate them. I have learned a lot about my successful husband these last two days. What a past he has had! While bringing up a family and preaching the virtues of family life, he has been consorting with whores and Jezebels and generally disgracing his family and his name! You marry off a sweet innocent girl – your daughter, *your* daughter – to a distinguished young deputy and we come away thinking only happy thoughts – and *look* what we have found here! – a cesspool of perversity, a vulgar hotel constantly shaken by earth tremors, a motor car so tiny that you can hardly *squeeze* into it, a luncheon with the Governor where no one any longer seems to understand the courtesies of behaviour!'

She was in tears now and he held up a hand. 'You have made your feelings clear. They are exaggerated but I have to admit there is a basis for your complaints.' He drew himself up. 'We shall go.'

She took out a tiny lace handkerchief and dabbed her eyes like a young girl.

'Where?' She was cooling off, admitting that he was the master.

'Where you wish. You were agreeable to come on this holiday. Now you want to end it. What do you wish? To go back to Paris? Do not forget Cecile and Armand are on holiday too. There will be no help in the house.'

Estrella considered the matter.

'Do you know Marrakech?'

'I have been once.'

'Is there a good hotel?'

'There is one. Very expensive. Where Winston Churchill stayed.'

'What do you think, then?' Tension had really gone now.

'We could leave here tomorrow. Or today if there is a flight. It is not a great way, but too far to drive in – in this car. I will enquire, if you wish.'

She sniffed. 'I should be glad if you would enquire.'

He straightened a picture on the wall. 'I must confess I had not imagined so disagreeable a climate as this. Even if one discounts the earth tremor the weather itself is so oppressive. Perhaps it would be for the best. I will go and see the manager and see what he can arrange.'

He noticed that the door was stiff to open, as if it had become wedged at the top.

V

AT THE TIME this decision was being made two men were boarding an Air France plane, AF 217, at Heathrow.

One was big, an inch or two over six feet and weighing probably 220lbs. He had streaky black hair very thin on the top and slicked back with brilliantine; his heavy jaw already needed another shave. Small eyes with pouches under them and a hint of scar tissue. At some stage his nose had been flattened. He was wearing a blue suit, black shoes, an MCC tie (which he had bought secondhand last week in Wolverhampton) and carried only hand luggage: a hold-all and an attaché case.

The other was short and dapper. Flint-coloured hair, flint-coloured eyes, a bland expression, almost boyish, unsophisticated. Only the absence of feeling in the eyes struck a chill. Double-breasted blue sports jacket with brass buttons, grey Daks trousers, suede shoes. A spotted yellow handkerchief flowed from his breast pocket.

It had been a frenetic few days. After the enormity of the betrayal had sunk in, Mr Artemis had put all his forces to work double time. He had not of course the almost unlimited resources of the police, the manpower, the criminal records, the fingerprint experts, the sniffer dogs, the cars, the informers. He only controlled, or had some influence over, a small corner of the underworld. But he had the supreme advantage over the police of knowing the identity of the culprit.

After Johnny Carpenter's flat had been taken to pieces inch by inch in search of any clue as to his likely whereabouts or destination, threatening enquiries had been made of his friends and cronies in London, of whom he seemed to have had very few and in whom he seemed to have confided little of his personal life. The nickname, Frère Jacques, had been fairly widely known, and this suggested a French connection, but no one knew what. He had taken part in a few minor robberies in the Home Counties in the last few years but had never been caught. Big Smith had enlisted him into this one because he was reputed to have a cool nerve, and just because it was necessary to use people without current form. (One didn't want the fuzz thundering on doors demanding alibis on pure hopeful guesswork within the first twenty-four hours.) He had apparently lived in London for the past few years, but one of the friends, suitably pressurized, had come up with the information that Johnny had been brought up in Wolverhampton.

Big Smith, accompanied by Greg Garrett, had rushed up there and there had found quite a goldmine of information. Johnny had arrived in England with his mother just before the war. His mother, who had begun life as a dancer, had died six years ago, but a neighbour provided them with some useful clues. Johnny was indeed half-French, sometimes had boasted of it. He had friends or relatives in Morocco, she thought, and went out there now and then. He had worked in the motor works until the factory closed in the post-war slump. Then for a long while he had been on the dole. After his mother died he sold the house and moved to London, and she had lost sight of him. Did he have any other name, they asked, other than Johnny Carpenter? What was his father's name? Was he still alive? Where abouts in Morocco did Johnny go? To these questions she had no answer.

Big Smith was very disappointed that there seemed to be no woman involved. He always believed if you were looking for a man in hiding you could spring him like as not by finding his woman first.

Some frantic hours later they ran to earth an old school-friend of Johnny's who told them that he had once or twice spoken of going to Agadir.

But no other name.

Johnny Carpenter flying off to Morocco, by himself.

By devious extra-legal connections they had a friendship

with an Air France official working in Piccadilly. He reported that no one called Carpenter had flown to Morocco in the last ten days. The last one was Sir Rowan Carpenter, who had taken plane to Marrakech with his wife on the 10th of February.

A dead end. Or did one fly to Agadir and stroll round the shops and hotels and bazaars looking for a familiar face?

They went back to the flat in Bulstrode Street. It was as they had left it. Everything in chaos. Drawers pulled out, linings torn, newspapers draped everywhere, letters torn apart, clothing ripped. Nothing new except a couple of circulars delivered since yesterday and a communication from *Reader's Digest* saying that the recipient was in the running for a £20,000 prize. The draw was to take place within a month, and all the recipient had to do was fill out the enclosed form, etc., etc. The envelope was addressed to John R. Frazier, Esq. at this address.

VI

BEING SUNDAY, the Air France offices in Piccadilly were closed, and the Air France official had said that on no account was he to be rung at his private number, which somehow these dubious acquaintances of his had got hold of. But Greg Garrett said, to hell with that, time is vital, so rang him immediately from Johnny's devastated flat.

The official was wary, irritable and said he was busy, but ultimately agreed to see what he could do. An hour later he rang back to say a Mr John Frazier had left England last Friday on an Air France flight, AF 217, for Bordeaux. This had on-going connections with Casablanca and Agadir.

Without hesitation Garrett told him to reserve two seats on tomorrow morning's flight. The Frenchman replied sourly that he could do nothing from his private address, but gave them the number to ring at Heathrow.

CHAPTER TEN

I

THE AFTERNOON was intensely sultry, thundery, though no
thunder rolled. The sun broke through just before sunset; a
half slice of a glowing disc: it was as if one looked into a
furnace of incandescent heat and trembled at the sight,
before a mass of curled grey cloud drifted across, shutting it
in like shutting a furnace door. Large spots of rain fell.

Dr Ibrahim Berrada was the senior doctor at the hospital.
A farmer's son, his parents had contrived to get him sent to
the Karaouine University in Fez, and from there he had gone
to Paris and returned to Morocco ten years ago, when he
had been appointed to run the Ben Ahmed Sanatorium for
tuberculosis. Four years ago, when Independence came, he
had been chosen as one of the purely Moroccan doctors
of distinction with a partly Western education to change
and rehabilitate the hospital at Agadir, giving it for the
first time a non-racial administration, yet maintaining its
Western traditions. He had made an outstanding success of
the job.

But Dr Berrada, though a good Muslim, was by race
pure Berber and therefore not without superstition. He knew
about *baraka*, the healing power possessed by some holy
men, and he understood about amulets, charms, evil signs
and taboos. While his European culture and his medical
knowledge suggested he should deride such things, a deeper

strain, born into him through generations of his Hamitic forebears, still carried old influences along.

Last night he had been up to the Kasbah on business and had stopped for a few minutes to listen to old El Ufrani speaking to a circle of elders around a smouldering fire; they leaned against walls, crouched on haunches, sat cross-legged, stood silently among the flickering shadows listening to him. El Ufrani's word was that there would come a vengeance on the town. It had become utterly ungodly, as accursed as Sodom and Gomorrah and Admah and Zebolim and all the cities of the plain and would as surely be overtaken and overthrown by the earth's convulsion and God's revulsion at so evil and carnal a way of life.

Of course in the light of day it was easy to throw off such prophecies of apocalypse as the ramblings of a crazed old man, but in the half-lit gloom of the old walled city with its narrow alleys and tattered roofs, amid the smell of the donkeys and the leather and the spices and the smoke, it was easy to be taken in, to remember childhood tales of holy men and curses and old women muttering in the dark.

Also, there had been signs and portents of another sort that Dr Berrada had observed. Two of his sister's cattle had died inexplicably and there had been strange marks upon their bodies. The five-pointed star over the door of the hospital had suddenly, inexplicably, become stained and cracked. Nothing to go on for a rational man.

But the weather was brooding, threatening, unseasonal. And there had been the earth tremor at midday. It had done no damage, but it was the heaviest that anyone in the hospital could remember.

At four o'clock Dr Berrada passed out into the rough compound of grass and gravel surrounding the hospital and looked at his charge.

Built in 1910, when the French, having recently taken over the country, were anxious to show the world and perhaps even themselves the civilizing effects of their dominion, the building was not much to look at either architecturally or structurally. While a fair amount of modernization had taken place inside, nothing had been spent on the exterior at all. The roof leaked, stucco peeled from walls, and there were cracks behind the stucco, window frames rattled, a door at the back was off its hinges. Since Independence the new Moroccan government, short of money, had yielded only to demands for new equipment, not for repairs.

Berrada strolled back and spoke to the almoner, a man called Sadeq.

'How many patients have we in the hospital at the moment?'

'It will be – yes, the man died – it will be eighty-nine.'

Berrada took off his glasses to polish them. 'If an order were given to evacuate the hospital, how long do you think it would take?'

Sadeq stared. 'I don't understand.'

'No ... It is probably nothing. I don't like the look of things ... But it was just a thought that crossed my mind. How long – an hour?'

'Oh yes, that and more. Wards three to six would all be stretcher cases. But I'm still not following you. Do you mean in case of fire?'

'That sort of thing.'

'But where could they be taken? We have only two ambulances.'

'Wherever it was safe. Or safer. In the grounds outside. It is such warm weather for the time of year. One would hope also to save blankets.'

Dr Sadeq watched his superior as he walked off towards

the dispensary. This was something he must tell his wife when he got home – that Ibrahim Berrada was becoming increasingly eccentric, while still relatively so young.

II

M. THIBAULT had told the manager, M. Taviscon, they were leaving. They would have liked to walk out, making something of a dramatic exit; but the one plane a day to Marrakech had long since gone and tomorrow's was fully booked. The manager said they were first on the waiting list and he would put pressure on the line to accept them. But the distance from here to Marrakech was not great, scarcely more than two hundred kilometres, and the roads were magnificent. They had a car. It would not surely be difficult to drive there?

M. Thibault said under no circumstances would he consider driving two hundred kilometres in that box on wheels which was all the hire company had seen fit to provide him with. If necessary he would hire a chauffeur-driven car. But in the meantime, if no seats were available on tomorrow's plane, he would complain personally to M. Bouamrani.

Taviscon bowed and said quite so, he understood how they felt, and should he in the meantime reserve them accommodation at the Mamounia in Marrakech from tomorrow? Thibault thought angrily of the extra amount this would cost him; but Estrella was so temperamental that only the height of luxury would ease her feelings now. He nodded to the manager. The plane left at twelve. By ten thirty they would leave the hotel by one means of transport or another. Meanwhile the bill, so far as their short stay at the Saada went . . .

The manager said it would be sent up on the breakfast tray.

In the late afternoon Johnny Carpenter went to see his father.

The old man looked better, and one of the monitoring units had been switched off.

'So you haven't trusted him,' he said, glancing at the case under Johnny's arm.

Johnny waited until the fat nurse was out of earshot.

'Not for that. He's getting me the other.'

'When?'

'Tomorrow or the next day.' It was always Johnny's habit to lie about his projected movements, even to the one man he could trust. Rational thought hardly came into it; it was instinct.

'They say I can't be moved for a week yet,' Tournelle said. 'It's up to you, but when I get home it'll be bed for maybe another week after that. If you can hang on that long. A fortnight, I'd say, at most.'

'I'll see,' said Johnny, sucking his teeth. There was no smoking in this hospital and he found it a deprivation.

'What you been up to?' his father demanded suddenly, his eyes straying again to the case. 'It's not like you to go for the big time.'

'Not all that big,' Johnny said uneasily. 'It was just a chance that came along.'

Tournelle breathed heavily for a moment or two, and the nurse came back.

'Ça va?' she asked.

'Ça va. Ça va. This is my son. We have a little private talk.'

'I know, I know. But do not excite yourself. *I* shall get the blame if all is not well.'

They waited until she had moved on again. An old man at the other end of the ward was having a fit of coughing.

'Is it all money?' asked Tournelle.

Johnny fidgeted. 'I will tell you soon enough. Now it's better maybe you shouldn't know any more than you do. In two weeks . . .'

In two weeks, he thought, I shall be in Rio. Never been there. Wonder what it's like. Known as a bolt-hole for robbers. Maybe that's not a bad thing. Easygoing laws. No extradition treaty. Or maybe I'll move on. The more hops I make the less likely to be traced. Buenos Aires is a good spot too. Or Santiago. They said Chile was one of the most beautiful countries in the world. As long as you had money you could go anywhere. Johnny had never had much to do with women. A tart now and then and that was enough. He had no intention of linking himself to some blonde gold-digger who would help him get rid of his hard-won money at a fabulous rate. Maybe when the chase had died away he would buy a little *hacienda* and find a pretty little servant girl as fresh as a peony and settle down with her . . .

'What are you thinking about?' Gaston Tournelle demanded in a harsh voice.

Johnny started. 'Oh . . . Just this and that. These flights from Casablanca to Agadir, are they pretty regular?'

'So far as I know. They've got their own line now, of course. Air Maroc. They're using French planes. Have to. France makes the loans, France takes the pick of the trade.'

'Well . . . This is damned funny weather for February, isn't it? Hot wind. Hot nights. Not the usual.' Johnny stood up as the nurse approached again. 'Time I was off. See you tomorrow.'

His father stared at him piercingly. 'Go easy, Jacques. Take your time. Don't jump at things. You've got to be cautious in this life.'

'Aye,' said Johnny. 'Dead right. You have to be cautious, don't you.'

III

NADINE HAD not seen Matthew since they returned. She had kept to her room expecting, she said, the call from Maurice Daumier, her agent. This was partly true, partly a diplomatic absence. She wanted to have time to breathe, time to think her own thoughts, to distance herself for a few hours from this importunate young man. He had an eager, cheerful, triumphant vitality that carried one away. She felt herself more circumspect, more clear-eyed than he was, and that she might have to think for them both.

The call did finally come about six. Maurice always began work late and ended his day late. Of all the Paris agents he had the closest connections with Hollywood; it was why she had joined him. The important part of Maurice's day began when his contacts in Hollywood were fully awake.

This time, however, he had another proposition. The part which might become available for her was in a French film, and the development was hanging fire. But another property had begun to stir itself. Rossellini was mounting a film to be called *Era Notte a Roma*, and hoped to begin shooting it at Cinecittà in the autumn. If she could contrive to find herself in Rome on the return from her holiday, he would join her there and take her along to meet the great man. How was her Italian? No, it need not be fluent; the part that she might play was of a Polish girl stranded in Rome and involved in the disturbances of last year.

Of course, said Nadine, she would be delighted. Or interested, she corrected. It never did to be too eager.

Keep in touch, Daumier said. He did not think there was any pressure for a week or so. Rossellini was in New York. But if the moment should come suddenly, he might want her to fly to Rome at short notice.

Of course, said Nadine, she would do that.

An hour later she went down to join Matthew for drinks.

He was standing at the foot of the stairs and saw her coming down. He went up three steps at a time to join her.

She knew as he came up to her, smiling, eager, eyes glinting, and took her hand, that she would sleep with him again tonight. It was a decision taken by her body rather than by her reasoning mind, but she never for a moment queried it. For tonight she had no doubts.

In the hall as they went down Lee and Letty were just coming in from the gardens. Darkness had fallen, but the grounds and all the paths were lighted by shaded lanterns. A sickle of new moon showed among the clouds over the sea. The three French ladies were wrangling with the concierge at the desk. M. and Mme Thibault were nowhere to be seen.

IV

THE SMALLER Caravelle flying from Casablanca was delayed leaving because of an electric storm. Ten o'clock was past before it touched down in Agadir.

It had been a long journey for Big Smith and Greg

Garrett, but their luggage was light and they were soon through to the waiting taxis outside. Greg Garrett had taken the risk of bringing a 9mm Luger with him, but no one had bothered at Casablanca.

Smith gave the address of the Hôtel Mahraba to the driver. While waiting in Casablanca Garrett, who knew a few words of French, had gone to the tourist agency at the airport and asked them to book them in at a hotel. The clerk had first tried the Saada but was told it was full. So they had been booked into the second best hotel, the Mahraba.

In a short time they were in, had surrendered their passports, had signed the register in the hotel and had stared back uncompromisingly at fellow guests who stared at them. They looked an unusual couple to be walking late at night into a holiday hotel. In a London street you would hardly have remarked them. Here they stood out like sore thumbs. One might have been a heavy-weight boxer and the other his promoter.

The clerk said dinner was over, but if they would like some soup and some crayfish sandwiches ... Or coffee and biscuits?

They'd have the lot, said Smith, and while the clerk's back was turned swivelled the guest book round to see the names of recent arrivals. The clerk, turning back, frowned disapprovingly at this manoeuvre and was about to protest, but Smith reversed the book again with a disagreeable grin and said: 'Was just looking. Thought a mate of mine might be here. Name of Frazier. That ring a bell?'

'No, sir,' said the clerk coldly. 'Supper will be in the dining-room in ten minutes. Would you care to see your room?'

'Nah,' said Smith. 'Eat first, I reckon. You got any beer?'

V

TRAVELLING IN the same aeroplane with the two Englishmen was a sharp-featured Moroccan wearing a blue skullcap. He was tall and thin and otherwise dressed entirely in black. On the left lapel of his long coat was the Star of David. He looked consumptive.

He had left Agadir on the morning flight, gone to a friend he knew in the port area of Casablanca, spent the day sipping coffee at a bar restaurant and wandering through the shops. He had bought a coral necklace for his wife, making sure it was the real thing, not artificial stones dyed pink. Then in the evening he had returned to his friend in the port and picked up a passport, which carried a photograph of Johnny Frazier but said that his name was Henri Delaware and stated that he was French Canadian, born in Chicoutimi, Quebec Province, in October 1924.

When he arrived in Agadir he took a taxi to the little photographic shop in the Rue Moulay Ismail and deposited the envelope containing the passport with his cousin. His cousin remarked on his lateness but said it would not affect the arrangement, as Benjamin would not be coming off duty at the Casino until eleven. He was then going to deliver the passport to the new Mr Henri Delaware personally and receive a cash payment on the spot.

VI

'CHRIST!' EXCLAIMED Big Smith. 'What the hell was that?'

While they were eating the table had fairly danced under them. At another table two glasses fell over, rolled to the edge and smashed. A ripple stirred the swimming-pool outside. It was as if an underground train very close below the surface had moved under them at speed.

'Damn me,' said Greg Garrett. 'Like the bloody Blitz back again.' He got up and stared around.

The only waiter left in the deserted dining-room hurried over. He said something to them in French and then, receiving uncomprehending stares, broke into English.

'It is but a little tremble, messieurs, a little tremble. Now and then in this country the earth gives a little tremble. It is like thunder but it comes from the earth and not from the sky. Do not disturb yourselves.'

Garrett didn't resume his seat. 'I've finished anyhow. Come on, Big, you'll do till morning. I've a fancy for a stroll.'

'Stroll? This time of night?'

'Why not? No time like the present. It's only eleven. Reckon I've a fancy to go round one or two of the other hotels, take a look at their visitors' books.'

'They won't let us look at them.'

'Well, then, just go round asking if they've a guest called Johnny Frazier. Dear friend of ours. Dear, dear friend. They can't refuse to say if they have a guest of that name.'

Big Smith belched. 'What was in that soup? I never do trust fish soup. Never know what the hell's in it.' He dragged himself reluctantly to his feet. 'God, I'm flaked out. I never was one for messing around at airports . . . I suppose you know, don't you, he'll likely have changed his name again.'

'Maybe. But he travelled under Frazier.'

'If it's the right Frazier.'

'Well, I've a mind to find out.'

VII

AFTER THE earth tremor, which seemed more pronounced inland than near the coast, Dr Ibrahim Berrada left his house and his wife and his son, whom he would never see again, got into his low-built dark blue Citroën, a car so beloved of the French police force, and drove a mile back to the hospital. Dr Sadeq was still on duty.

'Damage?' Berrada said brusquely.

'Yes, some. Superficial. But it alarmed some of the patients. We have been around to pacify them. All is quiet now.'

Berrada walked round. Nurses and wards were functioning normally. Colonel Tournelle had been taken off the danger list today, and Berrada nodded to him as he went past. In the laboratory two young dispensers were still picking things off the floor and rearranging them on the shelves. Berrada did not go up on to the roof, which he knew to be in poor condition, but screeched open a window to peer out at the hospital wall. It looked perfectly sound.

He was about to withdraw his head when he noticed an outside building used for storage. One wall had completely collapsed, and most of the contents of the hut had fallen out with it and lay on the gravel sand beside it.

He withdrew his head and shut the window. Sadeq had followed him all the way and was standing beside him.

'We'll evacuate the hospital.'

'What?'

'Begin on the top floor. Mobilize all the help you can get. There are – what, six, eight nurses? Have the patients brought down singly. Two of our staff should organize the blankets; bring down what mattresses are easily portable. No panic, take it slowly, but waste no time. I personally will speak to every patient as he is brought down.'

'But, do you want—'

'I have told you what I want,' Berrada said. 'No panic. But waste no time.'

VIII

WHEN THE tremor occurred Lee and Letty were in the Casino. The tables rocked, dice spilled, a woman screamed, some plaster dust floated down from the ceiling. A number of people got up, looked around, looked speculatively at the ceiling, talked among themselves, half-joking, half-alarmed. It was noticeably the Europeans, or those who had experienced wartime bombing, who were the more uneasy.

Letty said: 'Just when I was winning. Perhaps they are going to blow the place up.'

Lee said: 'Bombers are getting nearer. Maybe we should move to the dugout.'

She glanced up to see if he was also joking. But it wasn't really fun. A heavy rumbling like the sound of distant gunfire was too reminiscent for them both.

They went on playing for a further twenty minutes. At another table the three Frenchwomen were creating a disturbance. They were arguing with the *tailleur*, a man called Ardrossi, who had, they said, unfairly scooped in two of their chips.

The three ladies had become unpopular in the hotel because of their noisiness and general air of caring nothing for what other people thought, but they had got into conversation with Letty in a shop where they were all looking at leather slippers, and they had laughed and joked with her in an amiable fashion, and Lee had come in later on to see them all practising their broken English on Letty, so he had gone out of his way to be amiable in his turn.

When Lee and Letty left they saw that the ladies, having composed their differences with the croupier, were also on the point of leaving.

'Before the chandelier falls on our heads,' said Françoise in a loud voice, and waved a flapping hand at Lee and Letty.

Outside, Lee's car was reluctant to start, so by the time they were driving away the three Frenchwomen were piling into their own car, and presently the noise of it, and the wobbling yellow lights, showed that they were in hot pursuit.

They arrived within moments of each other in the drive of the Saada. There was the screeching of brakes, the slither of tyres, the slamming of tinny doors as the three women beat Lee and Letty to the steps.

'Get in a proper building,' said Vicky. 'Case there's another shake. *Mon Dieu*, that place, that Casino, it is built of wood and straw. One puff and it'll blow over!'

Lee and Letty stood for a few moments while he locked the car. The wind had dropped. Dogs were howling, almost it seemed in unison; a donkey, tethered near the hotel, cried out and tried to wrest itself free. A flight of big birds wafted low overhead.

Someone spoke to them as they moved towards the doors. A big-built man and a smaller dapper individual, neither of whom commended themselves to Lee's fastidious antennae, used as he was to law courts and their occupants.

''Scuse me,' said the big man. 'This the Saada?'

'The Saada Hotel,' said Lee. 'Yes.'

'Light's gone out over the bleeding sign,' said Smith. 'Must have been that earth shake we had. Thanks.'

They followed Lee and Letty into the hotel. As they got their keys they heard the big man say to the night porter: ''Scuse me. You got a guest here called Frazier, eh? Dear friend of ours. Just enquiring.'

The clerk glanced down at the book. 'Er . . . We have a Mr J. Frazier, who arrived on Friday.'

'That's the man,' said Big Smith heartily. 'That's 'im. Our old chum. Our old friend. That's likely 'im, isn't it, Greg?'

'I reckon,' said Greg.

'Would you let 'im know we're here? What's the number of 'is room?'

The clerk, a young man called Basri, glanced round nervously at the keys behind him.

'It isn't the policy of the hotel to – to give the numbers of rooms. I'm sorry. In fact Mr Frazier, whom you are enquiring for, has just gone up to his room. He has a guest with him, so I do not suppose—'

'Guest? You mean someone from the hotel?'

'Er – no. Just a friend, I presume.'

The doors of the lift closed to bear Lee and Letty up to their bedrooms on the third floor.

The two men at the desk had exchanged speculative glances. If this was their quarry they had no particular wish to run him to earth when there was an outsider present. Yet, having come so far today, they were slow to drop the scent here, to leave it hours to go cold again. Who knew what twists and turns the Judas bastard might get up to overnight? It was prime luck that they had apparently found their man at only the third hotel tried. Even if they could not bring their mission to a successful conclusion tonight, it would be of vital satisfaction just to be sure that this wasn't some innocent guy who happened to bear the same name.

Greg said: 'Know how long this other bloke is staying?'

'Bloke?' Basri blinked. 'Oh, I have no idea, sir. But it is so late I would not think he would stay very long.'

In that case, Frazier might come down with him to see him off.

Greg Garrett felt in his jacket and took out a crocodile wallet. From it he fished a fifty-franc French note.

'Can we have a cup of coffee here, eh? Not too late for that, is it?'

Basri was looking at the note. 'It – er – I think it could be arranged.'

'Could we wait, here in the hall?'

'Uh, er, I suppose so.'

'And if I give you this now, will you let us know, point him out, Mr Frazier's guest when he leaves?'

'It would have to be in the next hour, but I would think . . .'

The note changed hands.

Basri was becoming less uncooperative. 'If you were to sit in those leather armchairs under the indoor palms you could see the entrance to the hotel, and also I could see you.'

'OK. OK. And two black coffees. The real stuff, y'know.'

'Thank you, sir. I'll get that arranged for you.'

Big Smith trailed after Garrett, not quite convinced of his reasoning. Garrett winked as they sank down into the chairs.

'He's fixed,' he said. 'When this feller's gone I reckon another hundred-franc note and he'll be discreetly giving us the number of the bedroom.'

'Ah,' said Smith. 'And then what?'

'Dunno. See how the cookie crumbles. Could all be done tonight.'

. Basri was aware that all the dining-room staff were off, but there was always – or should be – one waiter on duty until midnight. He went in search of him and was annoyed to find the kitchens empty. He looked out over the lighted swimming-pool and heard voices in the staff pavilion that was used to service the pool for light refreshments and drinks. Basri knew what had happened. The waiter was out there chatting to a girl.

Swearing under his breath, he went out to call him, unaware that this action saved his life. He reached the pavilion, found the situation exactly as he had supposed, rebuked the sulky waiter, gave the order and started back.

As he did so there was a crackling crumbling roar and a belch of sulphur. As the ground hit him the swimming-pool broke in two, a piece of concrete briefly sticking up in the air. And then, scrambling to his knees, he saw the great six-storey hotel in front of him fall to pieces. First the roof came off, scattering tiles and slates and timbers, and then the walls followed, buckling and sinking quite slowly towards the ground, crumbling, breaking, splitting, powdering into a shapeless ruin.

The ground weaved and waved; hot air like a breath from hell blew over him. And then every light went out.

CHAPTER ELEVEN

I

THE EARTHQUAKE lasted twenty seconds. The Hôtel Saada, built only five years ago, collapsed entirely, going down as the ground opened under it. The Mahraba, where Smith and Garrett were staying, split down the centre but remained drunkenly upright, masonry from it falling all over the garden. The Préfecture, opposite the Saada but built on seismic-resisting principles, stood alone among the ruins round it. (Though, its being Ramadan, most of the police force were on leave and were killed piecemeal in cafés and in their own homes.) The hospital totally collapsed, as did the Chamber of Commerce and the Post Office. The Casino fell upon itself but, being built of wood, caused less injury to those still gambling, except for the unlucky few who were under the chandelier. The new central market – not yet opened – went with the rest.

The Taborit quarter, where thousands of Moroccans lived in blocks of flats, was laid waste. In the walled Kasbah on the hill its entire population of six hundred people were buried. The barracks collapsed and three companies of the Royal Moroccan Infantry were wiped out. The official residence of the Governor, M. Bouamrani, caved in upon itself, killing his three sons. Dr Berrada lost his wife and family. In pitch darkness in the space of half a minute four-fifths of the city was shaken to pieces. What was worse,

212

many of the victims were buried alive without hope of help.

Of the one hundred and fifty guests at the Hôtel Saada, nineteen survived.

II

MATTHEW WAS in Nadine's room. He was lying on the bed beside her, in a lovely comfortable state of lassitude, when the heavens cracked, the walls shook and gave way, the ceiling and part of the floor above fell upon them; the bed tipped, and they half slid off it as they tumbled into the abyss.

When they finished falling Matthew tried to struggle out from the remnants of a wardrobe that trapped his leg. Clothes from the wardrobe had spilled out, almost smothering him. He was dizzy and shaken, and there was something warm and wet on his arm. It was pitch dark, all lights having instantly gone.

'Nadine!' he called hoarsely. 'Where are you?' She did not reply, and he raised his voice. 'Nadine! Nadine!'

After the terrible roar accompanying the shock and the fall, silence seemed to settle on the building from which as minutes passed all the other noises began to emerge, to surface, to identify themselves. There were cries and shrieks and groans, and the crackle of wood and masonry as these continued to settle. And all in intense, murderous darkness.

He kicked his feet free, reached out across the sloping bed to touch Nadine. She was not there. He called her name a couple of times more. He was almost naked; but he had come into the room in trousers and jacket and had dropped them beside the bed. But where was the bed?

He stretched up, the other way, climbing the tilt, painfully pulled himself further from the wardrobe, attained the edge, reached down. Clothes. But they were not his. Then a pair of slacks. His. But nothing in the pockets except a handkerchief and a key-ring. A jacket.

Something settled with a great thunderous sigh quite near to him – some other part of the building coming down, murmuring and groaning, tons of masonry settling around him.

That day he had bought a rose, put it in his lapel. His fingers closed on it, still fragrant, identifying. Leaning like a man out of a sinking lifeboat, he reached with both hands and pulled his jacket to him. His head was swimming and he was out of breath, but trembling fingers found their way to his jacket pocket. A round cool cylinder with a thin band round the middle. Cigarette lighter. Flip. Flip. Flip. The third time it sparked, came to life. He stared round at a flickering yellow nightmare of slanting beams and heaped rubble, a bed tilted like an upended raft, and more rubble below him, eight feet below him, things sticking out of the rubble, a wash basin, a clock, an arm, a broken table, a chair . . .

Arm.

They had been on the third floor but must have fallen through to the second or further. He got hold of his shoes, his trousers, he pulled them on, then launched himself over the edge, thumped on to the rubble and slithered down it until a table stopped him. The lighter had gone out but re-sparked when he tried it. The thing would probably only last a few minutes. Desperate not to lose it. His only eyes.

Arm. He slithered down towards it, peered at the hand. Dear Christ, it was Nadine's.

There was a block of masonry which looked stable, too heavy to move again; stand the lighter on it, touch the hand, begin to pull the rubble away. Among the plaster and the powder there were great stones and blocks that he could hardly shift, roll them further down; someone was moaning; not Nadine, a man; someone else buried even deeper? How breathe? He unearthed more of the arm and a naked shoulder, reddish-black curling hair. He coughed out the smell of sulphur, plucked with bleeding fingertips at the mess, praying, half-crying: 'Oh God, oh God, oh God!'

The forehead, the face, the neck; the beautiful eyes had been open but were smothered in white dust. He put his hand to her mouth, to her neck, the pulse of the neck. There was no pulse in the neck. For some minutes he went on digging, careless of where his diggings were sliding to, uncovering the top quarter of her body. Then he stopped, face in hands. He could see it was no use, could be no further use. Nadine was dead.

III

HE SAT THERE for an unmeasured time, face in hands, tears trickling between fingers and mixing with his blood. Some time later he began to be aware again of shouts and groans around him. His light had gone out but there was now some sort of light flickering through the ruins. He forced himself to move. His own bedroom was on the second floor, so he was probably now on a level with that. Whoever had been in the room below this must also be dead. His own room was on the opposite side of the corridor.

Was there still a corridor? Did he have a room? If he

clawed his way through the ruins ... He staggered and slithered over the rubble to a piece of open flooring from which a draught of poisonous air seemed to be emanating. The door of this second-floor bedroom had gone altogether but an area of carpeted passageway existed beyond. A body lay across his path but no sound came from it, and he moved on. A door, actually his door, but it was jammed. Next to it was another gap, and he peered in.

This had been the next door bedroom, and all the floors above had collapsed upon it, carrying part of it down to ground level. He peered over a precipice and nearly fell. People were crawling about down there like maimed insects. Some were digging, clawing at the rubble and the wood and the stone. Stink of sulphur whose hot breath might have come from a volcano.

A quarter of this room had somehow survived, protected by a mighty concrete beam which had fallen diagonally across it. Part of the bed, a wardrobe; two bodies lying beside the bed, both dead, he could see by their sprawling limbs; it was the beam maybe that had crushed them, though on his way across he stumbled over a half-dozen lethal pieces which had also come down from the floors above.

The light coming through to what was left of the collapsed building derived from a fire in the staff pavilion where the swimming-pool used to be. Beyond the beam he could see this, for all the side of the hotel had gone; he was staring through piled masonry at the open beach and the sea. But there was no beach, and the sea occupied the gardens and lapped around a few stark figures struggling away to get help. No fire in the hotel.

His head and his heart were bursting. The enormity took his breath. He had no time to think of the rest of the town, or even to wonder about fellow guests: all he knew was that he had been struck as with a thunderbolt, and his love, his very own new love, just found, now lost after only three days: it was to be the love of his life; it was at an end. Nadine was gone, all that youth and entrancing beauty was lost, crushed under mighty tons of falling rubble, out of his life, out of all life.

Even his own life was still at risk. If he were to climb out upon the great beam which protruded into the air and drop eighteen feet or so onto the flooded garden – or even upon more rubble – he would break his leg or his neck. There seemed no way back. But time was not on his side. The whole ruin might at any moment settle still further, or – worse dread of all – there might come another earthquake.

He peered at the two dead people, then crawled back over the litter and wrecked furniture to the one apparently secure corner of the room. The fire was burning more brightly now; it had reached some fuel and a sharp flaring flame lit up the scene.

The first man, in a skullcap and a long black coat, whom he recognized as a croupier from the Casino, was dead. The other was Johnny Frazier, and he too was dead. A girder had broken his back.

Someone was shouting. It sounded like: 'Is anyone up there?' But it didn't seem to be directed towards him. The moans and groans had not died down. How many were buried alive?

But if they could be heard they must surely be reachable. If he could help, he must help, and at once.

On the bed he saw the small suitcase. It had been so obvious a part of Johnny Frazier's life and appearance that Matthew had come to speculate on what the case was likely to contain. It was no longer going to be of any use to Johnny Frazier.

Matthew picked it up and flipped the catches, but they were both locked.

On the bed was a wallet with some money in it. A newspaper. An empty brown leather bag. A passport. The light wasn't good enough to see the name, but he could recognize Johnny's photograph. He put it in his pocket, and the other bits and pieces as well. Then he took up the case. Should he try to take it with him? Better leave it for the police.

There was an explosion somewhere behind him, quite distant. Might be a gas main.

Behind the bed a smaller beam had fallen, also slantwise; it made a triangular corner between where its ends rested and what was left of the floor. He pushed Frazier's case into this corner, then stood up, head singing and swirling, wiped more blood from his arm. He set about trying to find a way down into the flooded gardens.

IV

As the Saada collapsed it took with it downwards the bedrooms occupied by Lee Burford and Letty Heinz, down almost two floors, crushing to death the people below them. The two floors above came on top of them but a freak of construction caused them to fall partly outwards, so that the occupants of this part of the third floor were buried but not crushed.

Lee was sitting on the bed pulling at his tie when the world screamed and thundered and gave way under him and he fell with an ear-bursting crash amid a miscellaneous hail of objects of all sizes, fell some eighteen feet, landing still on the bed, not physically injured but stunned with shock and noise. When he came to, clutching at sense and reason as if they were about to leave him, he at once began to push the plaster and the broken glass off his body and to peer over to the right to where Letty's room had been. There was no wall now, only a mountain of refuse and broken furniture.

'Letty!' he called.

There was no reply. He struggled up, took a cautious step upon the shards of glass.

'Letty!'

'Lee . . .' It was a faint cry, but it was hers.

'Where are you?'

'Down here. Half – buried. I cannot – get free.'

He found a match and struck it. Before it burned down it showed he was in a low cave created by the way the rafters from the upper floors had fallen, and beyond the low cave a black crevice, about three feet high.

'Can you see my light?'

'Yes.'

'Wait. Don't move. I'll try to get you.'

The matchbox was more than half full. In darkness he edged towards where he thought the crevice was. Then he struck another match. It was a sideways crevice slanting downwards at about twenty degrees. Before the match went out he caught a glimpse of fair hair.

'I can see you. I'm coming for you.'

Again in darkness, he edged his way under the overhanging weight of two floors, clawed at the debris, encountered a great lump of masonry that barred his path. He did not dare try to dislodge it lest it should cause a general collapse. Scrape at the rubble.

'This way!' Letty gasped. 'Wait! I think I have a light!'

He lay there prone and exhausted, and then a pencil of

light penetrated the devastation. He saw her lying under a pile of debris, half buried, her long fair hair white with plaster dust. Her face was bloodstained, and below the waist she disappeared into a tangle of broken pipes and fallen furniture.

He could now see a way round the boulder and edged himself nearer to her.

There was a narrow space about her, and he touched her; felt enormous relief at the grip of her hand. On hands and knees he pulled at the mountain of stuff that buried her. There was no way for this to fall into any further hole, so it had to be picked away piece by piece, gingerly lest it should dislodge something above, and put to one side where it was near her but no longer pressing on her.

However careful he was, other rubble edged down several times to take the place of what he pulled away, and once a pipe clanged down just missing her arm. But he made progress, and he saw with overwhelming relief that as the weight was taken off her legs, she was able to move them.

'Take a rest,' she said. 'You are injured yourself?'

'No, nothing.'

She said: 'I had just picked up my bag when this happened. And the torch was inside.'

'I have a few matches left. But we must economize. You've hurt your head?'

'I do not think it is bad.'

He began to dig and scrabble again. Both shoes were still on. As he uncovered them she lifted one knee and then the other.

'Your back?'

'No, I think it is OK. Oh, my God, what a thing! How deep are we buried?'

'Well, I think we've almost come down to ground floor. It seemed further!'

'The whole hotel has gone?'

'I guess so.'

A nasty wound on the crown of her head. A flap of skin hung loose; her hair was tangled and crimson. He saw this when, having taken most of the weight off her legs, he crouched behind her and put his hands under her arms to see if she could sit up.

She sat up, retched, shook her head trying to clear it.

'Can you get onto your knees, follow me back? There's more room and a bit more air where I was. And a bed!'

Inch by inch he began to return, making sure that she was following. Behind them there was a sudden thump and clatter as more of the debris settled, already filling the space where she had been.

V

PARTS OF THE town were blazing, but not many of the fires lasted the night. The tidal wave, which had followed the earthquakes and submerged parts of the town, began to recede, taking with it the bodies of those who had been drowned and sucking away many who had been killed as the buildings collapsed. A few lights glinted, where hurricane lamps and candle lamps had been found and lit. New pinpoints of light began to show where two companies of French marines, drafted hastily to help and the first to arrive, began to penetrate the town.

Dawn came quite late; but when it came it looked like atomic war. In many of the smaller streets, where buildings had been chiefly of baked clay and compressed stone, the structures had collapsed into piles of white dust, from which a piece of furniture, a rocking horse or a human arm or leg protruded as the only solids left.

The Saada, a luxury hotel, was a different matter. A mountain of rubble and metal, concrete, wood, plaster, beams, pillars, furniture and fittings had become compressed into the earth's crack which had opened below it, so that twenty feet was the highest point of what had been sixty. Over it, sardonically, stood the large sign which had normally been illuminated. The S was gone, but the AADA drunkenly remained.

Scratching among the ruins as light came were the manager, Paul Gaviscon, Basri, the receptionist and only other surviving member of the staff, and a half-dozen of the guests. Another half-dozen sat huddled on stones, clutching some garment round their shoulders against the cool of dawn.

One man working with a spade and doing something to direct operations was Matthew Morris. He was in a jacket and trousers and sandals, no shirt, a bloodstained cloth round his arm, his hands scarred and bruised with pulling pieces of debris away to get to the many dozens of people buried underneath.

They had found twelve dead, but one man had been heard shouting, and they got him out as dawn came. He had a broken arm but was otherwise uninjured. He had been buried for seven hours. He was a German, who said not to bother about him. But he had lost his wife.

Sounds, cries, had been heard very faintly, more in the centre of the hotel, where one could imagine the lift had been, and Matthew and two other men whom he knew by sight were trying to lift off a great piece of cable that twisted and twined among the wreckage. It was too heavy to pull out and too tough to cut through without a blow-torch; but by moving a piece of a mantelpiece and three splintered beams it might be possible to lift a loop of it far enough away to dig below. One of the men – called Jonathan Jones – had been reluctant to deal with the cable lest it should be live, but, in so far as he thought about it at all Matthew assumed that nothing electrically alive could still exist in this town.

Matthew wasn't reasoning much about anything. The loss of Nadine stood across his mind. But somehow that was fuelling his determination to rescue the survivors. The physical shock to himself had not yet filtered through. He did not feel the pain in his hands or his arm. One of his feet was also bleeding where he had caught it climbing over masonry.

He and Jones and Lavalle, a Frenchman, now proceeded to lift a desk, which might have been the reception desk, but it was too heavy even for three of them. So Lavalle and he began with a pick and a hammer to break it up. Once it had been splintered they could lever pieces off it.

When this was done they could reach the rubble below. Jones went down first and began to shovel the stuff away, cautiously lest he should come upon someone buried in it. After a few minutes he stopped and knelt down.

'I can hear a voice,' he said. 'A woman. I think she's French.'

Matthew went over into a corner and vomited. He knew it was not *his* Frenchwoman and the thought turned his stomach.

A great red sun was rising over the mountains, lighting up the heavy clouds that still lingered. It was going to be another boiling hot day.

'*Ça va?*' said Lavalle, coming up to him and putting a hand on his shoulder. "Ow are you?'

'*Ça va.*' Matthew returned to his task. Jones had gone another foot down and was pulling at a pile of bigger stones. As he got them away Matthew could hear a faint mewing cry, like a cat. They worked their way along in the direction of the call, and Matthew came on the wooden end of a bed. He reached under it and found a hand.

'*Sauvez-moi!*' said a frail voice. '*Je me suis enseveli.*'

He pulled gently, but the hand could not come. 'Wait!' he called. 'Lie still. We'll help you.' He turned round. 'Have to get all this stuff off first.'

A few more people were about now: some ragged children, a group of native women.

Matthew stared up at some overhanging girders. 'Take care. This lot mustn't fall. Is there another spade?'

A man whose name he didn't know and who had been sitting with his arm round his wife got up and went over to the shattered pool, came back with a large children's spade for use on the beach. Jones was about to reject it, but Matthew seized it. 'It will do.'

They returned to the ruins. While Lavalle used the heavy shovel and Jones pulled at the masonry, Matthew used the small shovel to scrape and scratch at the loose stuff around the hand. Then on his knees he began to pull and scrape. A dark frizzy head. It was Vicky Reynard.

VI

LEE AND LETTY lay together in the dark on the same bed. Two legs of the bed were broken, and the mattress was aslant, so that they lay with their feet against the bottom board of the bed to stop the tendency to slip down. Four feet above their heads the great girder had jammed itself, protecting them from a massive accumulation of floorboards, furniture, coping stones, carpets, washbasins and other things waiting to fall. They had some space around them, narrow but just enough to move a foot here and there. The air was full of dust and no light came.

They had found the stump of a candle in one of the crushed drawers of the dressing table. All the hotel bedrooms were so provided in case of a normal electrical failure. But so far they had economized, for it would not burn more than two hours. They had tried knocking and whistling and shouting, but without result. Once they heard an explosion, and then a vessel hooting out at sea.

As they lay there Lee could feel the warm blood dripping on to his hand.

'We've got to do something about that,' he said, sitting up.

'This is nothing. I am using a pad to stop it ... What time is it?'

He flicked on Letty's torch. 'Just after three o'clock.'

While the torch was on he looked around for some level place where if necessary one could put the candle. There was a piece of the dressing table, just a projection. He slithered a foot or so, took the candle out of his pocket and lit it with one of his precious matches. The flame flickered and lost hope and then gained it again and lit up their prison. Letty was half lying, half standing on the mattress, holding a folded nightdress to her head. The nightdress was already heavy with blood.

'Let me see.'

As the flame steadied he eased the nightdress away and

stared at the wound. A big flap of hair and skin, about five inches long, had been part removed by a glancing blow which had left the skin loose and the wound raw. Blood was oozing.

His year in the Ambulance Brigade during the war had given him a fair experience of wounds, and he remembered that head wounds bled copiously to begin but dried fairly quickly. Dried if they were encouraged to dry. But she was losing too much blood. And who knew how long they might have to wait for rescue?

'What is there in your bag?'

'Oh. The usual things. See.'

He opened the bag, careful not to pull anything out lest it should roll away into some unreachable corner.

Hair clips. Make-up. Pen. Comb. Pocket mirror. Bottle of Chanel. Handkerchief. Nail scissors. Tweezers. Diary. Needle and thread. Purse. Passport. Travellers' cheques.

Needle and thread. He took them out and looked at them. She looked up at him.

He said: 'I guess I have to do something.'

She said: 'It will stop soon.'

'Maybe. But this air is bad, so dusty, and the wound is not clean . . .'

They thought it out while the candle guttered. He picked up the tweezers. They were small, but if you were deft enough . . .

'I must try.'

'. . . If you say so.'

It was white cotton thread and there were two needles, both of serviceable size. He wondered if they would bend. It would be so much easier with a curved needle. He tried one but it resisted his efforts with his fingers. A pair of pliers – which he lacked – might do it, or the needle might simply snap. He reached over and held the needle in the candle flame, then tried again, guarding his fingers against the heat of the needle with his handkerchief. It bent a bit. He tried again. A second small bend. It would have to do. Any further pressure might break it. He wiped the needle to get any carbon deposits off it.

Hell. What to do next? How achieve any sort of asepsis. Better to leave ill alone? By morning they might be rescued.

But do a bit to begin. He took her nail scissors – which were bent, as the needle ought to have been – and began to cut away her luxuriant hair around the wound. 'Jennie of the Light Brown Hair'. Much of it was rust-coloured or crimson. She winced, and he said: 'Christ, I don't know whether to do this or not.'

At the ends of the wound the skin was ragged, and he trimmed a few pieces back.

'Cry out if you want,' he said.

She said: 'Perhaps that way I shall attract the rescuers.'

If there are any, he thought to himself. He could hear nothing. Were they perhaps the only ones left alive?

The bottle of Chanel was nearly full. He unstoppered it and immersed the needle in it, then the scissors: it would be a sort of antiseptic. Seeing what he was doing, she said: 'Lucky you bought me that in Paris.'

He cut more of her hair away until it was no more than half an inch long at the edges of the wound. Then he tried to thread the needle, but his hands were fumbling and unsteady.

'Let me,' she said.

In a moment she had sucked the end of the cotton and threaded it. 'Use the darning stitch,' she said.

'Christ, I wish you could do it.'

'It is no matter. It will soon be over.'

'I can't bear to hurt you.'

'Oh, hurt. That is not important.'

As he had been trained – though it had been mainly watching others – he began in the middle, so that the skin tissue should not be drawn off centre. For a few seconds after putting in the needle he thought he couldn't go on; but then his hand steadied. Once he had drawn the skin together over the oozing wound and secured it with what she called the darning stitch and cut the thread and seen that his clumsy stitch was holding, he gained confidence and went on. Sometimes she winced but she made no sound. Only by the sudden clutching of her hands could he tell when he hurt her most. Six stitches were done on one side. A surgeon would have used many more, but at least it sufficed to bring the torn flap of scalp back onto its proper place. Then he began working away from the middle again. In ten minutes more it was done. The thread had almost run out and looked as bloody as his hands.

'Is there cotton in your bag?'

'A little. I think. A moment.'

She fumbled and produced a small wad of cotton wool. He pulled off a piece, took out a match and rolled the wool round the blank end of the match. Once it was quite secure he plunged it into the Chanel bottle, shook off the extra scent and began to dab at each of the stitches he had put in. She took a sharp breath at each touch, the alcohol in the perfume acting as an antiseptic but burning like iodine.

He lay back on the bed, as exhausted as she was.

Minutes passed, perhaps five. The shock and the tension had left him inert. With a great effort he stirred himself again.

'I'll tear a sheet,' he said. 'Make a bandage.'

'No. A wound like this should not need it.'

'But the dust and the dirt floating . . .'

'I'll put my scarf over it. Something light like that will be better.'

'Did I hurt you a lot?'

'Yes. But it is over.'

'It will hurt now, of course.'

'Yes, it does.'

'Letty, I hope it will ease soon. I guess we can only lie and wait.'

'Put out the candle,' she said. 'We may need it later.'

He did as she suggested and now they were lying in the dark. He put out a hand and found hers and they lay together as in the darkness of a burial ground.

CHAPTER TWELVE

I

MATTHEW AND Jonathan Jones drew at Vicky Reynard. At first it was inch by inch, grudgingly, fearfully, for risk of injuring her further; but suddenly she came quite all of a piece, leaving a rattle of rubble and squeak of springs behind her. She was still wearing the dress in which she had been to the Casino. She was smothered in white plaster, and in pain, but after half an hour it seemed that most of the pain had been caused by cramp and a few nasty bruises. With no medical man to examine her, she presently sat up and then crouched, then stood up, rubbing her legs in agony, and swearing in soft French.

In the night the manager had been able to find coffee and a coffee pot and a few mugs and a Primus, so the rescue party stood around for a few minutes sipping at the hot unsweetened brew. The wife of the man who had brought the spade sat beside Vicky and helped her hold a mug to her lips.

'Where are your friends?' Matthew asked her.

Great tears began to blob out of her eyes, mixing with the mascara and the dust. 'In there,' she whimpered.

Daylight was now fully come, and just then four French marines arrived in a jeep and disembarked, picking their way among the fallen umbrella pines and the cracked Tarmac of what had yesterday been the drive.

They consulted with M. Gaviscon and two of them came over and spoke to Lavalle and then to Jonathan and Matthew. Directed by them, the marines went to that part of the ruin from which Vicky had just been salvaged.

Before settling to his task the elder of the soldiers, a corporal, stood for a moment with his hands on his hips and looked around him.

'*Mon Dieu*,' he said. 'I have been here one hour only and I am suffering from *shock* – I who in the war was twice blown up and have seen many devastated towns before. Agadir is – a desert. Whole districts have gone. Someone said – some press person – that there might be two thousand dead. What nonsense! He is insane! It will be ten thousand or more. The buildings have fallen into dust. Death is everywhere. *Mon Dieu*, what will it be like when the heat comes!'

With two more strong men to help they made quicker progress, but they did not dare hurry. Like archaeologists excavating an ancient city, something could be easily broken or spoiled; and in this case it was buried people.

What was left of the town was beginning to come alive again now. A few cars tried to manoeuvre along the broken streets and among the fallen trees. Mostly they were piled high with people and their belongings, anxious to get out of the place while they were still alive. Someone was broadcasting a message in French and Arabic by megaphone, but it was too far away to hear what was being said. A portable radio crackled. A helicopter flew overhead, and then a small two-seater biplane. Most of the ships in the harbour seemed to have ridden out the tidal wave, though all the port cranes had been toppled and there was a range of new and massive boulders further along the beach. And the Kasbah on the hill had quite gone, as if it had never been. The preacher, El

Ufrani, had perished with the flock he had warned and condemned.

A Frenchman, one of the guests, came excitedly past. 'They're bringing help! It says so on the radio. They are to use the airport as a hospital! Ambulance teams and doctors and nurses and tents. King Mohammed is on his way and Prince Hassan. They're bringing troops from Casablanca!'

But so what? There was nothing here yet to help the people still buried, and very little help that could be brought except relays of workers. No mechanical excavator could possibly be used.

By nine the two other soldiers, with the help of a few surviving village boys, had taken out fourteen corpses, and two others still alive but seriously injured. Matthew knew none of them. A French doctor turned up, and most of the injured were taken away in his jeep. He said before he left that the ruins would soon have to be sprayed with quicklime to prevent disease spreading.

Soon after nine Matthew and the team he was working with excavated the second of the French tarts, Françoise Grasset, but she was dead. Vicky, who had refused to leave the scene, let out a great wail at the sight of her friend.

Beyond the excavation that had brought Françoise Grasset's body to light the mangled remains of the hotel reached to its maximum height, like the head of a mountain range. The prospect of anyone else being alive in that sloping pile was remote, and there was danger if one picked at it of creating a landslide.

About this time Matthew began to feel lightheaded and to shiver. He had lost an amount of blood from his arm before, sometime during the night, a friendly Moroccan bound it up, and he had been on the go for nine hours, with only a pause for the coffee, and later a biscuit and a hunk of bread. But it was he who took the lead in attacking the dangerous rubble that almost overhung where the Frenchwoman's body had been found. Twice he had to jump clear as debris slithered down.

A small ambulance had arrived at the entrance to the hotel, and two nurses and a driver got out and began to look over the survivors, picking out those most seriously hurt and helping or carrying them back to the ambulance. It was going to be another stifling day, and there was virtually no protection from the sun, as the palm trees lay about like scattered and broken matchsticks all over the muddy gardens. One old stone-built cabin had survived, but this was already half-full of corpses, where they had been carried to store them until they could be taken away. Already two rats had been shot escaping from the broken sewers.

Matthew staggered and Lavalle grasped his arm. 'You have had enough, my friend. You must rest. Or go with the ambulance.'

'No. I'm – well enough.' Matthew was obsessed with the need to recover Nadine's body and have it laid decently to rest. He hadn't been reasoning coherently for some time, and later he was to wonder what had so driven him on. It was not as if he had any hope of finding her alive. But loss of blood, mild concussion and delayed shock were producing their own twisted logic.

All the same, his persistent attack on the great mound produced some good results. This time it was Jonathan Jones who heard the first cry. Gently, laboriously, they unearthed another woman. She was conscious, breathing and, when they finally got her out, able to sit up. It was Laura Legrand, the third French lady.

The first word she uttered was '*Merde!*'

II

By noon the King was in Agadir. Twice he had flown over the ravaged town. This time he had come to Inezgane, a couple of miles out, where the Crown Prince Moulay Hassan was in charge of all the rescue work and the maintenance of law and order. Agadir airport was little damaged, and helicopters were ferrying the wounded, the sick and the dying from the centre of the town. A forest of tents had been set up at one end of the airport to accommodate them, but there were far more people than could be taken in, and many of the less seriously injured lay out in the open, shielding themselves as best they could from the sun. The Fahrenheit shade temperature at noon in the airport was 104°.

Everything was still in short supply: clean drinking water was needed as much as blood plasma, and indeed a little food, not only for the survivors but for the soldiers, marines and sailors who had flooded in. As they came in, the inhabitants, those who had survived, were flooding out. Crossing with the ingoing rescue workers were trails of Moroccans, some in old cars, others walking, many on mule and donkey, carrying a few belongings, all seeking the safety of the countryside for fear of another earth tremor. Many were camping under the argan trees, still within sight of the smouldering city.

Radios were crackling everywhere now, issuing instructions, words of hope and comfort, promises of all possible speedy help. The King had already announced that the old Agadir had ceased to exist, and that a new Agadir would be at once inaugurated. Prince Moulay Hassan added that it should all be rebuilt within a year, and that on the 2nd of

March, 1961, the anniversary of Morocco's Independence, the new city would be opened.

Eighty doctors and nurses were being flown from Paris and would arrive later in the day. The whole of the French Mediterranean fleet was sailing for Agadir, plus the aircraft carrier *Lafayette*. A further cruiser and six destroyers were coming from the Canaries. The ships of other European nations were on their way. From their airbase the Americans were flying in six Hercules transports carrying emergency supplies and bulldozers, and would convey injured people out of the area, whence they could be distributed to Casablanca, Rabat, Safi and Marrakech. Drugs and stretchers and other supplies were being brought by the RAF from Gibraltar.

With the risk of every sort of pestilence breaking out in this heat, it was further announced that by tomorrow evening, Wednesday, all rescue operations would have to come to an end and the city be flattened and abandoned.

III

'WHAT TIME is it?' Letty asked.

He switched on the torch. 'Twelve, I reckon it must be midday.'

'That's twelve hours we've been here. I think we should start shouting again.'

'Let me. I suppose your head . . .'

'It is still throbbing. But I believe not quite so bad.'

Lee began to shout. The air was foul, but there must be a current somewhere.

After about ten minutes he stopped. There was a piece of

the bed he could bang with Letty's scissors and this made a thin piercing noise within the confined space.

'It's only a matter of time,' he said.

He did not ask if she was thirsty; useless to emphasize what they were both feeling.

'It's only a matter of time,' he said again.

She said: 'Well, I have been in more uncomfortable places.'

'Have you?'

'Even this is better than being in the hands of the Gestapo.'

'*Were* you?'

'Yes, twice. In 1941. They thought I knew where my brother was.'

'Was this in Oslo?'

'Yes. The infamous Victoria Terrace. Where my father went before me.'

He put his hand back over hers. 'How long were you kept there?'

'The first time a week. The second time two. Lying here with you, with company, buried but waiting, it is rather to be preferred.'

'You were, I suppose – interrogated?'

'Oh, yes. Oh, yes. I told them nothing. Or sometimes lies.'

'Did they . . .' He hesitated and stopped.

'Torture me? No. They were bullies: they shouted at me, became hysterical. Many of the Gestapo were hystericals, did you know? But the only time they touched me was to grasp my wrists. After two, three hours of questioning they would take me back to my cell, where I was alone, a single light, no window, not allowed to read, to write. I could just pace about – perhaps three metres each way – or sit or lie on the bed, which was not so soft as this one.'

'Though not sloping.'

'Not sloping.'

'Listen, was that something?'

A distant droning which might have been an aeroplane. They both began to shout, but when they stopped the aeroplane had gone.

To take her mind off their situation and to help the time to pass, he began to question her about her life in Norway under the Occupation. She talked more then than she had ever done before, and he suspected that she was playing the same game. She told of confiscated food, men arrested without warning, children picking flowers to put on the grave of an unknown British pilot, the tank parades through the main streets, a mutiny among the German soldiers and the firing squads that suppressed it, the banning of newspapers and radios, the sinking of the cruiser *Blücher*, the Lofoten raid and the reprisals and the burning of houses and the arrests of prominent men.

When she and her mother had finally reached Sweden they had worked their way south to Göteborg. This had taken a month. There they had boarded a Swedish vessel carrying a cargo of cotton and leather goods for Baltimore. Being neutral, they had not been searched.

'And your brother?' Lee asked.

'He was captured and shot near Bergen, attempting to blow up an oil refinery. They were all shot, all six of them ... There is only one thing I am thankful for, he was not interrogated. I am told the German officer who ordered the shooting was later sent to the Russian front – not for killing these brave men but for not handing them over to the Gestapo first ...'

'You cared much for your brother.'

'Oh, yes. Perhaps him most of all.'

Towards two he put on the torch and looked at her head. The stitches were holding, and the bleeding had almost stopped.

IV

THEY HAD pulled out nine more corpses and one man alive but with two broken legs. He was English and was a big man with a pugilist's face and manner. He said he was not a guest at the Saada but came from the Mahraba. His chum was dead, squashed obscenely flat like some frog caught under a tractor wheel. He and his chum had come to visit a chum of theirs, he said, and had been caught sitting in the lobby when the earthquake struck. He was taken by jeep to the quay, there to be lifted by helicopter to the airport.

Special attention was being given to Europeans caught in the collapse of the hotels. This was not merely because they were wealthy visitors, though that counted for a great deal, but because Prince Moulay Hassan, circling the scene in a helicopter, could see that whereas building built of the Moorish *pisé* had collapsed completely, burying the inhabitants without hope of survival, the more modern and up-to-date buildings, even if they had collapsed, had fallen into heaps of masonry and steel girders which might have fallen and trapped people without killing them. Therefore different techniques had to be applied for different parts of the city. By tomorrow morning the bulldozers and the dynamiters must go in, followed by the disinfectant squads; the coastal strip would have to be left as long as possible.

But how long would it be possible? The buzzards were already circling, the rats multiplying, the jackals were out, and the flies and bluebottles, in this heat, and with this smell, everywhere. There had been pressure on the Prince to delay the total destruction of the town by another day. But would it pay to save one or two more buried people at the expense of many others who might go down in a wave of typhoid, cholera and dysentery?

Tomorrow at dawn four hundred men had been commanded to advance on the town wearing damp antiseptic masks and would smother it in quicklime. That would be the end of a fine city. In a month or so another would begin to rise, not quite on the same site but within half a mile, perhaps built on more stable rock. At this stage one had to weigh the consequences of ruthlessness against the consequences of hesitation and a form of humanitarianism which might earn praise in the foreign press but might well lead to terrible outbreaks of disease.

About four they dug out Mme Thibault, uninjured except for a gashed ankle. The curious sight was to be seen of Vicky Reynard comforting the other woman with her arm round her shoulders while Estrella wept into a small sodden handkerchief. M. Thibault was not to be found. Mme Thibault, having had her ankle perfunctorily dressed, refused to leave the spot while her husband was unaccounted for. Laura Legrand, also uninjured in spite of her long entombment, came across with a cup of strong coffee and a piece of fruit cake, and Estrella did not refuse to take them from her.

At six Matthew's legs gave way. He was helped into the next jeep, but refused to leave the town. In spite of all his efforts and the efforts of soldiers under his direction, Nadine's body had not yet been recovered. There had been a further fall of masonry, and everyone was reluctant to do anything to start another collapse while a hope of life still lingered among the rubble.

They took him instead to the ruined hospital, where makeshift tents had been put up in the grounds, and Dr Berrada, trying to ignore his personal losses, and others were dealing with the less seriously injured.

A young medical attendant dressed his arm properly, he was given some wine and biscuits, and then they jabbed his other arm and he fell into a heavy sleep.

He only realized how long he had slept when, on opening his eyes, he saw there were streaks of daylight in the sky. He had been out for about sixteen hours.

He felt sick and ill and tired and sick at heart, but alert. He sat up, and a man lying beside him stirred and groaned. In the glimmering light a few people were moving about the tents. He tried to get up but his legs were still weak and he sat back, taking in long deep breaths. He rested his head against the tent pole.

The catastrophe was still too much for him to take in. A happy holiday – made suddenly vividly exciting by his meeting with Nadine – had collapsed into a nightmare of unguessable proportions. That girl, that beautiful girl, in the full flight of her youth and elegance, crushed, smothered, bludgeoned to death by a convulsion such as had never happened before in the history of western Africa. And hundreds of other people. *Thousands* of others. If Nadine had accepted his suggestion that they should drive to Marrakech they would have escaped it all and she would still be alive. Or if they had accepted the Baron de Blaye's invitation to spend another few nights there . . . If . . . if . . . It was unthinkable. It was insensate, an evil force striking out blindly and caring nothing what it hit. There was some poem by Hardy he vaguely remembered: 'Or come we of an Automaton unconscious of our pains?' This Automaton cared as little as any other robot; killing and crushing as it went.

Among those it had arbitrarily missed was Matthew Morris. Among those it had arbitrarily killed was Nadine Deschamps. He wondered what had happened to the other guests. Fat old Thibault and the pretty Italian woman, and the limping German and that American couple. Had they been brought out to safety, or brought out and lined up among the other dead, or not brought out at all? He would never know now. He would never go back.

Recovering his strength gradually, he gripped the tent pole and pulled himself to his feet. In the next tent they were bringing in a boy of about twelve who, a nurse said, had been buried standing up to his neck in rubble for thirty-one hours. He had no serious injury but his nerves had gone now he was rescued, and they were trying to get a teapot between his chattering teeth so that they could pour water into him after the dehydration. At a table not far away under the light of an acetylene lamp a surgeon was performing some sort of an operation on an unidentifiable figure. After a few minutes the male nurse beside the table dropped an amputated arm into a bucket.

Matthew's new strength went and he sat down. As daylight grew he could see people everywhere, many lying on the ground, some kneeling, others standing like lost souls not knowing which way to turn.

'Are you better, monsieur?' a voice said. It was the young doctor who had dressed his arm.

'Thank you. I – have been asleep a long time. Have you water – or any liquid?'

'I can get you some lemonade.'

'That would be wonderful.'

'Let me look at your arm.'

Matthew allowed him to examine the bandage and to sniff it. He seemed satisfied.

Matthew said: 'You have far too much to do. Perhaps I can look after myself.'

'Presently you shall. But you are – a visitor, and therefore we do our best for you.'

'How many people are there in this – this encampment?'

'Perhaps three thousand.'

'And doctors?'

'Eight. There were only three to begin, but many more are coming. I think you should not have come here, M. Delaware. You should have been lifted out to the airport.'

'I did not want to go. I have lost someone – very dear to me.'

'As have so many others, alas.'

As the doctor turned away to fetch the lemonade Matthew said: 'But why do you call me M. Delaware?'

The young doctor smiled. 'It was in your passport, monsieur. We are trying – the authorities are trying very hard to keep a tally of those who have survived and those who – who have been lost.'

'But it is – that is a mistake,' Matthew said. 'I am not . . .'

But the young doctor had turned away and did not hear him.

CHAPTER THIRTEEN

I

LEE HAD BEEN tunnelling. After a long time he looked at his watch and reckoned he had been working for four hours. He had made little progress, for the rubble was pressed hard down, and he had to go cautiously. The other great problem, which was insoluble, was how far they had fallen. Did safety lie upwards, or downwards, or tunnelling level away from where they lay?

Letty was asleep. She had fallen asleep just after he began digging, and his only break in his activities was every now and then to edge nearer to her and listen to her breathing. Often it was short and troubled as if she were dreaming. Once he shone a shaded light and saw that her face was flushed. Probably running a fever from the wound in her head. He wondered if he would have been wiser not to have touched it, but he did not dare to lift the scarf for fear of waking her. Let her sleep.

He was feeling lightheaded and feeble himself, and though he had progressed about two feet into the rubble there was nothing to gauge whether this sort of effort was bringing them any nearer the surface.

Actually there wasn't very much either of them could do but sleep. Perhaps this way they would sleep their lives away.

There was no sound of activity outside. Occasionally an

aircraft could be heard, but these sounded distant and remote, as if hearing them through an immensely thick wall. There was some current of air, otherwise they could not have lived. He thought it came from below, from the area from which he had dragged Letty, and that was the way he had been tunnelling.

It would be going dark outside, and soon they would have been buried two days. For half a day the air had been unpleasant because of their own faecal motions, which they had been unable to contain; but with no food or water taken in they had passed nothing, and the air was clearing again.

He was feeling sleepy himself, and after rubbing the blood off his fingers and fingernails, he tucked them inside his shirt and slid beside her, trying to find comfort in her presence.

Almost at once he dreamed. He was marrying Ann again, and was being constantly offered glasses of champagne which, as soon as he grasped them, turned into dry straw. Then they were driving away, just as they had done so many years ago, but were somewhere in Arizona on a road overlooking a lake. It was a mountain road with hairpin bends, and although it was climbing he felt certain that it would soon lead him down to the cool waters of the lake. Instead the road narrowed and the Tarmac was barely a car wide; then it tapered to a narrowness that made it impossible to go on. But now it was impossible to reverse, so they abandoned the car and decided to climb down to another road fifty feet below. They had rope, which Ann was carrying in her handbag, but it was in small lengths which had to be tied together. The descent was impeded by fallen columns of stones, great rocks and broken bedsteads.

Suddenly he felt the rope behind him go slack, and he could not see his wife.

'Ann!' he called, peering into the still water of the lake. 'Ann! Where are you? Ann!'

A hand was stroking his forehead and he woke.

'Not Ann,' Letty said. 'Not Ann. Only Letty.'

'Oh, Christ,' he muttered through parched lips. 'I was dreaming . . .'

'Never mind, Lee. Go back to dreaming. Perhaps this is what is left for us.'

He struggled fitfully to stir himself. 'How are you?'

'It is not good now, is it. We must face what we have to face.'

'I have been digging.'

'Yes, I know.'

'Digging before dreaming. Equally futile.'

He was lapsing into sleep again, a sort of sleep which was not far from loss of consciousness. Suddenly, though unhurt, because of his age he was becoming the weaker of the two.

Letty held his hand, looked at the broken fingernails, and dried blood.

She said: 'Sometimes I have not much wanted to live. When my brother died. And then again later once or twice . . . But now I do not think I want to die.'

II

MATTHEW LOOKED at the passport. It was Johnny Frazier's photograph, but an entirely different name. Henri Delaware.

Born in Canada. Aged thirty-six. The photograph stared guilelessly out of the passport. How could the doctor have made such a mistake? *Were* they all that different to look at, Matthew Morris and Johnny Frazier? They were both tall, dark, Frazier was thinner and older, but in the half-light the mistake could have been made. Anyway, finding the passport in Matthew's pocket, the doctor no doubt had jumped to the inevitable conclusion.

Matthew felt in his pocket for the few other bits of paper he had picked up from beside Frazier's body. There were provisional reservations for a berth on two ships: the *Merrimac*, leaving on Tuesday the 1st of March and the *Vesteraaven* on Friday the 4th, both in the name of Henri Delaware. M. Delaware, alas, would not be confirming either. What *had* been Frazier's game? No doubt the answer lay in the case he had carried around with him so zealously.

One ship was bound for Rio, the other was some sort of Scandinavian cruise ship. How could he have intended taking two ships? *Was* there such a person as Henri Delaware after all and did Frazier himself intend to take the other vessel? Then how explain the puzzle of Frazier's face in Delaware's passport? The document looked genuine enough.

The other thing he had picked up off the bed was a small pocket wallet. It contained money: 500 French francs, 1000 Moroccan dirhams, £40 in English fivers, a driving licence in the name of John Tournelle Frazier.

And a cutting from an English newspaper, the paper being of the flimsy quality used for air editions.

The police have so far made little progress in their efforts to catch the half-dozen armed and stocking-masked men who early yesterday morning broke into the offices of

Benson & Benson, merchant bankers of 12 St Mary's Gate, EC4 and gagged and bound the staff while getting away with money, bonds and valuables estimated to be worth half a million pounds. Two abandoned cars have been found, and a Red Cross worker, Miss Elsie Wardle, has been able to give a description of the men involved.

All that morning Matthew lay in the shade of the awning and recovered his strength. He ate a little and drank a lot of lemonade, and for a while helped look after a group of children who had lost their mothers and fathers. Then the order came through at noon that in conformity with the decision to abandon the city, this hospital site would be evacuated and a string of trucks and lorries and, for the badly wounded, helicopters, would be made available. The evacuation would begin at two and it was hoped would be completed by dusk.

With these instructions confusion became chaos, and again Matthew helped to organize the loading of the trucks as they came in. Twice he was offered a helping hand to climb on a lorry and be carried to the airport. Twice he refused. Now that it came to the point he was reluctant to leave. He was certain he would never go back to the Saada, yet its ruins drew him. He knew he should go to the airport and telephone Baron de Blaye, telling him the news of Nadine's death. He knew he should also telephone his mother, or at least get news to her that he was alive and uninjured. Uninjured except in spirit. But the ruins of the Saada were in the front of his mind.

By six it became clear that although most of the patients, orphans and refugees who had occupied the site would be gone before dusk, a residue of a few hundred, and much gear, would have to go after dark. Tomorrow morning the city was to be abandoned as a city of the dead. About seven he slipped away unnoticed and began to walk back to the Saada.

III

IT WAS A ghost city he walked through, with the stench of death and quicklime overpowering in the hot, heavy air. The streets could be picked out among the hillocks of rubble, with spurs sticking up here and there like skeletal elbows, the streets themselves split up and open, with fallen trees, smashed motor cars and earth and dead animals and dust. Sometimes one side of a street would have maintained its shape in a row of erratic ruins, while the other side had become powdered debris.

It was not quite dark yet, and a sickle of moon shone out of a clear sky. Here and there floodlights with portable generators were coming on where troops were continuing their bulldozing or their excavations.

There were a few dark-clad figures about, defying orders to leave and digging among the ruins, no doubt most of them trying to salvage something from their old homes, or even still beating at blocks of masonry in the search for a husband or wife or child who might still be alive under it all. There were scavengers too, but the soldiers had orders to shoot anyone suspicious.

The city had been out of bounds since the first day, and Matthew kept as much to the shadows as possible, aware that if he were challenged he would be forcibly taken away. Occasionally sub-machine-gun fire could be heard, but he thought this was likely to be to scare away the jackals which had come into the town from the hinterland. Now and then he saw a dog slinking like him in the shadows, but he kept well clear of them, knowing the danger of rabies.

He had tied a damp handkerchief across his face to try to keep out the stench of putrefaction, but the evening was still so hot that he took it off, and retched at the smell, and tried to hold his nose. An armoured car rattled past, all the men in it wearing gas masks and carrying rifles and spades. It looked as if the armoured car had been sprayed with some white disinfectant.

The wall he had stopped beside was part of a house, still standing but partly sunk so that everything was leaning towards the back like a ship going down by the stern. From here he could just pick out the dark mound that was the Saada silhouetted in crazy rectangles against the sulky sea.

He approached it cautiously. Two soldiers were on guard at the gates – otherwise the place was empty and dead, awaiting demolition.

Everyone was gone. All the hundred and fifty holiday guests, French, English, German, American, Swiss. The very few survivors like himself had been taken away. The rest were either piled one on another in the mortuary shed or remained buried for ever under thousands of tons of masonry. A holiday sepulchre. Ice-creams and buckets and spades and swimming-pools and sunbathing and orange vodkas and mint tea and death. All over Europe and America there would be the occasional family who happened to have decided to have a holiday in the sun and would not return.

Matthew went down a sandy passage that led to the beach, which was empty and desolate and strewed with debris. Cautiously he approached the hotel from the sea side. The moon had not yet set, and the sky was lit by it. So was this side of the hotel.

In the contour of the ruins very little had changed. The great beam which he had walked out on and jumped to safety from was still there. In the distortion of the tragedy he had thought the distance eighteen feet. In fact it was barely six. Others must have been up this way. They would only need a small ladder. Very unlikely that if he went up there he would find the two corpses, grinning at him in the most noisome stages of decay.

Nor Nadine. They would be sure to have found her too, for she had not been buried, only crushed to death. Did he even want to see if she was there? If she was, did he want to see what two days of heat and putrefaction had done to her beautiful body and face?

Yet he knew he must look. He was still not in the most logical state of mind and he knew he must look.

The great concrete beam was probably nearly seven feet over his head. He stretched up and could just touch it with his fingertips. He cast around, found a table but one of the legs was broken, then a hard bentwood chair. Careful not to make a noise which might attract the guards, he lifted the chair across and stood on it. Better, but it did not lift him high enough – not nearly high enough, for the beam was too thick for him to get his arms round. He climbed down and began to search among the debris by the pool. There was a light breeze, still from the land, and when it gusted he had to hold his nose.

What he found was the pool ladder. Almost twisted from its fastenings, it dangled above the empty broken concrete. He found an abandoned walking stick and looped the handle round a rung, pulled it up and once it was on ground level he only had to twist it a couple of times for the last bolt to snap.

A patrol car had stopped at the gates of the hotel, and an

American naval officer was talking in bad French to the two guards. Matthew waited until the car had driven away, then carried the ladder to the beam. The ladder was also short, but he was able to prop it against the broken table, the chair and a pile of broken furniture in such a way that he could go up it, balancing on the beam as he scrambled up to it, then expecting the ladder to fall behind him with a crash. It stayed in place.

He dusted his hands, tied the handkerchief round his face and went into the darkness of the ruin.

He at once found the half room where Johnny Frazier and the croupier had been lying. It was unchanged, but the two corpses had gone. Surely everyone who could be found up here had been taken away. He pulled off the handkerchief and the air, while bad, was only just touched with corruption.

He went past the twisted bed into the more secure corner of the room, just to check against the probability that Johnny Frazier's precious suitcase had been taken away. It was still there.

IV

HE PICKED it up, shook it. The locks were unbroken. Whatever had been in it was still in it. He turned to go back with it, along the girder to where the ladder still swung. But this was not what he had come for. He had to go back to see if Nadine . . .

He put the case down, picked his way past where the two men had been, pushed open the half-ajar door, looked into the passage and towards where his room had once existed. Of it not a trace remained. But a few feet of still carpeted corridor led back the way he had come on Monday night. This part was all open to the sky, but the moon was sinking and its shadows stretched everywhere. He had borrowed a pocket torch but did not use it for fear of attracting the attention of the guards.

A piece of wall crumbled under his hand as he groped his way forward. Any of this, though apparently tightly jammed, might collapse at any time. Tomorrow came the bulldozers, reducing it all finally to dust and disinfectant and quicklime.

He was peering through a tangle of pipes and wires and broken furniture into what had been Nadine's bedroom. There was still the part rectangle of the bed but he could not at this distance be sure she was not still lying on it. He had to get nearer.

He began pulling at one of the pipes: it trickled a drop of water, which somehow had not all evaporated in the heat. Some of this debris must have come down since he escaped this way, for he could hardly have come through such a tangle. Had the army ventured so far? He thought he detected a shape lumped at the end of the bed.

His hair prickled as he looked at it. He had to go and see.

The pipe stopped halfway but he could now bend under it. He scraped his knee on the sharp edge of an upturned plank, slid round a wardrobe, pushed his way past a slanting washbasin and stood before the bed.

It was not Nadine. It was not Nadine. It was a couple of pillows and one of her dresses. It was not Nadine. They had been for her, taken her away. Reverently, decently, he hoped. But what reverence could one hope for from soldiery or ambulance men in a catastrophe such as this? At least she was gone. Thank God, thank God, thank God. He turned away, strangely relieved, as if now he could bear his grief.

Back now. Back now. Nothing more to do. Nothing more really to hide. He could declare himself to the guards. Maybe they could get a jeep to pick him up, take him to the airport, where – registered no doubt, and very ironically, as Henri Delaware – he could make what provision he chose for his own future. It was bleak. Without Nadine everything was bleak.

He turned to go and heard a noise. He listened, disbelieving.

A tapping.

Obviously some animal or bird using its claws, its beak, to get at some horrible morsel of decay. There could be nothing else after all this time.

Careful how you went back. The floor was splintered but the carpet held it, made it just safe to step on. He stepped on it and again stopped. Clear but faint. Tap-tap-tap-*tap*. Tap-tap-tap-*tap*. He recognized the rhythm of Beethoven's Fifth Symphony. What rubbish. Just plain coincidence. But hadn't that been the agreed secret rhythm of all the Resistances during the war?

Where the hell was it coming from? Somewhere below. The water pipe was near his head. He took out a coin and rapped on it – the same rhythm.

The other tapping stopped, then began again, slightly louder, more urgent. He tapped back. As the other tapping ceased he called at the top of his voice. No reply. He shouted. No reply. Now the tapping continued.

He turned and went back the way to safety – the twelve square feet of corridor, the splintered bed that had been

Johnny Frazier's sepulchre, the beam. As he stepped onto the beam a bright light shone in his eyes. He stopped, silhouetted against the setting moon.

'Halt!' said a French voice. 'Or we fire.'

He put his hands above his head.

'Come up!' he said. 'There are people alive up here!'

A muttered conversation. The light wavered.

Another voice said: 'Who are you? What do you want?'

'I was a guest in this hotel!' Matthew shouted. 'I came back from the hospital tonight, to find some of my possessions. Now I hear this tapping.'

'Tapping?'

'Yes. On and on.'

'Impossible,' said the voice to someone on the ground. 'It could not be after all this time.'

'Remember the two little girls we found here this morning. But is this man genuine?'

'Of course I'm *genuine*!' Matthew shouted. 'My name is – is Henri Delaware. I am a French Canadian. Come up here. Or allow me to come down. There is someone here who can be saved!'

V

THEY WERE located below the surface of the ground – the pipe had carried the sound up. So it was necessary to dig down between the shattered walls of the hotel which were jammed in their present upright position but waiting to fall.

After two hours they were able to communicate. A woman only spoke – in English – saying there were two of them down there. Matthew heard her name, Letty Heinz.

And the man, who was either dead or unconscious, was Lee Burford, her friend.

By now more searchlights had been brought, and there were more helpers. Six steel props were brought to shore up the walls and to try to prevent another fall which might crush and bury the rescuers as well as the victims. Only two men could work at a time.

They found the woman first and brought her out. She had a gash on her head, but otherwise seemed unhurt; though terribly weak and dehydrated from fifty hours without food or drink.

At first she could not drink. They force-lifted her to greater safety and pressed water between her cracked lips.

The man was still more difficult and did not answer their calls. It looked as if, in spite of their efforts, some extra debris had fallen on him during the last hour. It was a different colour from all the rest and was piled across his chest. Matthew could do no more to help and sat on a fallen slab, watching a doctor and an ambulance man at work. They cautiously cleared away the rest of the rubble and began to pull the man out as gently as possible by his feet. As soon as he could reach, the doctor bent forward and listened at the man's chest. He shrugged and they slid the man further out. Matthew could hear the woman above him whispering.

He was brought up, face ashen, no perceptible breathing. The doctor used his stethoscope and then gave the man an injection.

'Well?' said Matthew.

Again the doctor shrugged.

'It is touch and go. We shall know in a few minutes. But even then . . .'

It seemed a long wait. The moon had set and the stars,

though brilliant in the sky, were hardly to be perceived behind the floodlights. After all the digging and the shouting and the revving of engines it was suddenly very quiet. Then a whispering drone could be heard in the sky.

A lieutenant in the Moroccan Army who was standing near Matthew and apparently took him to be one of the recently rescued said: 'We are flying in a helicopter to take you straight to the airport. We wish to save you the jolting in an ambulance.'

The drone was coming nearer and soon hovered overhead, picking its place to land.

The doctor said: 'He is coming round. Now at least he has a chance!'

The plane landed on the road outside the hotel. Stretchers were brought, and Lee Burford put on one, Letty, though now sitting up, on another. It was assumed as a matter of course that Matthew should go as well. He raised no objection. Glad now to be out of it all.

It was only as he was about to climb into the helicopter that he remembered Johnny Frazier's suitcase, and he insisted on keeping them waiting until he had gone back to fetch it.

AFTERWARDS

I

M. HENRI Thibault was one of twenty-six victims in the collapse of the Saada Hotel whose body was never recovered. Estrella returned sorrowing to France, for though more recently he had irritated her beyond endurance she had once been fond of him; and she had borne his children and kept his home and shared his eminence as a banker and a philanthropist.

She had one unmarried daughter and decided to continue to live in the same style as before. But soon she had something more to sorrow about. Her injured ankle would not heal. A poison had got into her blood, unidentifiable by modern medicine, derived perhaps from some sulphurs in the earth's explosive breath, which could not be got rid of. In the end French physicians did give it a name – for what good that was – but they could not cure it. Her old father sent her to an extravagantly expensive clinic in Switzerland where, in June 1961, she died.

Colonel Gaston Tournelle, evacuated with the other patients of the hospital, made a slow recovery. His house was levelled, but Maria and the two girls had had miraculous escapes. The family eventually moved in to one of the ground-floor apartments in a new block opened in 1961. This did not have the character of the old villa, but it was convenient and easy for him to get around.

Tournelle was still too ill at the time of the earthquake to have attention to spare for any other than his own health, but as he got better he grieved over Johnny's death, and it crossed his mind to wonder if there had been any foul play involved in it. The suitcase, which presumably contained money or jewellery or securities, had never been found. Almost his first walk when he returned to Agadir was around the ruins of the old Saada, just to spy out, just in case. But by then the Saada had been bulldozed and was no more than a heap of rubble; and the chance of finding a suitcase, or anything identifiable, was remote.

It was all very sad, especially as the contents of his secret safe in the bathroom of his old villa had been looted before he was well enough to claim them.

Laura Legrand returned to Paris. With her share of Vicky's money she set up in a small luxury apartment, and organized an escort agency of six select girls for whom she picked what she called 'an exclusive clientele'. She became noticeably fatter and still more interested in gin, but she never lost her business acumen or her eye for an attractive girl.

Vicky returned to Bordeaux, and, having failed in her early ambition to marry one doctor, now married another, an elderly widower, who doted on her, who had an apartment in the Place des Martyrs, and property as well as medicine to his name. There she became the height of respectability and presently bore him a daughter who delighted him far more than either of the two sons, now long since gone, of his first wife.

Laura and Vicky got together to discover the whereabouts of Françoise's son, and once traced, to pay him half of the share in their dealings that Françoise would have had. 'Half,' Laura said firmly to Vicky. 'We can be generous but not too generous. Fair's fair. He's only her son. He's lucky to get so much.'

Laura and Vicky continued to see each other once a year, but after her marriage to the doctor Vicky always insisted on coming to Paris to meet her old friend. Laura understood the reason and raised no objection: after all, it was Vicky who had laid the golden egg.

The new Mme Badoit never showed any further interest in camels.

II

IN LATE APRIL 1960 three men meet in a spacious Georgian house near the top of Hampstead village.

Mr Artemis is in his usual discreet charcoal grey, a gold watch-chain dangles in old-fashioned elegance across an expanse of stomach. The big man sitting opposite him is in a blue suit shiny with wear. He has come in on two sticks. The third man is also big, though less big; he is in a thick red jumper caught at the waist by a black belt. He is wearing corduroy trousers and tennis shoes.

'We know Johnny's dead,' Big Smith says. 'That's for certain. I seen his corpse. I was lying there waiting for the ambulance to take me away and they brought him out – him and another bloke.'

'You told us this,' Mr Artemis says. 'Did he have nothing with him? A bag or a case or even a mackintosh?'

'It's not likely they'd bring anything out with him, is it? They was just bringing out the dead and the wounded. Anyway I couldn't see nothing. I wasn't feeling in the best of health myself. Did you ever have two legs broke?'

'Did you know the man they brought out with him?' Rooney asks.

'Nah. Except that he was an A-rab.'

Mr Artemis licks his blood blister. 'I found out about him. My friend Digby Ephraim, who lives in Tangier. He went down for me last month, asked around. The Arab was a man called Ardrossi, Benjamin Ardrossi, worked in the casino. Maybe he was Johnny's contact. Anyway, Ardrossi's dead, so's his family. My friend Digby says all records have been destroyed. Makes life difficult.'

'I reckon. Not surprised,' says Smith.

'We don't know if Johnny parted with the slush to someone before the quake,' says Joe Rooney, 'whether this Andross – whatever it is – was negotiating or what.'

'Johnny'd been in Agadir for two days and a half. But I reckon he wouldn't let go of the stuff easy. That case could still be buried among the ruins.'

'I reckon.'

There is a pause.

Mr Artemis shifts his stomach. 'We have to keep looking. Keep asking. You never know.'

'One thing,' Big Smith says. 'I'm not going back to that fricking city, no, not for all the tea in China. D'ye ever see a man crushed, the way Greg was crushed? He was like a pancake – blood spurted everywhere – and jelly and entrails – you'd never believe what's inside a man. Why—'

'Enough,' says Mr Artemis. 'That's quite enough. I realize you've been through a very unpleasant ordeal. But it's necessary still to try to keep track of things.'

'Ask Rooney,' Big Smith says. 'Let Joe have a go!'

Joe grunts. 'How much we got, boss? I mean here. All the stuff Johnny left behind. It must be worth a tidy bit. And we've two less to share it with.'

Mr Artemis looks cautious. 'Oh, fair. Oh, fair. It is taking time and expense to negotiate. Johnny took the easy stuff. But it's in process . . .'

'How much?' demands Rooney.

'Er – can't say yet. It's still in process. A few thousand pounds each. Poor reward for all the effort, but some nevertheless.'

'Hm,' says Joe. 'So we got to think of something else soon.'

III

LETTY MARRIED Lee on the 19th of October, 1960.

The two divorces had gone through without complications, but he had taken much longer than she did to recover from the entombment. Indeed for a while he seemed to be suffering from a poison of the blood not dissimilar from that slowly killing Estrella Thibault. But towards the end of the summer he regained his health, and psychologically the prospect of his remarriage was a powerful boost.

Letty's hair grew quickly over the ugly scar left by the amateur stitchings, but for the rest of her life she would not be able to part her hair on the right side. Perhaps the tragedy of Agadir had been a crucible in which her reservations about marrying Lee had finally melted. Or conceivably it had happened on the Saturday night they had spent together before the earthquake. He strongly chose to believe that. When he came out of hospital for the second time in September, feeling recovered, it was not so much that she submitted to him as that she welcomed him with a degree of warmth she had not begun to show before.

On the 28th of October of that year Letty wrote to Ann.

Dearest Ann,

Well, it has happened, just as you suggested it might, and schemed it might, all those many, many months ago! I must refuse to believe it! Do you know, I held nothing but scorn for your idea, because, after Carl, I never wanted another man ever to *touch* me again. Ever. Nor was I in the least attracted to Lee – not in that way, though I thought him a worthy man you did ill to desert.

Well, we are married last week. Once or twice during this ceremony my blood turns to water as I think: What if Ann comes back right now and walks into this ceremony and says, 'I have changed my mind, I am tired of New Zealand and I wish to come back, and I want *him* back!' What would I have said? I will have collapsed, and my pride with me, like a pricked balloon!

We did not go away, for Lee was only just out of hospital after our ordeal in Morocco. But he *seems* well now, and I am grown ever more fond of him. I shall never take your place in his heart, but at present he seems quite fixated on me and seems to rely on me for his social life. How long will it last? He takes his bridge very seriously – much more than you ever did – and although he is not a very good player he is awfully good-mannered and appreciates everything I do right.

I do not find him dull – as I am *sure* you did not in most of your life together, isn't it so? – and dear Ann, dear wicked scheming Ann – I do not find him so unsympathetic in bed! Perhaps he has changed. Perhaps I expected too little. Certainly he has some ideas that I would not have thought of! Anyway I have found something in him that I have not known before, and it gradually obliterates the memory in me of Carl's coarseness and brutality. I can tell you it took an effort even to go near Lee in those first weeks after you had left.

Well now; well. What of the future? We plan to stay on here. I would dearly love to come out to see you, and it is in my thoughts that perhaps Lee would like to come – but I do not think he ever will because of the way the break occurred – and perhaps it is well that we should not meet. At least, not yet. After such a long interval – for he was in hospital three times – he has taken up his work again with zest and is already deep in two cases – which he brings home to me, as he used to carry them home to you; but I am much less clever than you and I can really only help by listening. He is very busy at the moment advocating the proposal of a bill in Congress which would no longer forbid a lawyer to conduct a case outside his own state. Apparently it is not a popular idea with some members of his profession.

What you tell me of your adventures in Canton – bicycle and all – fills me with no wish ever to do the same! I would have hated it and probably have fallen off my bicycle in terror! When are you returning to New Zealand? Soon, I hope. This letter will await you. Naturally you must not reply to it, for I could not dare that he should see your writing on an envelope and ask to see the contents!

Ever devoted,

Letty

In September of '61 Letty had a son, whom they named Thor, and two years later a daughter, Christine.

Letty settled well into her new life as Mrs Lee Burford. Lee's friends, most of whom she knew at least by sight already, accepted her, and the arrival of two children made everything more assured. Hannah stayed on, accepting the changes with scarcely the lifting of an Irish eyebrow. Henry and Jessie Hayward were the only two to look askance and to ask Lee privately when his wife was not there what *exactly* Letty's antecedents were. But the old man said it was all Ann's own damn silly fault, and drove over to meet his new grandchildren.

Ann continued to write, but the letters became more infrequent. There did not seem any hint at all that she was not happy in her new life or regretted her decision. When her father died she was trekking in North Borneo and word could not be got to her in time. So she wrote but did not come. As the years passed it became a Christmas letter, part of it Roneoed so that all her family should be able to read it at the same time. There was always a separate one for Letty, but only topped and tailed with affectionate messages.

Lee continued to practise law until he was seventy, and then for another five years went to the office three days a week as a consultant. He played more golf in his days off, and enjoyed his wife and children and his evenings at home.

Letty's only worry was for her son, Leon, who remained a drop-out and preached flower power until well into his twenties. He came to stay with them for a day or so every six months and looked with unconcealed contempt on the luxury and wastefulness of their life. Then when he was twenty-four he turned up one day and told them he was going to England, where he was to work for an Anglo-American company prospecting for new oilfields in the North Sea. Lee concealed his surprise and Letty her gratification until the weekend was past. It was clear that over the past year or so his views, unnoticed by them, had been gradually shifting, and that making love not war was no longer foremost in his mind.

Making love on a more permanent basis may have had more influence on his decision, for six months later he married a girl called Rachel Wightman, a pretty Jewess from Philadelphia whose common sense and stability impressed itself on both the older people the first time they met her.

Thor – not so called after the god of thunder but because he had been born on a Thursday – was a healthy, engaging boy and a joy to both his parents; Christine was more tetchy but early on showed she had inherited her mother's good looks and elegance. On his seventieth birthday Lee, after an evening out to celebrate, found himself sitting in front of the fire opposite Letty planning the schooling of their children.

'I'm looking forward to the next decade,' he said. 'It will be expensive but real fun – and it's the sort of fun I've never had before. Much of the snobbery has gone these days, but I'd still like Thor to go to one of the good schools like St Paul's or Groton – because it helps when you get to Harvard.'

'I wish you would let me do without Hannah. Now both children are at school there's little or nothing for her to do during the day that I cannot do. I think Hannah would not mind, as her own husband has not been well.'

'You have your painting and your pottery. Hannah will tell us if she wants to leave.'

'Still better,' Letty said, ignoring him. 'Keep Hannah on and allow me to go out to work. I am a good cook – you know; I am trained as a nurse. There is work enough, I'm sure, even if only part-time.'

'Certainly not,' Lee said. And then after a pause: 'You know I've settled money on you if I should suddenly drop off the branch.'

'I neither know nor care!'

'Well, I've been figuring all the angles. When I'm eighty Thor will be seventeen and Christine fifteen. Of course I might not achieve that age.' He went on before she could interrupt: 'Or I might live *years* after that. Golf keeps me fit, and you and the children keep me young. If, or when, as I say, I cease to be, there should be money enough. If it should run short, with inflation and things, *that* would be the time for you to look for work. Not now, not in the immediate future while I am still around to take care of you.'

Letty was aware of the fact that if she had had some professional skill he might not have minded. It was natural for many wives to work. But her skills were domestic. So.

'You do not mind staying home a bit longer?' he asked.

'Of course I don't mind staying home.'

'You do not think it a chore?'

'No, I do not.' Letty was aware that he was watching her, and gave a slight smile.

'It is not too much of a chore living with me?'

'No, I find much comfort in it.'

Both children were asleep and nothing stirred in the house.

He said: 'Letty, would you look on it as a chore if I asked you to come to bed with me right now?'

She was serious, thinking of it. Then she said: 'No, Lee, I would not consider it anything of a chore at all.'

IV

THE AIR France plane AF 1061 from Casablanca to Libreville on Monday the 7th of March, 1960, carried among its passengers one Henri Delaware. Had anyone taken the trouble to look at the photograph in his passport with a suspicious scrutiny they would have remarked that he looked younger in real life. But no one was that interested. In the chaos following the earthquake, people simply registered a name and address and took whatever means was available to leave the country. Most of the non-Moroccan survivors were flying to Paris or London or Hamburg or New York. Planes were crowded and places on them difficult to get. Almost all the civilized world had mustered its resources to help. No one was specially interested in a single young man who happened to want to fly off with a few businessmen and hardened travellers to Gabon.

In Casablanca Matthew had fitted himself out with underwear, shirts, shoes, a couple of new suits, a watch, a wallet and a pair of dark glasses. He stayed only two days in Libreville, during which he discovered there was a Thursday evening flight to Nairobi. From there he flew to Johannesburg, and a week later was in Cape Town. He stayed at the Mount Nelson Hotel, and proceeded to take stock. Until this point he had felt himself obliged to keep on the move lest his deception should be spotted. Now, it seemed, he was safe – or temporarily safe. At least safe to choose for himself.

Already he partly regretted his decision. He had had a varied career but had never ventured onto the wrong side of the law. (If one excepted one occasion when he had gone down the fire escape of a smart French hotel and left without paying his bill.) This, this impersonation of a man who was either dead or never existed, accompanied by his seizure of a small suitcase stuffed with stolen money, was out of his class. It put him among the serious felons, and he didn't like it.

But the money was there, in his hands. Three times he

spread it out on his bed and counted it. It was staggering. He could live for ten years – maybe much longer – out of it. Dollars, pounds, francs, Deutschmarks. He doubted the good sense of what he had done – there must be pitfalls that he didn't yet know of – but even if he had not been suffering from a sort of shell-shock at the time, combined with his awful unbelieving grief over Nadine, even then, if he had been stone-cold sober and totally in his right mind, would he have chosen otherwise? Would the temptation not have been too great? He had always been short of money. He had always wanted the things money could buy. Could he have resisted the sight of it piled on the bed and the knowledge that the person from whom he had taken it was dead, and anyway had no right to it in the first place?

He looked at himself in the mirror and said aloud: 'I can ring England tonight, say I'd lost my memory; my passport and belongings are buried in the ruins of the Hôtel Saada – can you come out?'

His mother would come, establish his identity, they would apply for a replacement passport, return to England together. And the money? It would go back to the merchant bank from which it had been stolen.

A grey area here? The police would be suspicious. He had travelled out all the way to Agadir on the same day as one of the robbers. How to prove that he had not been implicated in the robbery itself? The police would want to know what he knew of the identity of the other criminals. They would go on asking and asking questions. They would keep on calling on him, trying a new angle, a new approach.

But suppose he went back and still did not return the money? So far no one had bothered to open the case when he came through customs, but it was a risk each time. It would be in character for some fellow at Heathrow to question what he carried.

And if he got through? Put the money in a safe deposit, help himself when he needed a bit. There would still be questions, even if not from the police. How justify to his mother and stepfather, and indeed Rona, a gradual affluence? A perilous and worrying business. Say his second novel had brought him in much more than expected? It could hardly account for his buying an Aston Martin.

If he stayed here, who would question anything?

But he would be officially dead. Rona would be sad – she would not grieve, he was certain, in the way he was grieving about Nadine – but she would be sad. Then there was his mother. She was the main stumbling block. She had never shown him much affection after the children of her second marriage came along; but he knew she loved him in her critical but generous way. She would grieve. She would be the only one really upset by his death. But if he had been five years older she could well have lost him in the war.

And, when he eventually reappeared, would she not be all the more delighted to welcome him back?

At this stage it was never in his mind that he would not return to England at some later date, claiming loss of memory over a much more prolonged period, whatever it was, two years, five years, whatever he felt like making it. His mother would be all the more delighted to see him. Rona might have remarried – if so, good luck to her. But *after* he had wandered about the world for a while, *after* he had spent some of the money. In a few years, while he was living in Cape Town or Sydney or Rio, he would suddenly remember who he was, remember his real name, remember his past and make himself known.

In the second week in Cape Town he spent some time in the public library, reading up in encyclopaedias about the district he had come from in French-speaking Canada. He learned that Chicoutimi, on the River Saguenay, was a thriving little town exporting great quantities of timber and was the seat of a Roman Catholic bishop. Tadoussac, at the mouth of the river, was the oldest trading port in Canada. These and other facts he stored away in his memory in case of need. It was to be his excuse, if found wanting in information about it, that he had left in childhood.

As an experiment he did not at all mind changing his identity, inventing and experiencing a new life. He always found it stimulating and exciting. He had already changed his father and his name in childhood, and continued to use one name for his own life and the other for his writing. Not to mention when he had run off as a schoolboy of seventeen, using a third name which he had picked out of *The Times*. (Then he had been *brought* back, but hadn't minded that: he'd had his fun.)

After two weeks at the Mount Nelson he bought a smart new yellow Austin Healey. (He had found Johannesburg extremely convenient for the changing of currency – it seemed almost as good as Switzerland.) The following week he left the hotel and took an apartment in Constantia.

Already he was making friends: he was a cheerful, likeable, moneyed young Canadian. No one seemed to mind that he spoke English with an English accent and French with a French accent – it only showed how well he had been educated. He met a man who worked on the *Cape Times*, who introduced him to the editor, who took a liking to him and offered him a freelance job to observe the South African scene and write an occasional column about it. The *Cape Times* was bitterly and loudly anti-apartheid – it surprised

Matthew to find such freedom of expression in what he had been told was a police state – and he wrote a few articles, signed Visitor, deriding the absurdities of the racist system, by which people in the Post Office were segregated into Whites and Ne-Whites, but went next door to the supermarket and stood in the same queue to pay. His tone in writing was generally light and humorous, but sarcasm was wanting in the system, and his sarcasms became more telling than the outright hostility of the editorials. He was shown some of the townships, and commented on them in language that became increasingly acrid. Then he met a Boer girl, beautiful and intelligent and eloquent, and the next article he wrote put something of the Boer history and point of view: that South Africa was their country, that they had built it into its present state of great prosperity, that it was the only such prosperous state in the continent of Africa, that the Boers had lived there for three centuries, much longer than most of the blacks and coloured people who had flocked in to participate in the prosperity; that to expect them to renounce their right to their creation was like asking the Americans to hand back Chicago to the Red Indians. This brought him popularity and unpopularity in several directions.

The following year he moved on, taking an Italian cruise liner to Sydney. South Africa was about to leave the Empire and become a republic, and he sensed the irreconcilable ambitions of the whites and the blacks and foresaw trouble wherever he looked. Apart from this, as a writer of a weekly column in the *Cape Times*, he was becoming noticed. Though he wrote under a *nom de plume* his friends knew, and from them others who might be less well disposed towards him – particularly the government and the police. He couldn't yet afford to be noticed. It was not time for anyone in authority to start asking questions. Also he had an affair with the Boer girl. She was one of the prettiest and most charming girls he had ever met, but his loss of Nadine was too fresh. He found he could not bring himself to commit himself in this way. Although he was officially divorced and free to marry, what legality or sincerity was there in marrying under a false name? It was not quite like writing a column for a newspaper.

Was this, he wondered, a problem that was going to dog his footsteps for the rest of his exiled life?

1985

I

THE TWENTY-FIFTH anniversary of the earthquake of Agadir was not celebrated with any ceremonies of commemoration on the part of the authorities. It had been a profound tragedy with enormous loss of life, almost a mortal blow to the struggling Moroccan economy; but with help from many nations, chiefly the French and the American, it had survived. A new Agadir, as promised, had been inaugurated in 1961, and the town had mushroomed since. New hotels had been put up all along the sea front, new houses and flats and roads built, avenues replanted with palms, the port re-established, the municipal buildings set in attractive squares. It was not thought necessary to remind the inhabitants over again of the blood and tears of twenty-five years ago.

In the Town Hall large photographs, blown up to measure six feet square, served as sufficient of a permanent reminder, and the old Kasbah on the hill overlooking the bay had not been touched: it remained a monument, a graveyard, with irregular mounds of rubble like scurf on a giant's head.

The Hôtel Mahraba, which had split down the middle and lost most of its ornamentation without actually collapsing, had been entirely rebuilt, but time and fashion had marched on, and it had newer and more highly rated hotels to compete with. (The Saada had never risen from its ashes.)

But it was to the Mahraba that some people came in February 1985, drawn by a common impulse to see the scene they had last left in devastation and despair so long ago.

One was a good-looking Australian with glasses and a trim close-cut dark beard flecked with grey.

Another was an elderly French lady, a doctor's widow from Bordeaux, called Mme Vicky Badoit, with her daughter Janine and her daughter's fiancé Hector.

The hotel was almost full, the weather entirely different from that other time: sunshine most of the day with a strong fresh breeze rising off the sea each afternoon. Far from being too hot, the wind when it rose made it too cold for most people to remain on the beach, and the nights were chilly.

Complex considerations had decided Matthew to make this visit at long last. He had often thought he would like to return – pure nostalgia working on old wounds, never quite healed. But it is unlikely that any of the returning survivors would have come together except for the presence of a M. Aristide Voigt. M. Voigt was about sixty, stout, round-faced, with grey stubbly hair cropped close to his skull, chubby fingers, fat feet and a powerful voice. He came from Metz. Recently widowed, M. Voigt was an expert on Agadir, having come every year in February without fail; he had been staying with his wife in the Mahraba on the night of the earthquake.

Soon after he arrived he had spotted Mme Vicky Badoit, thought her a pretty widow taking a holiday with her children, and had scraped an acquaintance. When it became known that she too had been in Agadir on that dreadful night he claimed there was a bond between them, and when Janine and Hector were absent one evening, he invited Mme Badoit to join him for a drink after dinner.

She had no ambitions to find another man friend, certainly not to marry again, but she was feeling lonely so she accepted. Voigt was a cheerful, talkative man, and had no hesitation in telling her all about himself and his experience that night before asking for hers. He first of all informed her that he had begun life behind the counter of a shoe shop in Metz, had married the owner's only daughter, and in the course of time had inherited the shop and had opened four others. He had a handsome house in Verny, far too big for him now, two sons who were both married and in the business, and was thinking shortly of retiring, which he could now very comfortably do, and see rather more of the world than he had had time for. He had spent his honeymoon in Agadir in 1955 and had so much enjoyed it that they had returned every year except 1961, and last year when his wife had been too ill to travel. And always at the Mahraba, always at the Mahraba.

Yes, they had been here all through the earthquake: indeed, he and Mme Voigt had been playing bezique, one of his wife's great amusements of an evening; they had played a last hand and had been about to leave the lounge when the most terrible rending noise had occurred and they had both been thrown to the ground, when the very floor had seemed to oscillate, ornaments and chairs had fallen all about them, the lights had failed, and he had dragged Mme Voigt out of the hotel into the garden, where masonry and trees were falling everywhere. Some of the guests were injured, and it was a miracle that they had survived unscathed.

Eventually, after describing his situation in even greater detail, he said: 'And you, madame, you also were here? This is a great bond between us. Tell me of your experiences.'

Vicky sipped at her liqueur and demurely patted her lips with a lace handkerchief.

'I, monsieur? I was buried for twenty-four hours.'

At his expression of horror she began her modest story. She had been on holiday here with two schoolfriends – they had all been at the same convent together – they had stayed at the Saada, which completely collapsed, and they had all been buried. Laura, her oldest and dearest friend, had also been brought out alive and not seriously hurt, but her other friend, Françoise, had been killed.

M. Voigt was shocked and deeply sympathetic. The lady had deep blue eyes which were almost violet in the artificial light, and her thick brown hair, if necessarily tinted and waved, was very becoming. Altogether he liked the look of her. In the conversation which followed she let it be known that soon after returning to Bordeaux in 1960 she met and married Dr Badoit – the great Dr Badoit as he was to become known for his research into the adrenal gland – 'He was much older than I, monsieur, but we were very happy together. And we had one greatly beloved daughter, who has come away with me on this holiday.'

'Together with her "young man",' agreed Voigt. 'Yes, she is very handsome.'

'Not "young man",' corrected Vicky. 'Her fiancé. Perhaps I am old-fashioned, but morals today have become so lax. I am not in favour of casual relationships. Janine and Hector are properly affianced and will be married in October.'

'Splendid,' said Voigt. 'Splendid. I too am all in favour of moral discipline. A fine young man. Very suitable for such a fine young lady, who, if I may say so, takes her good looks from her mother.'

He looked at Mme Badoit, and received a glance from the violet eyes which was surprisingly astute and assessing.

'I am, of course,' she murmured, 'but recently widowed.'

'Yes, yes,' said Voigt. 'But it is important to avoid loneliness. I wish to travel round the globe and one day I shall look for a partner who can accompany me. Especially away from one's native land one needs conversation and companionship.'

Before she could reply to this, had she so intended, they were interrupted by the arrival of a tall, clean-cut, good-looking young man in his early twenties who stopped before them and said in fluent but heavily accented French:

'Pardon me, did I hear you speak about the earthquake? Were you here at the time? I am — interested in what happened.'

Voigt, not sure whether he welcomed the interruption, said: 'Just so. Madame was recounting her experiences. I am surprised you have heard of it, young man! Many of the guests at this hotel, I believe, know nothing of it whatever. One man yesterday said to me, oh yes, he had heard something but he thought it was a tidal wave. Imagine, a tidal wave!'

'No,' said the young man, 'it is almost forgotten.' As well as being tall he was also thin, with those prominent bones which convey the impression some young men give, quite mistakenly, of being underfed. 'As you no doubt guess, I was not here myself but my parents were here on their honeymoon. They were buried for four days!'

'In the Saada?' said Vicky.

'Yes. Was that where you were, madame?'

'Indeed.'

'She too was buried,' said Voigt. 'Was it for two days, madame?'

'Almost,' Vicky murmured.

'I am here with my half-brother. That is him, over there,

but he does not speak French. My mother was divorced and he is the son of her first marriage. Permit me to introduce myself: Thor Burford. I come from New England.'

'America, is that?' asked Vicky. 'Yes, I imagined so. I wonder if I knew your parents?'

'She is small and fair, he is dark – was dark . . . Leon, come on over here and meet these good people. Oh, and *you*, monsieur. I'm afraid I don't know your name. We met outside the Casino today, you remember?'

Thor was the outgoing type. Though half Anglo-Norwegian, he had grown up very much the All-American young man – friendly and frank and ready to mix, and a little naïve.

Clearly the bearded man who had been last addressed thought so, for he came over reluctantly and remained standing, a slight disclaiming smile of acknowledgement on his face, until M. Voigt got up and pulled a chair across. Leon Heinz, now a man of forty-five, whose sturdy build and breadth of shoulder made him look enormous, also came over reluctantly and took another seat. The conversation, although now fractured into two languages, mainly continued in French.

Mme Badoit was persuaded to recount again her story of the earthquake and her entombment and rescue.

Then Thor said: 'My father and mother were buried for four days. They were almost the last people to be rescued, certainly the last from the Hôtel Saada. They were buried under a fallen beam, just able to move. My mother was badly cut in the head, and my father, to staunch the bleeding, stitched up her scalp with an ordinary darning needle and thread. It still shows – the scar still shows – though normally it is hidden by her hair. She used to show it to me when I was a little boy and tell me the story.'

'And how were they rescued?' Voigt asked.

'A miracle. You'd never believe. My mother had been in the wartime Resistance and they always used the beginning of Beethoven's Fifth Symphony. Dar-dar-dar-*dar*. You know. Dar-dar-dar-*dar*. Well, she went on tapping this out on a water pipe, and the sound travelled, and some Frenchman who'd been in the French Resistance heard it and raised the alarm! When they were dug out my father was unconscious and they didn't think he'd live.'

'But he did?' asked Matthew.

'Oh, yes. Still is. He's in his middle eighties and still quite fit. Only gave up golf last year!'

Vicky was staring at Matthew. 'And you, monsieur? Did this gentleman say you were here at the time?'

'I was, yes. I was on my own, but I lost a dear friend.'

Vicky still stared at him, puckering her eyes. She exclaimed suddenly and then said: 'But were you not the – the man – the Englishman – who – who helped to pull me out?'

Matthew hesitated, then half smiled. 'I believe so.'

Vicky was on her feet. 'Monsieur, you saved my life! This gentleman saved my life! When I was completely buried. I was sure we should all die!'

'I only began to dig,' Matthew said. 'I was pretty shell-shocked myself. Then I heard you cry out . . .'

Vicky moved to him and kissed him on both cheeks. 'I thought we would never live. You saved me! And you saved Laura too! You were a great hero! I never knew your name! We too, as you can imagine, were shell-shocked at that time!'

'Actually,' said Matthew, 'I am not English, though I spent some years there. My name is Henri Delaware and I am French Canadian.'

'This makes it necessary for us to have further drinks,' said Voigt. 'M. Burford, could I ask you to oblige me by pressing the bell?'

Thor pressed the bell, came back, a thoughtful look on his face. He said to Matthew: 'Your name is Henri Delaware?'

'Yes.'

'D'you come from Australia, sir?'

'Yes, I do. I have made my home in Sydney for many years. But what made you think that?'

'Your name, sir. Delaware. Henri Delaware. It just seemed to me that you might – I suppose it's a long throw – you might be one of the Outbacks?'

Again Matthew hesitated. An extraordinary chance – or mischance – had thrown this up. Had he been wise even to come? But the risk was now so small.

'As a matter of fact, yes.'

'Gee, that's great! Really great! You're the leader of the group, then, aren't you?'

'I started it off – oh, what? – fifteen years ago. The three of us really began it together.'

'Henry, Floyd and Greener. A lot of the guys were mad about you at Law School. Now the CDs are coming out, it'll be wild. You ever been to the States? I mean recently?'

'No, not since we began the group. It was intended, you see, for the Australian market. We didn't really expect it to spread.'

'Well, it sure has! You're big everywhere now. America, England, fair bits of the rest of the world. I guess they've caught a new market right in between pop and country and western. This is great luck meeting you like this! I'd no idea what you look like; there's never pictures on the sleeves!'

'We decided we were all getting on a bit,' said Matthew evenly. 'Didn't think our photos would be much recommendation.' Not true: in the late 1970s when the music really took off they were all still in their forties and they had been under intense pressure from the record company to get a picture done, but they hadn't agreed. Green, the other guitarist, had sided with Matthew, clearly for some reason of his own which he had never divulged. Green had come from Manchester and had known the Beatles. He had come to be called Greener in Sydney because his broad Lancashire voice accentuated the last letter of his name so that it sounded like a second syllable. Floyd was a Tasmanian who had thrown up his job in a shipping office and settled in Sydney, as he said, 'to beat the drums'. They had all got fair voices, 'not Pavarotti', as Greener said, 'but better than Rex Harrison', and able enough to sing the simple lyrics of the songs they wrote.

Everybody was talking together now – except for Leon, who bit at his fingers and tried to catch the French. He had come back to America and was living and working in Philadelphia near his wife's parents. He had three children, all now almost grown up, and it had been a good marriage. Thor had always wanted to go to Agadir to see the site of the earthquake of which he had heard so much. His father not wanting to make such a long journey, he had arranged this holiday with his mother, but a week before they were due to leave his father had heard of the death of his first wife, Ann. She was eighty-three and had died of a heart attack after hauling a dinghy up the shingle in some seaside part of New Zealand where she was living. Although he had not seen her for many years (Thor had only ever seen photographs of her) this had upset Lee a lot, and Letty had felt she could not leave him on his own at this time. So sooner than cancel and waste their bookings, Thor had persuaded Leon to come in her place.

'And then,' said Thor, sitting on the arm of Matthew's chair, 'you built a hospital, didn't you. It was all in that magazine about what it had cost, the fact that you didn't want to be interviewed.'

Matthew smiled and made a dismissive gesture. 'All that was exaggerated. Good bit of PR, you know. I didn't build a hospital, for Pete's sake. They were building a new hospital, and I contributed to the children's wing. I meant it to be anonymous, but the hospital people leaked it. It was just one of those things.'

Shortly afterwards he excused himself and went up to bed. He had only arrived two days ago, and already was beset by ghosts. He was rather relieved that the woman he remembered as Vicky, after her spontaneous recognition and outburst of gratitude, had not pursued the subject in further detail. It occurred to him that perhaps she was not too keen to remember or have remembered in public some elements of her own past life.

As he reached his bedroom he wondered whether he should ring up Edouard de Blaye, see if he happened to be there. He already knew the answer. Pierre was dead and the house turned into a hotel. He had not heard of Edouard for years. It was all ghosts.

II

HE WAS UP early next morning as he was due to leave that day. A plane left for Paris at five this afternoon. He planned a couple of days there walking round his old haunts, then he was going to Madrid where there had been a special call for him. Not London. Even now he did not feel like facing London.

He had not thought it worthwhile to hire a car, but after

breakfast he took a taxi up to the Kasbah. He felt he would like to see what remained of it before he left.

In fact nothing remained of it but heaps of rubble and piled brick. He wondered how many of the six hundred buried here were unrecovered. Probably most. It was just a vast burial mound.

But there was a wonderful view. Below him stretched the great sweep of the bay and all the new white buildings along its perimeter. He remembered that first morning so long ago when he had swum along the beach and idly wished he had money to invest in buying land and building property in a region where growth – and profit – were an obvious proposition. And so, in spite of the great catastrophe, it had proved. Life had moved on. Agadir had become such a widely popular holiday resort that thousands flocked here regardless – and mostly ignorant – of what had happened a quarter of a century ago.

As it turned out he had needed no such property speculation to make him rich. Perhaps he hadn't even needed the contents of a suitcase – though without that he would never have gone to Australia, and all the rest would not have followed.

It had not happened at once: he had lived comfortably and well off the takings for more than five years, and it was the merest chance which had turned him into a rich man in his own right.

Years before that occurred he had one day been reading an English *Sunday Telegraph* two weeks old and had come upon an article devoted to him – 'a young man of great talent untimely lost in the Agadir earthquake'. Apparently someone had 'discovered' his two novels; they had been reprinted and become something of a cult. (He wondered sourly if this would have happened if he had still been alive.

There was nothing like an untimely death to interest literary critics.)

He had been spending his first years in Sydney chiefly surfing and sunning himself, and on bad days or in the winter he would sit for hours playing the expensive guitar he had bought. Evenings he socialized a bit, and had a number of brief friendships with friendly girls. But it occurred to him at this stage that he might take this as a suitable opportunity to recover his memory and return to England. It appealed very much to his self-esteem that his two novels were now being highly praised, and if he went back now, the money that remained to him – reduced now by more than half – could be left behind in Australia and he could capitalize on the new prestige by writing a third novel. Heaven knew, he had had plenty of new experience to draw on over the last five years!

He contemplated it, then thought of it, and at the last drew back. The explanations would be enormous, and even if he retreated into the excuse of a failed memory there seemed so many pitfalls. He agonized for a month.

One of the major obstacles to his return now was that he had just met a girl called Pola and fallen in love with her. If it was not the feeling that he had had for Nadine, it was the nearest he had ever come, and the thought of leaving her, or of trying to explain the situation to her and persuading her to return with him to England, was more than he could face.

So he decided to write another novel where he was and to write it under the name of Henry Delaware.

It took more than a year, and by the time it was finished he had asked Pola to marry him and she had accepted. Their marriage burned his boats. When the novel was finished he looked around for a publisher. He did not feel he could safely submit it to the firm who had issued his other two books. Australia remained almost exclusively within the English sphere. One or two English publishers had offices in Sydney and Melbourne, but they were outposts, the embassies of a friendly power. Times were in fact just beginning to change, and one or two publishers were issuing an Australian list, but he looked for a worldwide market.

Then someone told him of a firm of agents, a go-ahead group with their head office in Toronto, who already had offices in New York and London and were about to open a branch in Sydney. They had a reputation for being influential. With his pseudo link with Canada, Matthew would have preferred another provenance, but they said the head of the agency, a man called Chadwick, would be over next month and would be delighted to meet him.

They met, and Chadwick read the book, also Mather, who was to head the Australian office. They took a modest view of the book, but were happy to handle it at the usual commission; they thought their people in London would probably be able to place it with one of the smaller firms, and a copy of the typescript would certainly go to New York.

Over lunch, Mr Chadwick, a tall, big-boned man with heavy glasses, discussed the novel at greater length and Matthew drew a few extra criticisms from him which gave the impression that the book's chance of publication was not much more than 50/50. Matthew's experience of agents in England had taught him that optimism was not their most pronounced characteristic, so with the coffee he confessed to Mr Chadwick (Jim to you, Henry) that he had in part modelled his style on that suddenly popular novelist, the late Matthew Sorensen.

'Sorensen?' Chadwick put two lumps of sugar in his cup. 'Sorensen? That's the guy who was killed. Yep. Good writer.

I specially thought well of his first book. What was it called?
I can't remember.'

'*Chance Medley*,' said Matthew.

'That's it. You – more or less had those books in mind
when you wrote yours?'

'I admired his work. I thought it was a general style I
might adopt.'

Chadwick stirred his coffee, tested it with his spoon and
then put in another lump of sugar. 'Sorensen. Well . . .' He
shook his head. 'Can't see any great resemblance, Henry.
Honestly, I can't. I don't want to be depressing but Sorensen
is something rather special. D'you know? It's a matter of
personality, isn't it. It's all how you bring your own personality into the writing that matters, that marks what you might
call a good book from a not quite so good book. Sorensen
had a way of writing, you know. It isn't quite yours.'

III

MATTHEW HAD dismissed the taxi, and thought he would
walk back. The exercise would do him good.

Unnoticed by him while he was looking over the great
expanse of the bay, an old bus had ground its way up the
hill, and at the top a group of Moroccan women had climbed
out. Some were in white robes, others in black: they chattered in groups as they walked about, and some sat down to
look over the sea. Some just stood in the sun.

Along with them, the only Europeans in the bus, were
two big elderly people, a man and a woman, both in their
sixties. He wore a loud light check suit with two-toned shoes
and a white golfing cap. She was in a summery print dress of

over-floral design, hair dyed black, no hat but a hair net. Heavy earrings and a gold chain. He used a stick. They walked across the road and climbed the rubble not far from Matthew, staring down, as everyone was staring down, at the wonderfully picturesque scene and the water glinting and the ships moving like toys in the bay.

Matthew's luck had begun soon after the birth of his second child, Marya, named after Pola's grandmother. He often visited churches in Sydney, wherever there was a chance of decent music, of which there was not much, but this Sunday, going into the Greek Orthodox church, he had seen a bald youngish man and heard him accompanying the organ. After the service he had approached him, imagining him probably Russian or Polish, and found to his astonishment that he came from Manchester.

So his friendship with Henry Green, or Greener, had begun, and shortly after this Greener had introduced him to Floyd, and they had struck up instantly a musical affinity, which had led to their making a few records – financed by Matthew. Then Matthew – conscious of the lack of success of his book venture – had spent a couple of weeks in New York hawking the records round the record companies there. Presently one began to talk business.

And that was the way it had happened. In four years they were making LPs and selling in the States and England. In eight they were very rich.

His gesture in helping finance a hospital wing had been a later impulse, a final stirring of conscience over what he had picked up from Johnny Frazier's haul. It did not quite match that amount but went a fair way, and he felt he could sleep untroubled at night knowing that the banking firm of Benson & Benson had done more ultimate good with their money than if they had never lost it.

Not that he had suffered broken nights over the matter at any time.

His marriage to Pola had come adrift four years ago, for reasons very different from those which had brought him to his first divorce, yet with rather the same sort of outcome. He was still on friendly terms with Pola – just as he had been, or would have been, with Rona. They shared the children – to whom they were both devoted – and neither had so far shown any tendency to take another partner. For a while at least Matthew was content to live alone – so far, that was, as he was allowed to in his present high-profile situation – and, as he had done most of his life, keeping his own counsel, thinking his own thoughts, being his own man. In these circumstances he was pleasantly content, and he wondered now why he had felt impelled to come back to Agadir. Now he could not wait to return to Sydney.

IV

ON A SEPARATE pile of rubble not very far from Matthew, Big Smith stood with his wife, Madge, staring at the splendid panorama.

'Never been up here before,' he said. 'Never got the chance. Arrived one night, and *bang!* we was away the next.'

Madge licked her lips distastefully. 'Don't think that bacon was too good this morning. Bit rancid like. I ought to've sent it back.' She belched in a genteel fashion.

'Greg Garrett didn't stand a chance, poor bleeder,' Smith said. 'Squashed, he was, just like a frog under a stone. Blood and guts and brains everywhere.'

'You've told me forty times,' said his wife. 'Don't know

why you ordered bacon. They don't eat it themselves. We could've done without for a morning or two.'

'Mine was OK,' said Smith. 'You want to taste what it's like in stir; that's if you're lucky enough to get any of any sort.'

'I've never been "in stir", as you well know. Nor you for twenty years.'

'Eighteen,' said Smith. 'I wonder when that bleeding bus is starting back.'

'It's already gone.'

'Gone? Why didn't you tell me?'

'You was too busy talking about your old earthquake. Any road, we can walk. Do you good.'

'Hell. And I don't suppose we can raise a taxi.'

For two years Big Smith had needed a hip replacement, but he wouldn't trust the Spanish doctors and didn't fancy to return to England. They had a nice little place now on the Costa del Sol, to which Smith had retreated with his wife in 1977, and they lived there eating and drinking comfortably with a few cronies. After another foray under Mr Artemis, which had gone wrong and Smith had served a stretch, he had come out and teamed up with a man called Jones who had been in jail at the same time. Jones didn't have the class of Mr Artemis but he was a quick thinker and a spry mover, and they had successfully pulled off a couple of audacious small jobs together. In some of the Soho joints they frequented together they became known as 'Alias Smith and Jones'. Smith began to walk with more of a swagger.

Then together they had got away with a clever robbery at Gatwick Airport. It had all depended on effrontery and split-second timing. 'Got away' was a relative term, and Smith had decided that the moment had come to take his wife off and live in Spain, where extradition laws were interpreted leniently. There was no charge actually out against him but he knew what the British police were like when they held deep suspicions and had got their fingers on a man with a record. He had enough to live on and thought it time to quit.

Jones was too clever for that and stayed in Rotherhithe with his common-law family, but he had been nobbled a few years later and was still serving a long stretch. Bad luck, Jonesy, Smith had said to himself, sitting in the sun of Fuengirola. This might be a bit boring, but it was better than working for a living.

'Excuse me,' said Madge, addressing a tall bearded man who was passing by in European clothes. 'Do you speak English?'

The tall man looked from one to the other of the strange couple and stopped.

'Spika da English?' said Smith, making his point.

'Oh, yes, I do.'

'We was wondering,' Madge said, 'we was wondering what time the next bus back was.'

'Afraid I don't know,' said Matthew. Then he addressed in French a stout young Arab in a long black jellaba. Conversation took place, the Arab bowed and walked on.

'He says there is one at noon.'

'Stone me,' said Smith. 'That's – that's an hour and a half . . .'

'Come on, Big,' Madge said. 'We can walk. Isn't far, is it, mister?'

Matthew smiled. 'Mile. Mile and a half. It's all downhill.'

Smith said: 'Going down hurts my bleedin' hip more than going up.'

They started off. It had been on the tip of Madge's

tongue to ask: 'Are you English, then?' and maybe get into conversation, but the man did not look very friendly, so what the hell.

Matthew took a deep breath and looked about him for the last time. Perhaps he should have gone to Taroudant, where all his greatest happiness had been. But he could not face it. He could not face going to stay in a hotel which he had known as a private residence and where he had loved with such fervour so long ago.

Although yet only fifty-three this visit had made him feel old. His youth was gone. He might, he supposed, now call himself middle middle-aged. Time for another, a final change? Return to England at last? Seeking a youth that couldn't come back. Did he seek anything else? Not long ago he had met a man on Bondi Beach who came from Hampstead and knew the general area pretty well. Coincidentally this man had met a Mrs Patterson, one-time widow of this writer chap whose novels had been all the rage a few years ago. Patterson, her husband, was in law, he thought, quite a bit older than her, looking to become a QC. They had three children: one was autistic. Had he ever known the author? Matthew enquired. No, before my time. I was at school in the sixties.

From another source Matthew learned that his mother had died in 1975. His two half-sisters were married with families of their own.

So what to go back to? His third novel, published in London and Melbourne, and later in New York, had not done much. Of course it was not by Matthew Sorensen. Only a literary unknown called Henry Delaware.

Matthew began to walk down the hill following behind the odd couple who had spoken to him. Loud, unsuitable clothes, Bermondsey accents, what had brought them here? They didn't look like people who would sit on the beach all day and bathe.

As he went down he began to catch up this pair. Some sense of not wanting to get involved – and for God's sake he had got involved far more than he had ever expected last night, what with the little Frenchwoman, now all respectable, recognizing him, and the young American recognizing his name and knowing his recordings – that was more than enough. This afternoon he would be on his way to Paris.

So Big Smith and Matthew Morris walked down the hill almost together. They did not know each other and they had never known each other. They would never speak again.

They walked in tandem all the way back to the town.